FATAL CATCH

A DI Andy Horton Mystery

Pauline Rowson

This first world edition published 2015
in Great Britain and the USA by
SEVERN HOUSE PUBLISHERS LTD of
19 Cedar Road, Sutton, Surrey, England, SM2 5DA.
Trade paperback edition first published
in Great Britain and the USA 2015 by
SEVERN HOUSE PUBLISHERS LTD.

British Library Cataloguing in Publication Data

Rowson, Pauline author.
  Fatal catch. – (An Andy Horton mystery)
  1. Horton, Andy (Fictitious character)–Fiction.
  2. Police–England-Portsmouth-Fiction. 3. Murder-
  Investigation–Fiction. 4. Detective and mystery stories.
  I. Title II. Series
  823.9'2-dc23

ISBN-13: 978-07278-8497-8 (cased)
ISBN-13: 978-1-84751-660-2 (trade paper)
ISBN-13: 978-1-78010-714-1 (e-book)

All Severn House titles are printed on acid-free paper.

Severn House Publishers support The Forest Stewardship Council™ [FSC™],
the leading international forest certification organisation. All our titles that
are printed on FSC certified paper carry the FSC logo.

Typeset by Palimpsest Book Production Ltd.,
Falkirk, Stirlingshire, Scotland.
Printed and bound in Great Britain by
TJ International, Padstow, Cornwall

ACKNOWLEDGEMENT

With grateful thanks, as always, to Hampshire Police, the Hampshire Police Marine Unit, the Fingerprint Bureau and the Crime Scene Investigations team for all their continued support and assistance.

ONE

The call came through just as Nat King Cole was about to roast his chestnuts on an open fire, and just as Horton reached the head of the long supermarket queue. He scrabbled for his mobile phone inside his leather jacket, drawing a loud exhalation of disapproval from the woman behind him, while he threw an apologetic smile at the twenty-something cashier processing the toys and books he was buying for his daughter, Emma. It was Sergeant Cantelli and he'd only call if it was important.

'I'll call you back in two minutes,' Horton said hastily. He pushed his phone back in his jacket pocket and stuffed the Christmas presents into three plastic carrier bags. He hoped Emma would like them. The thought that he no longer knew his nine-year-old daughter's tastes caused him a surge of anger towards his ex-wife, Catherine, who seemed determined to keep him as far away as possible from Emma as she could. Catherine had begrudgingly allowed him to see their daughter on the day before Christmas Eve after which she was whisking her off to spend Christmas on the Côte d'Azur on board her new boyfriend's luxury yacht. Peter Jarvis was chief executive of an international packaging company, divorced, and the fact that he was watching Emma grow up, while he was being shoved out, made the bile rise in Horton's throat.

He hurried out of the supermarket feeling irritable. The grey sky was heavy with the threat of sleet and there was an icy edge to the north-westerly wind. Predictions of a white Christmas were coming thick and fast but his experience of living on the south coast of England told him that by Christmas it would be mild, wet and windy. He didn't care either way. He'd be on duty. Much better to work than sit on his boat alone thinking of what he'd lost. He crossed the crowded car park to his Harley, where he put the goods into the pannier, and called Cantelli.

'Elkins has got a Christmas present for us,' Cantelli announced.

That didn't sound good. Dai Elkins was the sergeant in charge of the marine unit.

'It's not a body washed up on the beach, is it?' asked Horton, thinking about the last time he'd been called to view one, not by Elkins on that occasion but by former DCI Mike Danby who now ran a private close protection security company. That body had been found on the private beach of Lord Richard Eames' extensive Isle of Wight holiday property, five miles across the Solent from Portsmouth, in mid-October, and the investigation had led Horton further in his quest to discover the truth behind his mother's disappearance over thirty years ago. Not that anyone knew that, unless he counted Lord Eames, a client of Mike Danby, and the man Horton believed was involved in Jennifer's disappearance. He quickly shelved his thoughts on the progress of his own private investigations as Cantelli said, 'It's not a body, exactly.'

'What do you mean, "exactly"?'

'Don't know. Dai said we had to see it. I'm on my way to Oyster Quays Marina. Hope it doesn't mean I have to go on a boat,' Cantelli added warily.

'Probably. I'll meet you there.' Cantelli could get sick just looking at the sea, a decided drawback when living in a city surrounded by it.

Heading towards the popular waterfront development of shops, cafés, bars, restaurants and leisure outlets Horton was glad to let his troubled thoughts find refuge in work. He speculated as to what Elkins might have in store for them which warranted the summoning of CID, and why he was being so mysterious. A stash of drugs? But then he'd have called the drug squad. Perhaps he'd retrieved some stolen goods. But neither of those things matched with not 'exactly'. Well he'd find out soon enough he thought, swinging into the underground car park and riding the escalator to the shopping malls. A brisk walk through the crowded centre brought him to the waterfront where Cantelli was waiting by the marina gate. He was talking to a bulky, balding, uniformed officer.

'OK, so why the mystery?' Horton asked Elkins as he keyed a number into the security pad to admit them to the pontoons. An icy blast of wind billowed off the sea from the narrow entrance of Portsmouth Harbour. Horton could see the small green and white ferry crossing to the town of Gosport opposite and an orange and black pilot boat was making its way into the Solent, probably to escort a container ship or continental ferry into the port.

Elkins' expression was grave. 'You'll see.'

Horton's eyes flicked over the small marina but he could see nothing to warrant Elkins' gravity or the reason for his reticence. Whatever it was though he knew it had to be connected with the two men huddled in the cockpit of the police launch, which was moored up on the outlying pontoon facing on to the harbour. In front of the police launch was a blue-hulled motor cruiser and on board Horton could see PC Ripley. Elkins couldn't have arrested a couple of drug runners because he'd never have let them sit meekly on the powerful police launch awaiting arrest.

Cantelli pushed a hand into the pocket of his rain jacket and pulled out a packet of chewing gum. He offered it around. Horton declined but Elkins took a strip, saying, 'The thin guy with receding hair and the stoop is Lesley Nugent, the other fatter man is the owner of the boat Ripley's on; Clive Westerbrook. He suffers from high blood pressure and has a dickie heart.'

Then he should lose weight, thought Horton, but that was Westerbrook's business, not his.

Elkins said, 'They were fishing for bream off Boulder Bank, just off Selsey Bill, east of here,' he explained for Cantelli's benefit. Horton, being a sailor, knew exactly where it was, in fact he knew practically every nautical mile of the Solent. 'The tide runs hard over the Bank and floating weed can be a problem,' Elkins explained. 'Lesley Nugent says his line caught on some seaweed wrapped around a container. He reeled it in and was disentangling it when he noticed how heavy the container was. He opened it, with Clive Westerbrook watching, who said he nearly had a seizure when he saw what was inside.'

'And that was?' asked Horton, as they walked past the two men on the police launch. They both appeared nervous.

Elkins didn't answer but climbed on board the blue-hulled motor-boat. Horton followed suit while Cantelli elected to remain on the pontoon. The canvas awning had been rolled back from the cockpit and velcroed into place, exposing them to the biting wind sweeping off a grey choppy Solent beyond the harbour entrance. Swiftly Horton registered the fishing rods, reels, bait, tackle box containing long-nosed pliers, a filleting knife, elastic, hooks and other odds and ends. It was a bitterly cold day for fishing but he guessed the weather hardly mattered if you were a fanatic.

There were two seats at the helm and between the seats Horton could see down the hatch into the single cabin. On the right was a small galley. In the centre of the cabin was a table with nothing on it and seating either side of it which he knew, from the design of this type of boat, made up into a double bunk. To the left was the heads which would contain a sea toilet and sink. This boat was fine for an overnight stay, or for a few days if you weren't too fussy, but not for much more, although he had lived on a smaller boat than this after Catherine had thrown him out following those false rape allegations while he'd been working undercover two years ago. That little yacht had been destroyed in a fire, almost with him on board, and the yacht he now sailed and lived on board was luxury in comparison, and a great deal newer than this boat which was about twenty years old. But this was solidly built and classically designed, and would still be ploughing the Solent and the English Channel in another twenty years when its flashier and more modern and expensive cousins had been consigned to the boat scrapyard.

'This is what they fished up.' Elkins indicated the dirty white plastic container lying on the floor of the cockpit. It looked to Horton like the type used for containing ice cream or margarine bought from the wholesalers only there were no labels or markings on it and inside he could see the vague shape of something that caused him a puzzled frown. Elkins nodded at Ripley, who, with latex-covered fingers, prised open the lid. Horton started with surprise but it was Cantelli, peering over the side of the boat, who voiced his initial thoughts.

'My God! Is it real?'

'It's real all right,' Elkins said solemnly. 'You can see the arteries where it's been severed at the wrist.'

And the blackened exposed tissue, thought Horton, quickly recovering from his initial shock, staring at the human hand. The flesh, although a yellowish colour and emitting a sickly odour, was intact, no sea creatures or insect life had eaten into it, and there was no decomposition, which meant it couldn't have been in the sea for very long. The container could have protected it he supposed, it looked fairly waterproof. There were slithers of water in the bottom but they could have been caused when the container had been opened by the two fishermen. The hand was fairly broad but the fingers were thin, ringless and quite long. A man's hand he thought, though he'd leave that for Dr Gaye Clayton, the pathologist, to confirm. Mentally he measured it against his own hand and decided that whoever it had once been part of had been leaner than him. The nails were short, possibly bitten. He couldn't see any tattoos and he wasn't going to turn it over to find out if there were any on the palm.

'Could a boat propeller have sliced it off?' asked Cantelli.

'It could but that hardly accounts for it being in a container. And where's the rest of him?'

Cantelli shrugged and reached for his mobile phone inside his jacket pocket. 'I'll call in and check for missing persons over the last couple of weeks.'

Hopefully Dr Clayton would be able to lift fingerprints from the hand which might give them a quicker ID than waiting for DNA. Horton nodded at Ripley to replace the cover and instructed him to put the container in a plain brown paper evidence bag. He didn't want anyone ogling it as they transported it to Cantelli's car. Ripley disembarked and Horton addressed Elkins. 'Did the fishermen touch it or lift it out of the container?'

'They said they were too shocked to do anything except call the coastguard. When the coastguard received the panic stricken call from Clive Westerbrook at ten thirty-five they immediately thought that someone on board had chopped his hand off by accident. They rushed out, found this and called us.'

'Let's have a word with them.'

Clive Westerbrook looked haggard, his dark eyes were haunted and fearful, which was understandable given the circumstances thought Horton. His companion, Nugent, didn't look much better. Hunched into the collar of his waterproof jacket with his hands thrust deep in the pockets he eyed them like a man about to be executed.

'Is it some kind of sick joke?' Nugent asked, agitatedly.

'I'm afraid not,' Horton answered solemnly.

Nugent looked as though he was about to throw up. Elkins eyed him with alarm, probably at the thought that he'd have to clean up the vomit.

Horton quickly continued. 'We'd prefer it if you would say nothing about this for now especially to the media.' Leanne Payne, the local crime reporter, would love this, and so too would the national media. He added, 'We don't want to distress anyone unnecessarily.'

Nugent swallowed hard as he fought to get a grip on his nerves and his stomach. But Westerbrook's breathing became a little more laboured. 'I won't keep you long,' Horton said with genuine sympathy. 'You've both had a shock. Just a couple of questions. I understand the boat belongs to you, Mr Westerbrook?'

'Yes. I wish to God we'd just thrown the bloody thing back in without looking.'

And if they had perhaps someone else would have fished it up or it might have washed up along the south coast or across the Solent on the shores of the Isle of Wight for another person to discover. But when, and in what state, was anyone's guess. There probably wouldn't have been any fingers left, let alone prints, but there might still have been enough of the hand to extract DNA.

'Do you remember seeing anything else floating around the boat?' Horton could see by the nervous glance they exchanged that they were both following his train of thought, the body could have been close by, or certainly the remains of it either in or out of containers. Nugent shook his head. Westerbrook's skin turned a paler shade of grey. There was a thin film of perspiration on his brow. He looked ill and Horton was concerned about him. 'If you could give your contact details to Sergeant Elkins that will be all for now but we'll need a statement from both of you. You can come into the station and make it later.'

'No. I'll do it now,' Nugent hurriedly said. 'I can't face going back on that boat even if that thing has gone.'

'And I need to take my boat back to the marina,' Westerbrook said.

'And that is where?'

'Fareham.'

Horton had sailed into there a few times. It was a small marina nine miles to the west of Portsmouth by car and situated at the top and north-westerly end of the harbour. He didn't see any reason why Westerbrook shouldn't do that. His boat wasn't a crime scene so there was no need to seal it off and call in the Scene of Crime Officers. He was more concerned about Westerbrook being fit enough to handle the boat.

'Will you be all right?' he asked. 'PC Ripley could pilot it for you.'

'No. Thanks. My car's there. I'll call in at the police station on my way back home. I live here, in Portsmouth.'

Horton offered to get a car to take Nugent to the police station to make his statement but Nugent declined. 'I'll walk. I need the air.'

Horton understood that. Alighting, and out of earshot of the two men, Elkins said he and Ripley would take a look around the area where the hand had been found. 'Not that I'm expecting to find any more surprise packages, the tide will have shifted anything, but you never know.'

Horton joined Cantelli and together they headed back towards the boardwalk, Cantelli carrying the gruesome cargo.

'No reports of anyone missing over the last fortnight,' Cantelli reported. 'But that's only in this area. This,' he jiggled the bag, 'could have been thrown from the side of the Isle of Wight ferry or one of the continental ferries, or a container ship or cruise liner, which means it could have been brought from anywhere in the country and then dumped in the sea.'

'That's right, cheer me up.'

Cantelli smiled. 'And the hand could be older than a few days. It might have been stuffed in a freezer before being thrown in the sea, hence the container. It reminds me of a 1951 film *The Thing from Another World*. A space ship crashes in the North Pole with a humanoid alien on board and the Air Force sends in a team to investigate. They sever the creature's hand. It feeds on human blood and comes to life.'

'I don't think you're in danger of that, Barney, but if you don't show at the mortuary in thirty minutes I'll put a call out for you.'

Horton arrived at the mortuary ahead of Cantelli where he was told that Dr Clayton was at a medical conference in London and wouldn't be back until late afternoon. He stifled his disappointment and sought out her much respected mortuary attendant, Tom, by which time Cantelli had safely arrived. He placed the container on a mortuary slab in front of the burly, auburn-haired Tom, and Horton waited with keenness to hear the mortician's analysis.

'It's human all right,' Tom pronounced cheerfully, peering at it. 'Caucasian male.'

They'd got that far themselves. 'Any idea how it was severed?' asked Horton.

Tom shook his head. 'No, though I'd say expertly and cleanly. I'll take some photographs and email them over. There's very little decomposition, and although the skin is a bit dry, I should still be able to lift some decent fingerprints. I'll send them over to the fingerprint bureau.'

That might give them a match, always given that the victim was on the database, and Horton wasn't sure they'd be that lucky. 'Any idea on how long it's been parted from its owner?'

'Two, possibly three days. Dr Clayton will be able to give you more.'

They had to be content with that. Horton gave instructions for Tom to send the container to the lab for forensic examination and headed for the station mulling over the discovery. The hand could belong to a villain who'd had it hacked off as retribution for a crime perpetrated against some innocent person. Wasn't there something in the Bible about that? He'd ask Cantelli, him being a good Catholic boy, he should know. Religion had never featured in Horton's life. The only times he'd been to church had been in the course of work and when he'd got married and look where those vows had taken him. Catherine certainly hadn't stuck to him for better or worse.

Or perhaps the hand was that of a villain severed by a villain, possibly a rival gang member. And what had happened to the rest of the remains? How had the victim died? Had it been quick and painless? Or had he been beaten and tortured first? Had he been alive and conscious when the hand had been severed? What kind of person could do that? A heartless bastard was the answer, but then Horton quickly revised that, it could be someone fuelled with rage and hatred, someone intent on revenge, or someone mentally deranged. And although these were questions that Detective Superintendent Uckfield, head of the Major Crime Team, would ask, without more to go on Horton thought he was unlikely to get the answers.

Uckfield's BMW was in its allotted space but the head of CID and his boss, DCI Lorraine Bliss's sports car wasn't. Good. That suited Horton fine. No need to report to the ice maiden first. He made for Uckfield's office in the major incident suite and was surprised to find it a hive of activity. For a moment he wondered if the rest of the corpse had turned up but Trueman quickly put him right on that.

'It's Alfie Wright, he's done a bunk.'

That wasn't likely to put Uckfield in a very good mood. Horton knocked and entered the Super's office on his sharp command.

'What happened?' Horton asked, taking the seat across the desk and eyeing Uckfield's craggy face, flushed with fury.

'The bastard didn't show in court.'

Horton frowned, annoyed. 'Can't think why he wasn't remanded into custody in the first place.'

'Because Ewan Stringer pleaded mental health issues so damn well that it blew Tim Shearer's pathetic prosecution to pieces. Makes you wonder why we do this job. Might as well make us all redundant and let the low-life scum criminals do what they want.'

Horton wouldn't like to be in Shearer or Stringer's shoes.

Uckfield continued. 'If Tim Shearer had got more of a grip on the case Wright wouldn't have walked out of that court on conditional bail. If this is the standard of his work I wish he'd bugger off back to London where he came from.'

Horton disagreed about Shearer. He found him a breath of fresh air after the last Chief Crown Prosecutor, who had grown cynical and disillusioned, not that Horton blamed him for that, but he'd also grown careless. Shearer, however, was keen, intelligent and dedicated to his work, but now was obviously not the time to point this out.

Uckfield continued his rant. 'And as for that weedy nerd Stringer, of course Alfie Wright's got mental health issues, he's a bloody nutter.'

Stringer was a forensic mental health practitioner, who provided assessments on offenders for the courts. Horton knew that many offenders desperately needed psychiatric medical help rather than a prison stretch but not in Wright's case, he was a persistent and violent offender. And prison was what he fully deserved after his vicious attack on David Jewson, a family man in his forties, a bus driver, who'd been having a quiet pint with his family in a pub until Wright had taken a dislike to him. But instead of being remanded until the trial Wright had been given bail on the condition that he remain at his address, a bedsit in the centre of the city.

'When did Wright go missing?' Horton asked, wondering if the severed hand could be his. Perhaps the Jewson family had seen fit to dish out their own form of punishment, though from what Horton knew of them he thought it unlikely.

'No idea. Dennings and Marsden are out making enquiries but you know what they'll get from Wright's known associates – sod all.'

'Are any of his clothes and belongings missing?'

'Hard to tell because we've no idea what he had to begin with. There's nothing in his bedsit to indicate where he's gone, but a passport was issued to him four years ago and that's missing. There's an all ports alert out for him and I've got an officer at the international port showing his photograph around.'

Horton knew though, just as Uckfield did, that Alfie didn't necessarily have to board one of the continental or Channel Island ferries, it would be easy for him to slip across to the continent on a private boat if he knew anyone who owned one, and Horton doubted that. And although he could have stolen one Alfie knew as much about seafaring as he did about space travel. Then it suddenly occurred to Horton that Alfie might have been enticed on to a private boat by the promise of escaping prison, and once there its owner had killed and mutilated him, as revenge for a crime Alfie had previously committed against the boat owner. Was the hand Alfie Wright's? He was about to relay the news of the gruesome discovery but Uckfield hadn't finished yet.

'Stringer said he was most disappointed that Alfie had decided not to show. Disappointed! I told him that Alfie would be more than disappointed when I got hold of him and I will.'

Horton hoped so too. 'And he's no idea where Alfie's gone?'

'He says not,' Uckfield replied, his tone making it perfectly clear he didn't believe that. 'And that skinny bint from the local rag was there. So you can imagine the headlines in tomorrow's newspaper.'

Uckfield was referring to Leanne Payne, the crime reporter. Wright's disappearance might distract her from news of the severed hand but he wasn't counting on it.

'Wonder Boy's wetting his pants over it, says we should have had more evidence to have Wright remanded,' Uckfield continued with disgust. 'He bloody well reviewed all the evidence himself and said it was watertight. He's covering his arse quicker than a patient faced with an enema. Scared it will bugger up his promotion chances.'

ACC Dean's claims came as no surprise to Horton, he was passing the buck just as Uckfield and DCI Bliss frequently did when it suited them but Horton wasn't going to say. It was time to break the news. 'We've got a severed hand, Steve.'

Uckfield blinked then scowled. 'I hope it's Alfie Wright's,' he said sourly.

'That depends when he went walkabout. The mortuary attendant reckons it's about two to three days old. Dr Clayton is in London but should be back later this afternoon to give us more. It's not an accidental death,' and Horton explained why. 'Who would want to hack off Alfie's hand?'

'Me for starters,' Uckfield growled. 'And I'd throw the rest of his scrawny body to the fish. Reckon David Jewson's family would too, we'd better ask them when they last saw the runt.' He hauled himself up. 'If the fingerprints match Alfie Wright's then I'll buy everyone a pint, even that drippy git, Stringer. I might even stretch to include that incompetent Crown Prosecutor.' He crossed to his door, threw it open, and bellowed for Trueman to join them. When he arrived within seconds, Uckfield said, 'The Inspector's found some body parts. Tell him.'

Horton did. Uckfield gave instructions for Trueman to set up another crime board and for Horton to get everything over to them. Dismissed, Horton diverted to the canteen and bought a packet of sandwiches. He stopped off at the vending machine outside CID and fetched a black coffee for himself and a tea for Cantelli. There was no sign of DC Walters in CID which meant he was still following up Tuesday's petrol station robbery. The perpetrators had bored a large hole in the rear wall of a garage situated on one of the roads heading north out of the city and had then forced their way through to gain access to the shop where thousands of pounds of cigarettes and hundreds of pounds of alcohol had been stolen. It was the first of this kind of robbery and Horton hoped it would be the last, but he wasn't banking on it.

He gave Cantelli his paper cup of tea and took the seat at the desk alongside him. Cantelli's plastic container that usually held his sandwiches was empty. The gruesome discovery hadn't put him off his delayed lunch but then both of them had seen worse. 'So why hack off a hand?' Horton asked, after relaying that Alfie Wright had gone walkabout. 'Isn't there something in the Bible about it? An eye for an eye and a tooth for a tooth, could it be revenge?'

'That's the right hand.'

'It is a right hand.'

'Matthew chapter five verse thirty,' Cantelli said. '"And if thy right hand offend thee, cut it off, and cast it from thee."'

'I'm impressed. What does it mean?' Horton peeled back the plastic film on his ham salad sandwiches.

'Some say it's to do with adultery, others claim it refers to masturbation.'

'How?' Horton asked surprised, biting into his sandwich.

'The right hand is said to be one of the most important members of the body and therefore should be sacrificed rather than that we should commit sin and be poisoned by unholy thoughts and impure desires. The right hand is the organ of action to which the eye excites.'

Horton raised his eyebrows. 'What if you're left-handed,' he replied somewhat cynically.

'Or ambidextrous. Matthew's well into this stuff. Chapter eighteen verse eight: "If thy hand or thy foot offend thee, cut them off and cast them from thee."'

Horton continued eating with a troubled frown. 'Hope we're not going to find his feet.'

'Or eyes, because the next verse urges sinners to pluck out their eye and cast it out.'

Horton groaned. 'Don't tell me we've got a religious nutter on the patch.'

'Probably got several of them.'

'But mad enough to kill?'

'If driven hard enough or insane, yep.' Cantelli answered. Walters ambled in eating a jam doughnut. Cantelli continued. 'Alfie's got some nasty associates. I wouldn't put it past one of them to lop off his hand. But I can't see why they'd put it in a container, although there aren't many brain cells amongst them so they probably thought it would sink.'

'What would sink?' Walters asked, flopping on to the chair at his desk and wiping the jam from his chin. Cantelli told him while Horton finished his lunch. Cantelli asked Walters what he'd turned up on the petrol station robbery.

'No witnesses, no one heard anything, or saw anything, and there are no prints, a phantom petrol station robber.'

Except the theft wasn't imaginary, thought Horton. He wasn't surprised that Walters had gleaned nothing. The Golden Hour following the crime, when evidence was fresh and witnesses could come forward with useful information, wasn't much help in this instance because it had taken place between one and two a.m. Tuesday morning, which meant there were very few people about. In fact none given that it had been a bitterly cold morning, and the garage wasn't in a fashionable area of the town so no one around to take and post photographs and videos on the internet.

Walters said he'd take another look at the social media websites in case anyone had posted anything or one of the villains had been stupid enough to brag about it. Horton thought it unlikely given that it appeared to be a professional job but then villains could and often did behave foolishly, thankfully.

He rose and entered his office. Pulling open his slatted blinds he glanced up at the leaden sky. It certainly looked as though it was going to snow. He flicked on his computer and turned his attention to his emails. There was one from the Centre for the Study of Missing Persons, which was part of Portsmouth University. He knew the centre well from the research it conducted, the workshops and conferences it held and the information it published. Also with regards to the work it did with police forces around the UK and overseas. It was thirty years too late to help find his mother, Jennifer, and even if it had existed in some crude form then, Horton doubted anyone attached to it would have been allowed to discover any vital information about her disappearance because his own recent research had unearthed the fact that, incredible as it seemed, Jennifer had been working for British Intelligence.

He thought the email must be an invitation to a seminar. He didn't recognize the name of the sender, a Dr Carolyn Grantham, but then he didn't know everyone who worked there. His body stiffened as, scanning it, a name leapt out at him. Holding his breath he rapidly read that Dr Grantham was conducting research into missing persons cases of over twenty-five years standing and she wondered if she could meet him to discuss the disappearance of his mother, Jennifer Horton.

His heart skipped several beats. Why Jennifer? Why now when no one had been the slightest bit interested in her for just over thirty years? How much did Dr Grantham know? If it was just what was on the official file then it would be practically nothing because Jennifer's disappearance had only been cursorily investigated in 1978 and never since, not even by him until a year ago, when a case he'd been working on had led him to question the validity of what he'd been told as a child, that she'd grown tired of having a kid in tow and had run off with a man.

In January, Detective Chief Superintendent Sawyer of the Intelligence Directorate had entered the fray. He'd been, and was still as far as Horton knew, very keen to enlist Horton's help in flushing out the man Jennifer was believed to have absconded with, a master criminal wanted for several international jewellery and art thefts across the continent whom the Intelligence Directorate had code-named Zeus. Horton hadn't played ball. Sawyer could make a request for him to be seconded but so far he hadn't and he couldn't force him to work on the case because he'd be emotionally compromised. Perhaps Sawyer had instructed this Dr Grantham to make contact. It was Sawyer's way of getting more information and Horton's cooperation. Equally Lord Eames could have set this particular chain of enquiry in motion in order to discover how far Horton had got with his investigations, because Horton firmly believed that Eames was connected with British Intelligence and he knew Eames had been acquainted with Jennifer. Horton wouldn't put it past either of them. There was only one way to find out.

He punched the number into his mobile phone and with a racing heart waited for her to answer. She did and quickly. Horton announced himself and said a little stiffly, 'I received your email.'

'I know how painful this must be for you.'

Did she? Horton doubted it.

'And of course you don't have to tell me anything but if we could meet up and I could explain why I'm interested then you can tell me to get lost.'

His first reaction was to refuse, but that was an emotional response and the wrong one. 'When?' he asked, keeping his tone neutral.

'Tonight if you're not busy?'

How could he be when every night was the same except for when he was working on a serious crime and the severed hand was not his investigation and neither was the hunt for Alfie Wright.

'Where?'

'I'll buy you a drink. The Reef at Oyster Quays.'

It was a trendy bar on the waterfront which was frequented by students.

'Eight o'clock,' she suggested.

'How will I recognize you?'

'I'll be the only person over the age of thirty-four,' she said lightly.

'OK.'

He rang off and immediately called up the internet. First he checked the University of Portsmouth website but she wasn't listed as being a member of staff either at the University or at the Centre for the Study of Missing Persons. Next he entered her name in the general search engine and found she was mentioned on a number of professional and social media websites. There were a few photographs of her and he found himself studying an attractive dark-haired woman in her mid-thirties with an engaging smile and a long list of academic qualifications, as well as published research papers and articles to her name. She had a BA in Criminology and a PhD in Investigative Psychology. Her specialist areas and the papers and articles she'd had published were on missing persons and media bias; the costs of missing persons investigations and the repeat reports to the police of missing people, their locations and characteristics. Jennifer's disappearance didn't fit with any of those, there had been no media coverage, the investigation had cost nothing because only one police officer had been sent to follow it up, PC Adrian Stanley, and he was now dead, and there were certainly no repeated reports of her missing because she'd only vanished the once, on a foggy November day in 1978.

Work intruded, and Horton spent the next four hours answering phone calls, replying to emails, reading reports and briefing Bliss, who had returned from a meeting. She wasn't best pleased with the lack of progress on the petrol station robbery. He wasn't either but she regarded any failure on his part as a sign of his incompetence. Ever since her promotion and transfer from a station outside the city to Portsmouth and CID just over a year ago she'd been looking for a way to get him out of her ponytail. So far she hadn't succeeded but Horton knew it would only be a matter of time, unless she managed to wangle herself a higher profile position in another unit and the sooner the better as far as he was concerned. He told her about the discovery of the hand and that he had reported it to

Uckfield and that they were awaiting Dr Clayton's further examination of it.

At six thirty Cantelli popped his head around the door to say he was off home and that Clive Westerbrook hadn't been in to make his statement. That surprised Horton. Westerbrook had had plenty of time to return his boat to the marina and drive back to Portsmouth.

'I've tried the mobile number he gave Elkins, there's no answer. Do you want me to send a unit round to his flat? He lives at Spring Court.'

That wasn't very far from the station. Horton said he'd call in on his way home or rather before his meeting with Dr Grantham. The more he considered Westerbrook's no show though the more concerned he grew. He'd certainly looked unwell at Oyster Quays and Elkins had said Westerbrook had a weak heart. Perhaps he'd been taken ill heading back to Fareham Marina but if that was the case then his boat would have been found in the harbour and reported to the harbour master. Maybe it had been.

He rang through to them but there had been no such incidents. There was no point enquiring at the marina to see if Westerbrook's boat was there because the marina office was closed now and Horton certainly wasn't going to walk the dark pontoons searching for it. Perhaps Westerbrook needed more time to recover from the shock of his discovery and intended to come into the station tomorrow morning.

Just before eight, Horton headed north towards Spring Court. Light flakes of snow were falling. He could see several lights, including coloured Christmas ones, shining and blinking in the windows of some of the flats. The building backed on to a band of trees and the motorway. Horton could hear the roar of the traffic as he pressed the buzzer to flat sixteen. Still no answer. He tried again with the same result. Maybe he should call up and effect an entry, but surely that wasn't necessary. Westerbrook had probably gone out for something to eat, or was with a friend or partner, talking over his ordeal. He glanced at his watch. It was five past eight and he was late for his meeting. He climbed on the Harley and with a mixture of anticipation and apprehension made for The Reef at Oyster Quays, hoping that Dr Grantham would still be there.

TWO

The heat and noise hit him like a shockwave. The bar was packed and the Christmas music so loud that Horton thought they'd be able to hear it in France, ninety miles across the Channel. Why Dr Grantham had chosen this as a meeting place was a mystery because he'd never be able to make himself heard above the racket, let alone hear what she had to say. He stood at the entrance wondering if the best course of action would be to leave, if only to protect his eardrums. He could telephone her and rearrange their meeting at a more suitable place, but that would delay matters and now that he was here, he guessed he might as well press on.

He quickly scanned the crowded bar, wondering if perhaps she'd already given up on him. Despite what she had said about being the only one under the age of thirty-four, there were several people older. He registered a couple of men in their early forties in amongst the groups of students. There was also a man in his mid-fifties at the bar, drinking alone, and four women in their fifties, plied with bling and make-up, clustered around one of the many high tables dotted about the place. Then he spotted her on the far right of the bar. Her photographs hadn't done her justice, she was far more attractive in the flesh and even from where he was standing he could see there was a lot of it on show.

He thrust his way towards her feeling ridiculously overdressed and overheated in his motorbike leathers. She was talking to a blonde man in his early twenties wearing jeans and a wide smile along with a T-shirt and a close cropped beard. Or rather the man was talking and Dr Grantham was looking bored. She glanced beyond the youth and her eyes locked with his. Horton caught a fleeting hint of surprise before recognition, perhaps he too looked different to what she had expected.

Raising his voice above the clamorous crowd, he bellowed, 'Dr Grantham?'

'Yes,' she shouted back.

The fair young man swung round and studied Horton coolly and assessingly with pale blue eyes. Then he shrugged, smiled pleasantly and said, 'See you around Dr Grantham,' and walked off with a slight swagger.

'One of your students?' Horton again shouted.

'I don't have students. I'm conducting a research project. I think that young man was trying to chat me up.'

That was Horton's cue to say that he had good taste, but he didn't. He formally introduced himself, offering his hand to establish the business nature of the meeting. She took it with a smile. Her handshake was dry and firm, and her eye contact confident with a hint of sensuality that caused him his second quickening of pulse since spotting her. He steeled himself against her obvious charms.

'Can I get you a drink?' he bawled above a sudden burst of raucous laughter and a sing-along to one of the Christmas songs being pumped out. He'd rather have said can we get the hell out of here.

'Brandy and soda,' she shouted back.

Good job he could lip read he thought, pushing his way to the bar. He'd been given to understand that students were hard up but judging by what he could see here they must have been saving up their student grant, unless they had wealthy parents to subsidize their drinking.

He bellowed his request for a brandy and soda and a Diet Coke to the pubescent barmaid who looked as though she had a hangover along with a skin problem. She had to be over eighteen to work behind the bar but she looked more like fifteen. Horton made a mental note to ask uniform to check out the place.

'I could have chosen somewhere quieter to talk,' Carolyn Grantham said, taking her drink from him on his return. 'But I thought this might not make you feel obliged to talk to me whereas a quieter less frenetic environment might have done.'

So there was method in her madness. No one would hear a word he said here. He removed his jacket and thrust it on the floor by his feet. Carolyn Grantham had already done the same with her black coat and red scarf, and there was a computer case beside them. He thought the sooner they got this over with the better. 'You wanted to talk about Jennifer Horton.'

She took a large pull at her brandy before answering. She didn't look nervous but maybe she was. 'Yes. Your mother.'

She eyed him closely but he made sure not to betray any reaction. He was after all an expert at hiding his emotions, he'd had years of practice. Catherine had accused him of being too cold, too distant, but then she would say that to assuage her guilt over deserting him, and having an affair while they were married, although he had no proof of the latter, just suspicions. It didn't matter now anyway.

'I realize that this must be difficult for you,' Dr Grantham continued. She moved closer to him to make herself heard and Horton caught the soft smell of her musky perfume, not to mention an eyeful of her cleavage, encased in a figure-hugging dress, and it was a figure worth hugging. Did her words have a double meaning because he was finding it difficult not to respond to her physically? But again he made sure to hide his emotions. She continued, 'And I know this is not the right place to discuss such a sensitive matter but if you feel able to talk about Jennifer's disappearance then I'd be very happy to meet you in a more relaxed, quiet and private environment.'

'There isn't anything to talk about,' he said evenly and loudly. 'She vanished on the 30 November 1978 and that's it.'

'Have you ever tried to find out what happened to her?'

He eyed her steadily. Did she already know the answer to that question? He wasn't sure. 'It's the past. It won't change things,' he said neutrally.

'But it leaves a gap.'

Of course it did he wanted to snap, a great yawning chasm that he had tried to learn to live with until a year ago when an investigation had opened the lid on it.

Hastily she continued. 'Look, if you decide you'd like to cooperate in my research or just talk to me then call or email me. If you don't that's fine. If you want more information about me then I'd be happy to provide it and references. I don't expect you to take me on trust.'

He took a pull at his drink. 'How many other cases are you examining?'

'I'm focusing on five, all from the 1970s.'

'Why then?'

'Pardon?' she cried, leaning even closer to him as more loud laughter rang out behind her.

'I said why the 1970s?'

'Because the date is far enough back to make a good comparison between the way such cases were treated then compared with now. I'll explain,' she quickly added to his puzzled and probably sceptical glance. 'If I can make myself heard. Do you want to continue this outside?'

'Go on.' She'd been right. Outside was cold and quiet. There would be more pressure on him to confide. Even though he knew he could resist that, he'd still feel obliged to offer that they go somewhere warm and quiet, perhaps for a meal, and that could lead to him relaxing his guard. He wasn't ready to do that yet. Maybe never. And why should he play easy to get, especially if she was in Sawyer or Lord Eames' pocket.

She smiled as though reading his thoughts. 'I'm looking at missing adults as opposed to children. Two of the five adults I'm focusing on are from Hampshire, Jennifer Horton from Portsmouth and Brenda Myers from Andover. There's more information on Brenda than on Jennifer and Brenda still has a sister and two brothers living but there's only the skimpiest of reports on Jennifer's disappearance but then you'd know that. I'm not investigating the cases but examining how they were reported and managed; the experiences of the relatives then and their views now; and what, if anything, they did to try and locate the missing person along with the emotional and psychological effect on the family, but my key area of research is how the media portrayed such cases then and how that compares with similar cases today.'

Horton took a swig at his Coke.

She continued. 'In Jennifer's case there was zero media coverage because of you being a child, I suspect, and, so far as I can see from the file, she had no living relatives to kick up a fuss. Is that correct?'

'Yes.' He took another pull at his Coke while watching her. A burst of laughter and another chorus of out-of-tune singing to one of the Christmas songs caused Carolyn Grantham to frown. He said, 'I can't tell you anything other than what's in the file.'

She would know from it that PC Adrian Stanley had interviewed two people at the casino where Jennifer had worked as a croupier, her boss, George Warner and a fellow croupier Irene Ebury, both of whom were dead. Stanley had also taken a statement from their neighbour at the council tower block where they had lived. Mrs Cobden at Jensen House had reported that Jennifer had last been seen leaving their flat at about one o'clock on 30 November 1978 wearing her best clothes and make-up, and in good spirits. There had been no further investigation, or if there had been the evidence of it had been destroyed.

'I can't help you.'

There was a short pause before she smiled again and tossed back her brandy. 'OK.' Bending down and treating him to another eyeful of cleavage she retrieved her computer bag, coat and scarf. Straightening up she added, 'If you change your mind then you know how to contact me.' She stretched out her hand. 'Thanks for coming anyway and for the drink.'

He watched her leave, then swallowed the rest of his drink and got out of the hellhole as quickly as he could. The cold air struck him a welcoming icy blast and he could see her shapely figure ahead as it swung on to the escalator down to the car park. It was still snowing. He followed more slowly. There was no sign of her by the time he reached his Harley. She was already heading home, wherever that was. Time he was too.

The thin sharp flakes beat into his visor as he rode carefully along the seafront eastwards to the marina. Perhaps he'd been too abrupt. He certainly hadn't discovered anything from her but then the choice of her meeting place had made that impossible, deliberately so he wondered? Or was he just too suspicious. The questions that had formed in his mind when he'd first seen the email and again before his meeting were still there. How genuine was she? If he'd been smart he would have played along with her slightly flirtatious and seductive manner and got the answers. But he wasn't ready for that yet. Maybe he wasn't ready or willing to play that game at all. Perhaps it was time to draw a line under the whole thing and move on.

The dark night swallowed up the sea on his right leaving a black abyss. He felt as though he was stuck in one. There were no lights visible on any passing ships because there weren't any sailors foolish enough to be at sea in this weather, but neither could he see the lights of boats anchored up off the Isle of Wight or any life form itself on the island five miles across the Solent. There weren't even any lovers in their parked cars with steamed up windows. It was as though he had the world to himself, or rather as though he was alone in the world. He tried to push the thought aside and yet

Catherine's refusal to let him spend time with Emma, the thought of the lonely Christmas ahead and his daughter growing up without him depressed him. He'd always been alone.

The snow was thickening and beginning to form a light dusting on the pavements and on the only car in the marina car park, which belonged to Eddie in the marina office. Horton drew to a halt and silenced the engine. Everything was quiet except for the soft moan of the wind through the rigging of the yachts. He made for his yacht scanning the car park and road as he went but there was nothing untoward and no one sitting in a parked car, watching him. But then why should they be, Eames and the intelligence services knew where he lived.

His yacht was cold. Catherine's assertion that it was completely unsuitable for Emma to stay on overnight depressed him further because she was right. But it wasn't quite the Dark Ages he thought crossly, tossing the bags containing Emma's Christmas presents on to the table. He had access to electricity on the pontoon and he had heaters on the boat. He didn't feel the cold but a nine-year-old girl would. *Not in the Riviera on Peter Jarvis's yacht.* And his gifts would look puny alongside Catherine's and her boyfriend's. Emma probably wouldn't even be permitted to take them with her.

Dejected he made a black coffee and sat at the table. His thoughts drifted back to his meeting with Carolyn Grantham. She hadn't conjured up painful memories because they were there anyway, all the time, only he'd learned how to shut them out, until last Christmas when he'd got the first hint that what he'd been told about Jennifer running off with a man wasn't true.

His mind flashed back to the first Christmas without his mother. He'd been ten. His stomach constricted at the agonizing memory of his isolation and desolation. Despite his best efforts the pain never went away, it was as intense now as it had been then. Even Bernard and Eileen Litchfield's attempts to make Christmas happy for him after he'd gone to live with them at the age of fourteen hadn't succeeded. By then he'd had four years of Christmases spent in children's homes and with other foster parents who wouldn't have known the true meaning of Christmas if it had slapped them in the face. After his marriage he'd spent twelve years with Catherine, seven of them with her and his daughter, trying so very hard to make up for those lonely despairing Christmases and look where that had got him? Alone. Again.

A noise outside made him start. He listened for it, unable to define exactly what it had been, but there was only silence. Even the soft wind had dropped, and the snow was muffling everything. He was tempted to take a look but resisted. It was probably something out to sea.

Had he gone as far as he could with trying to discover the truth behind Jennifer's disappearance? He reached into his pocket and retrieved his wallet. From inside he removed a worn and creased black and white photograph taken in 1967 during the student sit-in protest at the London School of Economics, where Jennifer had worked as a typist.

He'd studied it so many times that he knew every feature of the six men in it by heart. He'd discovered who they all were. Five of them were dead: Timothy Wilson had been killed in a motorbike accident in 1969 on a deserted road on Salisbury Plain on a calm, clear April night. James Royston had died of a heroin overdose in a sordid bedsit in 1970. Zachary Benham had perished, along with twenty-three other men, in a fire that had raged through the ward of a psychiatric hospital in Surrey in 1968. Rory Mortimer had been killed by Antony Dormand who had been alive when Horton had last seen him on a dark wet October night on a beach on the Isle of Wight. It was Dormand who had confessed to Horton that he had killed Rory Mortimer under orders from the intelligence services because Mortimer, like Royston and Wilson, had been a traitor, selling his country's secrets to the Russians. When Horton had asked if Dormand had also killed Wilson and Royston he hadn't answered. Was that an admission in itself? And Horton recalled Dormand's chilling words before he'd boarded a small boat and motored away into the dark night of the Solent. Jennifer had disappeared in 1978 when there had been a spate of bombs set off by the IRA in Northern Ireland and Britain. Dormand had claimed she was involved with British Intelligence and the IRA. But Horton wasn't sure if he could believe that. The sixth man, Lord Richard Eames, was very much alive.

His thoughts veered to the well-built, athletic man in his mid-sixties who had left this picture stuffed behind the cushion on his boat in June. He'd introduced himself to Horton as Edward Ballard, except Ballard didn't exist, certainly not on any databases Horton had checked. It was an alias. Ballard had told Horton he was sailing to Guernsey but, according to Inspector John Guilbert of the States of Guernsey police, a good friend of Horton's, Ballard had never arrived, or at least not in any of the official marinas. He could have moored up at a private house but finding which one would take police resources, which meant making it an official enquiry and Horton hadn't wanted that. He'd since discovered that Eileen Litchfield, his foster mother, had come from Guernsey. So too did a lot of people but Horton was convinced that Ballard had rescued him from the horror of those children's homes and placed him with Bernard and Eileen Litchfield when he was fourteen. And that it was Ballard he'd seen hand his foster father a tin which Bernard had given to him containing his birth certificate, with no mention of who his father was, and a photograph of Jennifer. Both had been destroyed in that fire on his previous boat.

Guilbert had made some enquiries about Eileen and mentally Horton replayed the telephone conversation that had taken place between them last Wednesday.

'Eileen Litchfield, née Ducale, was a twin,' Guilbert had relayed.

And that had been a complete shock to Horton. She'd never mentioned that, or any other living relative even when she had been dying of cancer, and none had attended the funeral, only a handful of neighbours, because he'd had no list of names or contacts to invite. Eileen had been a very private person.

Horton's interest had deepened as Guilbert had continued with his unofficial report.

'She and her brother, Andrew, were born in 1942 on Guernsey and both left the island in 1961. Eileen to join the Civil Service in London and Andrew to study at Cambridge.'

Lord Eames had been at Cambridge between 1964 and 1967. Had their paths crossed?

Horton had asked Guilbert what Andrew Ducale had studied but Guilbert didn't know. He'd continued, 'Their father, William, was a police officer and remained one throughout the German occupation. He died in 1967 and their mother, Florence, died in 1958. There's an aged aunt living on the island, Violet Ducale, sister of the twins' father.'

Horton had asked Guilbert to find out if the aunt had any photographs of the twins. He was very keen to see pictures of Andrew

Ducale, feeling certain that he'd recognize him if it was the man who had called himself Edward Ballard. He'd told Guilbert it was a personal matter and Guilbert had accepted that, as Horton knew he would. Horton trusted him as much as he trusted Cantelli, which was completely. He hadn't had the opportunity to dig into Andrew Ducale's background. Maybe soon he would. He was due a few days off and if he wasn't needed to help find Alfie Wright and the owner of the severed hand, which again he thought might be one and the same, then he'd take some leave.

He stuffed the photograph back in his wallet wondering what to do about Dr Carolyn Grantham. If he stuck to his decision not to co-operate with her research what would she do? Respect it or find some other reason to contact him? The answer depended on how genuine she was and perhaps how desperate she, or the person she reported to, was to know just how much he'd discovered about his mother's disappearance. Maybe tomorrow he'd have the answer.

THREE

Thursday

'Any news of Alfie Wright?' Horton asked Sergeant Warren the next morning. He'd risen early and despite the fine layer of snow had gone for a run along the promenade to clear his head after a restless troubled night of lustful dreams of Carolyn Grantham, who alarmingly became Jennifer, who in turn became Alfie Wright and in amongst all three was the sweating florid face of Clive Westerbrook and the severed hand that had taken on a life of its own. He blamed Cantelli for the latter. He'd called at Westerbrook's flat before heading for the station. There had been no answer when he'd rang the bell and he'd been reluctant to trouble the neighbours. He didn't want to alarm them unnecessarily. Westerbrook could have decided to stay with a friend. But if so then why wasn't he answering his mobile?

Warren said, 'Not unless Alfie's using an alias and has had a face transplant, which would save us from looking at his ugly mug again.'

Horton asked if Clive Westerbrook had been in to make his statement. And as he expected was told he hadn't.

Grabbing a coffee on his way to his office, Horton rang through to the Accident and Emergency department at the hospital and enquired if Clive Westerbrook had been admitted. The answer was no, and no unidentified males had been either. Next he called up the vehicle licensing database and keyed in Westerbrook's name. He obtained the registration number of his car and rang it through to Fareham police station with a request that an officer visit the marina car park to see if the vehicle was there but to do nothing except report back. He was told it might be a while before they could get someone over there, resources were tied up dealing with a multiple accident on the motorway. Horton then rang through to Warren and asked him to send a uniformed officer round to Spring Court to check if the vehicle was parked anywhere in the vicinity. Horton couldn't remember seeing it out front but it could be in a nearby street.

Putting his concerns about Westerbrook on hold, Horton focused on Dr Grantham. He called up the Missing Persons database and found the details on Brenda Myers. It was as she had said, but he hadn't doubted that part of her story. Brenda Myers had been living in Andover in the family home with her mother, sister and two brothers. She'd left for where she worked, a shoe shop in the centre of the town, on Saturday morning and had never arrived. She had been twenty-three when she had disappeared and had no boyfriend. Horton didn't call up the full report, there was no connection between Brenda and Jennifer's disappearance apart from the fact that Dr Grantham claimed to be interested in both for her research. If her research was fake, a cover designed to find out from him what he knew about Jennifer's disappearance, then whoever had sent her would have made sure that it would check out. And that meant the university would also have been primed with all the correct details.

He turned his attention to the reports of crimes that had come in overnight. It had been remarkably quiet, the snow always kept the villains at home. And there had been no further petrol station raids. His phone rang and from the display he could see it was Bliss.

'Your team, in the incident suite, immediately, Inspector,' she commanded with her usual curtness and rang off. She'd never been one for small talk, and Horton couldn't recall her ever having uttered the words 'good morning', 'well done' or 'thank you' but then she wasn't alone in that respect. Both Uckfield and ACC Dean's vocabulary seemed to be sadly lacking those phrases. He wondered if the summons meant that further body parts had been found, except he'd seen nothing in the reports to say they had been and Sergeant Warren hadn't mentioned it. He rose and entered CID as Cantelli arrived carrying the local newspaper. 'The witch in the wardrobe requests our pleasure in the incident suite. She didn't say why.'

'It could be in connection with this.' Cantelli handed Horton the newspaper.

Horton winced at the headline, 'Police allow violent criminal to abscond'. *Thanks, Leanne*, though to be fair she wouldn't have penned the headline. But anyone reading this would think they'd either failed to arrest Wright or had simply patted him on the head and let him go. Uckfield was going to be very pissed off about this and the ACC would give, or might already have given, the Super a bollocking. The full article was on page three. Horton turned to it and quickly read it. Uckfield had been right. Leanne Payne had gone to town on Alfie Wright absconding. There was a photograph of his lean-featured face, looking slightly cocky, taken after he had appeared in court and been granted conditional bail, along with details of the vicious assault he'd committed on David Jewson. The article implied that the police had let him escape their clutches, she was wrong on that score but she was correct in describing Alfie Wright as a dangerous man. He had a quick temper which accelerated to hyper speed when fuelled by alcohol.

She'd also backed up her article by listing other criminals who had evaded the law including two men from the Portsmouth area: Wayne Naughton who had been awaiting trial for conspiracy to supply cocaine and Gordon Penlee, a phoney art dealer granted unconditional bail on 26 November and due to appear before Portsmouth Magistrates on Wednesday 5 December, only he'd vanished as had Naughton. Horton's feelings echoed Uckfield's fury. It beggared belief that a criminal could be convicted then allowed to roam free before being sentenced. Most were remanded when committing a serious crime but that was dependent on the barristers' ability and the magistrate or judge sitting at the time. And Alfie had been very lucky in the judge who had sat at his hearing, Nigel Appley, and the barrister who had defended him, Douglas Pylam.

Horton didn't know how Tim Shearer had squared up against them, he hadn't been in court, maybe Shearer had been unlucky, or had had an off day. He'd certainly not been as sharp as Pylam.

Alongside the list of the local men who had disappeared was a list of six other wanted criminals, most of them on drugs related offences, and one who had been tried at the Royal Courts of Justice, in the Strand, London for bankruptcy but was wanted for fraud on a massive scale, Jesse Stanhope, whose relatives lived in Portsmouth, all of whom categorically denied any knowledge of where he was or any part in his disappearing act. Horton wouldn't be surprised if this made the national media, and tomorrow Leanne might have another big story to add to her CV, that of the severed hand, which could belong to Alfie Wright.

'Not good,' Horton said, handing the paper back to Cantelli and heading into the corridor. 'Where's Walters?'

'Where do you think?'

'We'll collect him on our way.'

Walters looked bereft at being parted from his fried breakfast, which he'd only just started. Horton told him his arteries would probably be relieved at the reprieve.

Bliss greeted them with her usual scowl and glanced pointedly at her watch as they entered the crowded incident suite. What had she expected? For them to have been tele-transported? Clearly, her 'immediately' was not the same as his but then they disagreed on almost everything, especially the manner of catching criminals. Bliss was strictly a 'by the book' copper, and while Horton recognized they were operating in a tough climate that had to bear rigid scrutiny, much of the heaps of paperwork they were forced to deal with he considered a waste of time. Uckfield, legs akimbo, stood at the head of the room by the crime board, beside him was the muscle-bound, short-necked and cropped-haired DI Dennings. The room fell silent, as, with one deepening glare, Uckfield called it to order.

'The fingerprints on the severed hand are not Alfie Wright's,' he announced.

Horton thought there was a hint of disappointment or perhaps it was frustration in Uckfield's voice.

'But we do have a match.'

Horton's pulse quickened.

'They're Graham Langham's.'

'Langham!' Horton repeated, surprised. 'Are you sure?'

Bliss glared at Horton for daring to question a senior officer. She didn't know Langham, not having worked the patch, otherwise she would have understood his surprise. She'd also have understood Cantelli's and Walters' shocked expression, and Uckfield's irritation. They were all very familiar with Graham Langham.

'There's no doubt,' Uckfield declared. 'Langham's done his last job. He was a crook, and not a very good one, spent more time in prison than out of it, petty theft was his speciality, not serious crime, so why would someone hack off his hand?'

'Perhaps he helped himself to something he shouldn't have done and the owner took revenge,' Dennings suggested.

Horton thought of what he and Cantelli had discussed about the Bible but that didn't fit because Cantelli had said the hacking off of the right hand had something to do with masturbation or adultery, and Horton couldn't see any woman wanting to have sex with the scrawny weed that Langham had been, except his wife Moira. Someone would have to break the news to her. But of course the person who had committed such an atrocity might not know his Bible, probably didn't.

Cantelli said, 'He never took anything very valuable. His usual MO was quick in and out: usually garages, garden sheds, anything that looked an easy target. He'd take what he could, no matter what it was.'

Walters chipped in. 'Perhaps the householder Langham stole from chopped off Langham's hand in self-defence, thinking he was going to be attacked, then seeing what he'd done he got scared. He had to get rid of the body so he chopped it up, stuffed the body parts in kitchen containers and disposed of it as best he could by chucking it in the sea when he went out along the beach or in a boat.'

Dennings took it up. 'And if he did it piecemeal perhaps he thought no one would notice.'

Walters continued, 'He could even have left the containers on the shore, while no one was looking. Sort of taken them with him pretending they contained his sandwiches, and then acted absent-mindedly as though he'd forgotten it.'

'Must be pretty big sandwiches,' quipped Uckfield.

Walters shrugged. 'Depends on how small you can cut up a body. Maybe he cut it into tiny bits.'

Uckfield eyed him sceptically. 'Ask Dr Clayton, she'll know all about corpse dismemberment.' There was a moment's silence while everybody contemplated the grisly thought.

Cantelli broke it. 'Perhaps Langham got into a fight and someone hacked his hand off with a knife.'

Horton answered, 'But why not just leave it by the body, or ditch it without putting it in a container?'

Uckfield crisply continued. 'OK so what else do we know about Langham?'

He'd made no mention of the newspaper article but Horton knew he had seen it. There was a copy on Trueman's desk.

Cantelli answered. 'Married to Moira, a former prostitute and drug addict. Three kids the last I heard, could be more by now but if there are they're not Langham's, he got sent down for burglary for four years.'

Trueman looked up. 'He served just under three in Winchester Prison. He was released two months ago.'

Horton said, 'He didn't live long to enjoy his new-found freedom. It could be the act of a villain who was banged up with him intent on revenge who took it as soon as he was out. Perhaps Langham put his nose out of joint while inside.'

Trueman said he'd checked who else had been released in the last two months and if Langham had antagonized anyone while inside.

'Could be a long list,' muttered Cantelli.

Horton addressed Dennings. 'Did Langham know Alfie Wright?'

'Not that we know of.'

'Then bloody well check,' roared Uckfield.

A fraught silence followed Uckfield's outburst. It was as though everyone was holding their breath. Dennings' lips tightened as he threw Horton a look that would have felled ten sword-wielding Samurai in seconds.

Horton said, 'Perhaps Graham had pissed Alfie off and he killed him and has gone on the run. Alfie's vicious enough to have done it, although I can't see him putting the hand in a container and then throwing it in the sea, unless he did it while on board a boat, owned by someone helping him to make his escape, but why would Alfie kill Langham?'

Bliss said, '*They* could have served time together.'

Trueman said he'd check that.

Horton added, 'I suppose Graham Langham could have been in the Jolly Sailor when Wright attacked David Jewson. Langham saw what happened and threatened to tell unless Wright paid up. Wright's not having that and kills him.'

Dennings quickly addressed Uckfield, 'I'll get some officers down to the Jolly Sailor asking if they remember seeing Langham there on the night Jewson was attacked. They can show his picture around. And we'll reinterview members of the Jewson family.'

Horton asked if they had anything further on the last sighting of Alfie Wright.

Dennings curtly replied, 'We've placed him in The Trafalgar Arms in Fratton Road on Saturday morning. But we can't find anyone who knows what time he left. The landlord didn't see him go, said it was too busy because of the football match that afternoon. No one saw him return to his flat.'

'Did Dr Clayton provide any more information about the hand?' Horton asked.

Trueman answered. 'She got held up in London. She's looking at it this morning.'

Horton said, 'If it's two to three days old, as the mortician claimed, then why didn't Moira report him missing?'

'Well, you can ask her,' said Uckfield. 'Take Cantelli with you for protection. If I remember rightly Moira's bite is certainly worse than her bark and unless she's cut her fingernails you could end up scarred for life.'

Cantelli had nicked Graham Langham more times than anyone.

'Perhaps she's relieved he's gone,' Bliss said.

Maybe, thought Horton. 'I could talk to Ewan Stringer, he might know if Alfie had ever come across Langham.'

Uckfield nodded assent. He scratched his crotch and sniffed loudly before continuing. 'No doubt some of you have seen the local rag, and if you haven't then you soon will or someone will delight in pointing it out to you. Finding that scum bag Wright is our priority.'

Not who killed Langham then, thought Horton, but didn't say. Maybe they were one and the same, anyway.

'We go all out to locate him. DI Dennings will head the team with full resources while DCI Bliss will oversee the investigation into Langham's suspected murder. And I want that kept firmly under wraps, no leaks to the media.' Uckfield glowered at everyone. Bliss's narrow mouth tightened. To Horton, Uckfield said, 'Will the two men who fished it up talk to the press?'

'I don't think so.' Horton didn't think now was the best time to mention that they couldn't find one of them to ask him. 'But I'm not sure that Moira will keep quiet about it.'

'Then tell her it will hinder us finding who killed her old man.'

Horton wasn't convinced that would be enough of an incentive.

Uckfield continued. 'If the media come sniffing around, refer them to me or DCI Bliss. Is that understood?'

Everyone solemnly and rapidly agreed.

Uckfield added, 'We treat these as two separate investigations unless we obtain evidence that says otherwise. Well get to it.' Uckfield stomped off to his office.

Bliss turned to Walters, crisply she said, 'Check out the fights reported over the last few nights to see if any of them involved Langham. And get everything you can on him? I'll tell Sergeant Trueman that you'll contact the prison and obtain information on Langham's sentence and inmates. I'll contact Beverley Attworth at the Probation Office and find out who Langham's offender manager is and the rules of his probation, when his last meeting was and when the next one was scheduled.' Addressing Horton she continued. 'Break the news to Moira Langham, find out when she last saw him and who his associates were and then report back.'

Horton refrained from saying that he knew how to do his job. The sooner he and Cantelli got out of the station the better. Any delay might make her ask to see Nugent and Westerbrook's statements, and then he'd have to admit that Westerbrook hadn't yet made one. As she turned to Trueman, Horton quickly made his escape with Cantelli and Walters.

In the corridor he asked Walters to contact Elkins. 'Find out from him what time Westerbrook headed up Portsmouth Harbour from Oyster Quays and get him to check with the marina manager when he arrived. I've got an officer from Fareham checking if his car is in the marina car park, find out if they've reported back yet, if not ask Elkins if he can get that information from the marina manager. Brief him about Graham Langham. Ask if he knows where Westerbrook and Nugent work.' To Cantelli he said, 'I'll call Stringer on the way to Moira's and find out when he's available. Have you got Moira Langham's address?'

Cantelli nodded.

'Then let's go and break the bad news to her.'

FOUR

'W ell, don't just stand there. Come in. Otherwise the nosy bugger neighbours will be wetting themselves with excitement, thinking you're on a drugs bust,' Moira greeted them twenty minutes later.

It had taken them longer than expected to reach the flat, which backed on to a busy road leading into the city centre. The chaos even the light smattering of snow earlier had caused on the roads had left its legacy of vehicle shunts. But Horton was pleased to see that the snow had vanished, the temperature had risen dramatically and the morning had turned damp, cloudy and clammy. On the way he'd called Stringer who said he would be in the CPS offices next to the law courts for the remainder of the morning. Horton hadn't mentioned why he wanted to see him but it wouldn't take much for Stringer to guess his purpose. He'd also received a call to say that Westerbrook's car was not parked outside Spring Court or in any of the adjacent roads. Horton would wait until he heard back from Elkins before raising the alarm. He hoped he wouldn't have to. But as he'd said to Cantelli, it was worrying that there was still no answer on his mobile phone.

As they had walked from the car to Moira's flat Horton had wondered if Langham owned a vehicle. They hadn't checked before coming out but even if they had Horton doubted it would show up on the vehicle licensing database because it was unlikely that Langham would have gone to the expense of insuring and taxing it. Cantelli agreed.

'Should we be looking for drugs?' Horton said mildly, following Moira's sloppily dressed figure into the small hallway that was yellow with nicotine and smelt like a fishmongers on a bad day. Paradise Mews hardly lived up to its name, and while some of the occupants had made an effort to keep their flats presentable Moira was not one of them. Situated on the ground floor in the middle of the brick-built block, the inside was as filthy as the outside.

She flashed him a resentful glance and her thin lips tightened. Horton knew she was in her forties but she looked more like sixty. Faded tight jeans clung to her skinny legs and a shabby, dirty jumper hung off her flat chest.

'What do you want?' She eyed them with open hostility and suspicion before crossing to a worn sofa in the middle of the small, untidy, dirty room. Heaped upon it were clothes, magazines and some Christmas cards, there were no Christmas decorations. Toys were strewn over the filthy carpet, along with more clothes. There were the remnants of a meal on a plate on the floor by an electric fire set into the wall and two lager cans in front of the television set, which was on. Horton hadn't smelt alcohol on her breath, but then she might have drunk the contents of the cans last night, or had a visitor while her old man was having his hand cut off somewhere.

'Where are the children?' Cantelli asked.

'School, where do you think?' she snapped. She picked up the remote control and punched down the volume on the television. Grabbing a packet of cigarettes from the arm of the sofa she added, 'Thought they'd bum a day off school because of the snow but I don't want the little bleeders hanging round here getting under my feet.'

Horton couldn't imagine how they could possibly do that because housework didn't seem to be high on Moira's agenda. She lit up. Through the grimy windows Horton saw the small rear courtyard strewn with rubbish and some broken toys. He felt suffocated by the poverty and the hopelessness of Moira Langham's life and that of her children.

As though picking up on his thoughts Cantelli asked how many children she had. His enquiry had been made pleasantly and with genuine interest but it drew the customary scowl of suspicion and her smart retort. 'Three, why? What's it to you?' She inhaled as though it was her last cigarette on earth.

Cantelli shrugged indifference and gave a weary smile. He knew, just as Horton did, that polite expressions of interest without any ulterior motive were alien concepts to the likes of Moira who treated every copper and every official as the enemy.

'OK, so what's the bastard done now?' she demanded. She didn't invite them to sit. Horton wouldn't have done so even if she had.

'Moira, we have some bad news for you,' he began but she interrupted.

'Oh yeah? Bugger got nicked again, has he? Well bloody good riddance, that's not bad news. I'll put the bloody flags out.' She puffed on her cigarette while scrutinizing their faces with an air of defiance and hostility. But then her brow knitted as she obviously saw something in their expressions. Her anaemic face paled. 'Jesus! Don't tell me he's killed someone!'

'No, Moira. I'm sorry to tell you that Graham is dead.'

'Dead? Graham? You're having me on.' She smiled and shifted as her expression flicked between them. 'You're not, are you?' she said slowly. 'Bloody hell. He's dead? Shit.' She sank down on to the sofa.

Cantelli said, 'Is there anyone we can call for you?'

'Of course there isn't,' she snapped.

No, thought Horton with sadness recalling Moira's background. A young life spent in care, no knowledge of who her parents were, two spells in a young offenders institute for thieving while under the influence of drugs, prostitution, another spell in prison for theft and assault and then life with Graham, sometimes with her kids and sometimes without them when they were periodically taken into care for their own good. Graham Langham hadn't been much, but he'd been all she'd had, except for her kids.

'Was it a fight?' she asked.

Horton answered. 'That's what we're trying to find out.' There was no easy way to say we've found your husband's severed hand. But first he thought he'd ask some questions and see if he could get some straight answers before the shock and even deeper suspicion set in.

'When did you last see him, Moira?'

She drew on her cigarette and then stubbed it out in the small tin ashtray on the arm of the sofa. Was that to give her time to concoct a lie or was she genuinely trying to remember and to come to terms with the news. 'Monday.'

'What time?'

'Dunno. Afternoon. After the kids got home from school.'

'So about half past three?'

'If you say so, could have been later.'

'Did he say where he was going?'

She eyed him as though he'd spoken in Arabic.

'Has he contacted you since then?' Horton persisted.

'No.'

Cantelli looked up from his notebook. 'Weren't you worried?'

'No.'

'Why didn't you report him missing?'

She snorted with derision. 'If I did that every time he went off you lot would bang me up for wasting police time.'

Horton said, 'Where do you *think* he went?'

'No idea.'

But Horton thought she probably had. 'Could he have gone to another woman?' he asked, again thinking of Cantelli's remarks about the hand being severed on adulterous grounds.

'I'd cut his balls off if he did.'

And Horton wondered if those particular body parts would be found parcelled up. He didn't think Moira was responsible for her husband's death and certainly not on the grounds of adultery. She was as likely to be familiar with the Bible as he was of the Koran. He'd asked if Langham had had another woman, but perhaps he should ask if she had another man, or several come to that. Perhaps she'd resorted to her former profession. If she had then her clients weren't choosy. Could one of these men have killed Langham? He'd save that question for another time. She was still talking about her husband in the present. That was understandable.

'Has Graham ever mentioned a man called Alfie Wright?' He watched her reaction closely.

'No.'

'Do *you* know him?'

'No.'

Cantelli handed across his phone showing a photograph of Alfie Wright, which Walters had sent over from their files.

'Never seen him before.'

'Where did Graham drink? Which pub?' asked Cantelli.

She shrugged.

'You didn't go out with him?'

'How the hell can I with three kids?'

Horton didn't think that would have stopped her. She held his gaze, defying him to contradict her, but he didn't. Instead he asked who Graham associated with.

'No bleeding idea. He's only just come out of the nick.'

It was clear they were going to get nothing from her on that score. Horton reverted to his original line of questioning. 'How did Graham seem on Monday when he went out?'

'OK,' she said.

Horton eyed her closely, forcing her to add, a little reluctantly, 'He was in a good mood.'

'And he isn't normally?' asked Cantelli, pencil poised over his notebook.

'Well who would be the state this fucking country's in?' She glared at them, her bony lined hands twirling the cigarette packet.

'But there was something that made him happier than usual?' Horton probed.

Again she shrugged her thin shoulders.

Cantelli said, 'And he said nothing else to you?'

'Like what?

'Like where he was going, what he was doing?'

'No and I didn't ask because I knew he'd tell me to stop nagging and if I didn't he'd lay one on me.'

Horton wasn't sure he believed her but he let it go. She opened the cigarette packet and found it empty. She eyed Horton hopefully, but he shook his head and so did Cantelli. She sighed and tossed the packet on the sofa. The sound of a lorry grinding past on the main road rattled the windows.

Horton studied her carefully. Now was the time to break the news. 'Moira, we believe Graham was killed. We're investigating how he died. All that we have discovered of his body is his hand.'

'His what?' Her bloodshot eyes widened.

'It *is* Graham's hand,' Horton swiftly continued. 'The fingerprints match. There's no doubt. He couldn't have survived his hand being severed.'

'Christ!' She sprang up and ran a hand through her straggly brown hair and then turned feverish eyes on them. 'Maybe he did survive? Maybe someone took him to hospital.'

'We'll give you a liaison officer,' Horton said.

'No!' she cried, alarmed. 'I don't want no bloody policewoman in here poking her nose about. How the hell do I tell the kids their dad's hand's been found but not his body? Where was it found?'

'In the sea?'

'What the fuck was it doing there, and where's his van?' she added belligerently.

So Langham had had a vehicle. A car revved up outside, Horton could hear the deep bass of a stereo pounding. It faded as the car drove off. His phone vibrated in his pocket. Probably Bliss. Cantelli asked for details of the van.

'White. I don't know the registration number.' But her gaze was shifty.

That meant it wasn't registered, as he'd suspected. 'Please, Moira we need to find it.'

After a moment she sighed and told them. Cantelli wrote it down. 'Where does he keep it?' he asked.

'Eh?'

'Does he park it in the street?'

'Where else would he park it?'

'He might have a garage or a lock-up.'

'If he has he never told me about it.'

'What about a mobile phone?'

'He hasn't got one. I have but he doesn't use it.'

'How about a computer or a laptop?'

She looked at him as if he were mad. 'Do we look as though we can afford that?' she said derisively.

Horton said, 'We'll need to see his things?'

She looked alarmed and then resigned. 'Do what you bloody well want. I'm going out to get some fags.' She moved into the kitchen and picked up a purse and set of keys. Returning she added, 'That should give you time to search the flat but if you find anything, I'll say you planted it or it was Graham's.'

'Of course,' Horton acknowledged, as she strode out and slammed the door behind her.

Cantelli sighed and put away his notebook. 'Not quite the grieving widow.'

'Maybe she was fond of him in her own way. It might hit home later.'

'Guess so.'

'You take here, the kitchen and bathroom. I'll do the bedrooms.'

Horton stepped into the children's bedroom on his right off the hall. It looked as though a nuclear explosion had hit it. Toys and clothes were strewn around the grubby foetid smelling room. The sheets and duvets on the bunk bed and the single bed looked as though they'd never seen the inside of a washing machine, the same for the curtains half hanging off hooks at the filthy windows.

He checked his mobile phone and saw that the call he'd missed had been Dr Clayton. She'd left a message to say that she was examining the hand and would have some information for him if he'd like to call her or visit the mortuary in about an hour's time.

He pulled on his latex gloves not because he was worried about leaving prints but because he was more concerned with catching something. It was raining heavily now, bashing against the window. Swiftly, he searched the cheap plywood wardrobe and broken and chipped chest of drawers and found nothing to give him any indication of what had happened to Langham. Neither did he find anything illegal stashed away.

He crossed to the Langham's bedroom and found the same chaos. It smelt of sweat, sleep and dust. Again he checked the usual places: under the mattress, the inside and top of the broken down wardrobe, dressing table drawers and the space behind them and under them, but Langham hadn't brought his work home and Moira didn't have any drugs hidden away. It was a relief to be out of it. He joined Cantelli in the sitting room.

'Nothing but dirt, used crockery and stale food in the kitchen,' Cantelli reported, 'I'm surprised they haven't all contracted bubonic plague.'

'Probably immune to it.' Horton noted that like him Cantelli had put on his gloves.

Cantelli added, 'I don't think anyone's taken a bath for weeks. That bathroom is enough to make you throw up. There are the usual medicines in the cabinet, no evidence of any illegal substances, unless Moira took them out with her.'

That was possible but Horton wasn't concerned about that for the moment.

The front door opened and she swept in, her wet hair plastered around her bony face. She had a packet of cigarettes in her hand and a cigarette in her mouth. She didn't bother removing her wet jacket or taking the cigarette from her mouth. 'Well?'

Cantelli answered. 'We didn't find anything.'

'Didn't think you would.' But Horton noted her relief.

He said, 'We'll need a photograph of Graham.' She rolled her eyes at him, causing him to add, 'I know we've got him on file but a recent picture might help when we make enquiries. We need to establish who saw him after you on Monday afternoon and where he went.'

She reached for her mobile phone, scrolled through it and then handed it to him. 'I took that two months ago just after he came out.'

Langham was outside a pub holding a pint of beer in his hand. Horton swiftly studied the narrow face, hooded dark eyes, pitted complexion, wide mouth and weak chin. He'd last seen Langham five years ago. His hair had got thinner and greyer, his face was more lined and there was a feral look about his eyes. He handed Moira his business card and she sent the photograph to his mobile number.

On the doorstep he said, 'We'll do everything we can to find out what happened to Graham, but it would help if this was kept from the press for a while, so as not to warn whoever did this. Either I or Sergeant Cantelli will keep you informed of progress but if you think of anything that can help us call me.'

'You'll tell me if you find the van,' she said.

Horton said he would.

As they returned to the car, Cantelli said, 'She seems more worried about the van than Graham.'

'Probably thinks she can sell it.'

Cantelli headed for the CPS offices a short distance away and parked in the small car park behind the casino. Ewan Stringer was waiting for them with an anxious and slightly hostile expression on his fair, slender face. Horton knew he was mid-thirties but he appeared younger with a remarkably smooth skin that looked as though it rarely required a razor.

'If you've come to ask me where Alfie Wright is I've already told Detective Superintendent Uckfield and that thug who was with him that I have no idea,' Stringer said defensively. They were alone in one of the small private rooms off the main area where witnesses waited and tried to remain calm before being called to court. Taking a seat across the low coffee table, Horton interpreted Stringer's 'thug' as being DI Dennings, who Dr Clayton had nicknamed Neanderthal Man not because of his fifteen-stone build, mainly muscle, but because he was crude, blunt and not too bright as far as detective work went. But Horton was biased and his opinion, and that of Gaye Clayton, wasn't shared by the powers that be who had seen fit to promote Dennings and appoint him to the Major Crime Team. But then Dennings hadn't blotted his copybook by being falsely accused of rape as he had been.

Tetchily Stringer continued. 'We need open discussion to analyse and learn from incidences like these, not accusations and hurling blame at the professionals. That's not going to help anyone, and neither will it find Alfie Wright. It hasn't even occurred to Detective Superintendent Uckfield that Alfie, angry with himself and despairing of his life and future, could have resorted to drink and drugs and might even have attempted and successfully committed suicide.'

'Is that likely?' Horton asked, thinking it was highly improbable, Alfie loved himself too much. Cantelli also thought it incredulous judging by the way his dark eyebrows shot up. But then Stringer hadn't known Alfie Wright as long as they had. Stringer, like Tim Shearer, had only recently moved to Portsmouth. Stringer had been here ten months, while Shearer only since October, both had transferred from London.

'We need to know if Alfie Wright knew a man called Graham Langham,' Horton said.

Stringer frowned and pushed a hand through his unkempt wavy hair. 'I don't recognize the name, why do you ask?'

Cantelli told him. Stringer's hazel eyes widened with surprise. 'You can't think Alfie did that?'

Horton answered, 'Why not? He's got a history of violence.'

Stringer stiffened. 'And he'll continue to have one unless he's offered proper psychiatric help.'

'He's been given it before, more than once,' Horton said tersely and with an edge of weariness, 'both in and out of prison and it's not made a blind bit of difference. And neither will it. Alfie enjoys being violent and that's not because of an abusive childhood, despite what he might have told you, quite the contrary. His poor but very hardworking, honest parents gave their only son everything he asked for that was within their powers to give, but it was never enough, not for Alfie who thought he deserved more.' And maybe that was partly the trouble, thought Horton. They spoiled a child who had a quick temper, a short attention span and an inherently cruel nature. 'But we're not here to debate that, we need to find him, Ewan, and we need to know if he and Langham knew one another.'

'Then I can't help you, Inspector.' Stringer rose.

But Horton refused to be hurried. 'When did you last see him?'

Stringer gave a resigned sigh and sat down. 'Friday morning. We had a meeting to discuss the case. He agreed to plead guilty to assault occasioning actual bodily harm but not to unlawful wounding or inflicting grievous bodily harm.'

'He broke David Jewson's jaw!' Horton stressed.

'I know, but that wasn't his intention.'

'Oh, that's OK then,' Horton replied flippantly.

Stringer's face flushed.

The difference in plea meant how much time Alfie Wright would serve in prison and he knew that full well. Cantelli was right when he'd said Alfie's associates were dim but Alfie was far from it.

'As part of his bail condition he had to stay off alcohol and he assured me he had.'

'And you believed him?' Horton scoffed. He recalled that Dennings said Alfie had been in The Trafalgar Arms on Saturday afternoon, perhaps he'd been drinking mineral water. He thought not.

'He didn't smell of drink and he didn't appear bleary-eyed or hung over. I had to trust what he said.'

Cantelli coughed, earning himself a scowl from Stringer.

Horton quickly interjected. 'What did Alfie do after your meeting?'

'He said he was going back to his bedsit. I telephoned him on Tuesday afternoon to make sure he was OK for his court appearance. He has a pay-as-you-go phone, but there was no answer. I left a message. I didn't expect him to return the call and he didn't. I've tried him several times since he didn't show up at court but the phone's dead. I guess he must have ditched it.'

And obviously Uckfield's team had drawn the same result. The severed hand wasn't Alfie's but perhaps he was dead, killed by one of his victims or by a violent and disgruntled associate. At a nod from Horton, Cantelli reached for his phone and showed Stringer Langham's photograph and asked if he'd seen him.

Stringer studied it for a few moments but shook his head. 'No. He doesn't look familiar.'

Horton asked him to keep the news about finding Langham's hand to himself, adding that they wanted to keep it from the media for a while.

'After what I've seen in today's local newspaper I agree. Why do you think that man and Alfie might be connected?'

Cantelli answered. 'They both have criminal records and they could have served time together.'

Stringer looked concerned. He seemed to have calmed down now. 'It's dreadful what you say about that man having his hand . . . but I can't help you. I have no idea where Alfie is and I don't think he'd have done that.'

Horton rose. Cantelli followed suit, tucking his phone back in his jacket. Outside, he said, 'His heart's in the right place.'

'Pity his head isn't. Alfie's taken him in completely. I thought Ewan Stringer was brighter than that.'

'Sometimes our hearts rule our heads, despite all our best efforts.'

Horton flashed him a look. Should he tell Barney about his meeting with Carolyn Grantham and how far he'd got with his research into his mother's disappearance? Cantelli was the only one who knew about Jennifer or rather how he felt about her desertion and his childhood. He'd barely said anything to Catherine about his mother and never about how he felt, even from the start of their relationship he'd sensed she would quickly dismiss it. But Carolyn Grantham was a different matter, she'd be very keen to know his inner most thoughts, but for the wrong reasons. Even if she wasn't connected with Sawyer or Eames, he didn't much care for having his emotions put under the microscope, analysed and then paraded in a paper for everyone to read. But he knew that he wanted to see her again and not solely because he was curious about her.

In the car, on the way to the mortuary, he rang Bliss and relayed what Moira Langham and Ewan Stringer had said. 'I asked Moira not to talk to the press but I can't guarantee that she won't or that one of her friends might not let it slip.'

'I'll let DCS Uckfield know. I've spoken to Beverley Attworth at the probation service. Langham's offender manager was Dennis Popham. The rules of Langham's probation were that he met with Popham once a fortnight during the first three months of his release after which it was to be reviewed. Their last meeting was on Friday. Beverley's going to talk to Popham, review the file on Langham, and let me have all the details shortly.'

'Ask her if Popham knew that Langham had a van.'

Horton was betting he didn't.

Abruptly Bliss rang off and as soon as she did Horton's phone rang. It was Elkins and he sounded worried.

'Westerbrook's boat's not in Fareham Marina, Andy. The manager said he hasn't seen or heard from him since he left to go fishing yesterday morning. He assumed Westerbrook had gone away overnight. His car is still in the car park. He certainly set off in the direction of the marina from Oyster Quays yesterday because I saw him head up through Portsmouth Harbour. There are no reports of a boat adrift so he's either moored up somewhere else in this area or he turned round after we had left Oyster Quays and headed out into the Solent. I'm putting out a call to all the harbour masters and marina managers to check for sightings of his boat.'

With concern, Horton relayed the news to Cantelli.

'Perhaps he was too upset over finding the hand and needed some time to himself.'

Maybe, thought Horton, only he wished he'd made his statement before taking off. Hopefully, Elkins' unit would locate him.

He rang Langham's vehicle registration number through to Walters and asked him to put out a call for it. His thoughts flicked back to Dr Carolyn Grantham and Cantelli's remark about the heart ruling the head. Despite his reservations about the genuineness of her research Horton knew he was attracted to her. He wasn't sure how she felt about him and even if she showed an interest could he trust that to be real? Did it matter if it wasn't? Some men would take what was on offer, perhaps he should. No one was forcing him to reveal his darkest fears and secrets, he didn't have to tell her anything. He was well able to resist sexual pressure if it came to it and maybe it would. Maybe he should play along to see just how far she was prepared to go to discover what he knew of Jennifer's disappearance. And perhaps she'd reveal more about her real purpose and interest in a post coital glow. That thought made his mind veer to the woman he was about to see. He'd never considered Gaye Clayton in a sexual sense before, at least not until October when he'd found himself inordinately pleased she'd accepted his dinner date. But that hadn't come off because they'd both been involved in a murder investigation. He hadn't repeated the invitation – why not? And she hadn't chased him up about it. Why hadn't she? Perhaps she'd thought twice about it just as he had done, reluctant to move their relationship on to a more personal level. Perhaps like him she was reticent about becoming involved with someone. She too was divorced, though beyond that he knew nothing of her personal circumstances. But having been hurt once perhaps she was afraid of being hurt again. Or was that his fear, not hers? Sod it. Angrily he thrust the thoughts aside. He had a job to do and that was to find out everything he could about Graham Langham's death and how he'd become separated from his hand.

FIVE

' I 've been told we have an ID,' Gaye said, sitting forward at her desk in her small office behind the mortuary and turning her clear green eyes on them. The fingerprint bureau had informed her.

Cantelli relayed what they knew of Langham while Horton steeled himself to concentrate on the task in hand, not the best of phrases in the circumstances, and trying not to speculate what had delayed her in London last night. The thought that she might have been with a lover disturbed him before he chastized himself for being two-faced. Hadn't he considered Carolyn Grantham in that sense? But Carolyn Grantham was totally unlike Gaye in looks, build and dress. Horton studied her petite boyish figure in a T-shirt and jeans, her short spiky auburn hair and felt a lustful stirring in his loins that annoyed him. How could he be attracted by two complete opposites? Was he that frustrated and sex-starved?

Irritated with himself he gazed around her office bedecked with Christmas cards, wondering who sent a pathologist a Christmas card. Not grateful patients or relatives. Must be colleagues, which meant she was clearly very popular, and why not. Maybe he should give her a Christmas card. Cantelli and his family were the only recipients of his seasonal greetings except for Emma and he'd give her a Christmas card and her presents on the day before Christmas Eve. But the memory of what had happened last Christmas flashed into his mind, causing his gut to tighten. He'd been due to see Emma on Christmas Eve only he'd had a call from his solicitor to say that Catherine had decided against it and had flown with Emma to Cyprus to stay with her parents. He could do nothing about it. Would she repeat the exercise this year, deciding that she and Emma needed to be with this Peter Jarvis earlier than she'd told him? He hoped to God not.

He turned his attention back to the investigation. Cantelli had finished bringing Gaye Clayton up to speed.

Springing up, she said brightly, 'I can't help you find the rest of him but I can tell you what I've got. Follow me.'

They did. Horton felt a mixture of reluctance and eagerness at the prospect of viewing the hand. He sensed the same in Cantelli. In an area just off the mortuary Gaye opened a refrigerated drawer and Horton stared at the remains of Graham Langham. It seemed hard to associate the hand with the thin, anaemic, shifty-eyed bugger he remembered. In fact it was hard to think of it coming from a living breathing human being, the father of three young boys. Horton felt sorry for the kids. Despite the fact Langham had been a criminal and useless he was still their dad.

Staring at the hand he wondered if the remains of Jennifer had been discovered or washed up somewhere and were lying like this in a cold mortuary, or perhaps had even been buried in an unnamed grave. He shuddered at the thought. There was no national database of unclaimed bodies or body parts, so he couldn't trace her that way. Her prints weren't on file, he'd checked, and she'd disappeared long before DNA had come into use.

Cantelli's voice broke through his thoughts, echoing Horton's sentiments. 'It still doesn't seem real.' And Horton knew that until they found Langham, or rather the rest of him, it wouldn't, certainly not for Moira and her kids.

Gaye said, 'I can assure you it is flesh and blood or rather it was once. As Tom has already told you it is a right hand, Caucasian, male. It measures eight inches from the tip of the middle finger to the point of separation and weighs just under two pounds. It is in the very early stages of putrefaction and hasn't been embalmed. The fingernails, which are bitten, are intact. There are no residual scars or tattoos. It's difficult to give a timescale of when it was amputated because it could have been refrigerated and then thawed out before being placed in the container. The hand is covered by a light layer of salt, probably from immersion in the sea. I've sent skin samples for analysis as there could be other substances on it which you might be able to match with a location. It was severed just above the wrist.'

'Any idea how?' asked Horton.

She studied him with that candid, slightly teasing gaze that always sent his pulse racing. 'The shape of the amputation is interesting, it's slightly curved which suggests you need to be looking for a curved knife with a sharp non-serrated blade. It's also a clean cut with no evidence that the hand was pulled away after a first or second blow, so it could have been done after the victim was dead, or executed in one very quick and expert blow by someone fit and strong taking the victim by surprise. It's a traumatic amputation, although not typically fatal, however the condition of the hand and the decomposition suggests that it most probably was fatal.'

Cantelli chipped in, 'Someone without conscience then if he could look the guy in the eye and chop his hand off while doing so.'

Horton added, 'Or someone very angry who struck out instinctively.'

Gaye shrugged. 'Possibly. I think it more likely the victim was unconscious when the hand was severed.'

Horton hoped so. 'Which means it was executed as a gesture, a message.'

'Meaning what?' posed Cantelli thoughtfully, chewing his gum. 'It wasn't sent to anyone but dumped in the sea and would have stayed there if Nugent and Westerbrook hadn't fished it up.'

'And one of them seems to have gone missing.'

Cantelli nodded, thinking along the same lines as Horton. 'So did they really fish it up?'

Gaye answered. 'It might not be the only body part to have been placed in a container, perhaps some of the other parts have been sent to others as a warning.'

'For what though?' asked Horton

'To keep silent about something,' Gaye suggested.

'But why Langham?' asked Cantelli.

Exactly, thought Horton. 'We need to talk to Lesley Nugent to see if there is a connection between him and Langham, or between

Westerbrook and Langham. And we need to find Westerbrook. Is there anything else you can tell us, Dr Clayton?'

She raised her eyebrows slightly, perhaps at his formal mode of address or his slightly tense tone, but said pleasantly, 'You're looking for a knife with a blade of at least four inches. I'll let you have my full report.'

As they headed for the car, Horton called in and asked Walters for Lesley Nugent's contact details.

'According to his statement he lives at Lee-on-the-Solent but he works for Jamesons the wholesale meat suppliers at the Hilsea Industrial Estate.'

'And Westerbrook?'

'Elkins doesn't know where he works, all he had was his address and mobile phone number. I've checked out the fights in the city before Moira's last contact with her old man. Langham wasn't involved in any fights or if he was then he wasn't caught.'

'Has Bliss asked for Westerbrook's statement yet?'

'No.'

Good. 'Stall her if she does and don't tell her he's missing. We'll see what we can get from Nugent.'

Horton told Cantelli to make for Jamesons, which was situated on the northern outskirts of the city and only a short distance heading south from the mortuary.

'Plenty of knives at a wholesale meat suppliers,' Cantelli said, negotiating the busy roundabouts.

'Not to mention freezers and facilities for cutting up and disposing of a body,' added Horton. 'And possibly containers like the one the hand was found in.'

Jamesons occupied a large site tucked away on the edge of the industrial estate not far from the Hilsea Lines, a nature reserve that faced on to the Creek that had once separated the island city from the mainland. In reception Cantelli asked to speak to Lesley Nugent. He didn't say why and neither did he show his ID. The receptionist seemed remarkably lacking in curiosity. Perhaps Nugent had many visitors requesting to see him, thought Horton, wondering what his position here was.

While they waited for Nugent to appear, Horton gazed around at the pictures and information on the walls. Jamesons had been established in 1986 by Simon Jameson and his brother Kevin. Their father, Duncan, had owned a chain of butchers in the city but they had closed once the brothers had seen that wholesale rather than retail supply was the way forward. The company claimed to supply the best quality meat from farms in Hampshire, the Isle of Wight and the neighbouring county of Dorset to the catering and retail trade in Portsmouth, Southampton and the Isle of Wight. Judging by the photographs the Jameson brothers enjoyed their meat, both were very well built and ruddy-cheeked, and in their early fifties. And the company had prospered, winning a number of national awards over the years.

Nugent shuffled into reception looking pale and nervous. He showed no sign of surprise at their visit, which made Horton wonder if he'd seen them arrive from one of the windows that faced the front visitors' car park, or perhaps he'd been expecting them to question him further at some stage.

'We can talk outside,' Nugent said pushing open the door, leaving them little option but to follow. Cantelli looked as though he was about to suggest the interview be held in the car because of the chill damp wind that seemed to delight in swirling around them but Nugent lit a cigarette, putting paid to that idea. At least it had stopped raining, Horton thought, as they walked to the rear of the building and across the yard to a ramshackle structure with a buckled roof, open on three sides. They had the place to themselves, apart from two cycles and a moped. It was well away from the rear entrance where Horton could see a refrigerated van being loaded.

As though reading his thoughts, Nugent said, 'It's a busy time of year so better make this quick before the boss notices I'm missing. There's nothing I can add to the statement I made yesterday.'

Cantelli said, 'Just a few points we'd like some clarification on, Mr Nugent. We won't keep you long.'

Nugent sniffed and sucked on his cigarette. He hunched his shoulders into his dark blue anorak and shuffled his scruffy trainers as though cold, but Horton wondered if his body language was more on account of nervousness. That didn't necessarily mean he had anything to hide, Horton knew a police presence could make even innocent people apprehensive.

Cantelli continued. 'Have you seen or heard from Clive Westerbrook since you left him yesterday morning?'

'No. Why? Should I have done?' Nugent said defensively and warily.

'I thought he might have been in touch to discuss your ordeal. Not a very pleasant thing to have fished up, a human hand,' Cantelli said with concern.

Horton thought Nugent turned a little paler. 'You can say that again. Turned my stomach over.'

Horton said, 'I wouldn't have thought a butcher would have worried about finding a severed hand.' Or chopping one off. Could Nugent have done it? He looked nervous enough for it. And, as he and Cantelli had already speculated, the knife could easily have come from here.

'You do when it's human,' Nugent retorted.

Was he lying?

'Anyway I'm not a butcher,' Nugent swiftly continued. 'I work in order processing and despatch. I take the orders and organize the deliveries for the hotels, cafes and restaurants we supply. I haven't told the boss about finding the hand.'

'Why not?' asked Horton.

That shifty look was there again. 'Because he doesn't know that I went fishing yesterday. I phoned in sick. Bloody well was after finding that thing. Will he have to know that I was skiving off?'

Perhaps that was the cause of his apprehension. Horton said, 'We've identified the victim and it's possible the press could pick up on it.'

'Shit.'

So clearly Nugent wasn't going to go running to them. 'We might be able to keep your name out of the press reports but journalists have a way of unearthing things.'

Nugent frowned and drew heavily on his cigarette. The wind howled through the shed making Horton wish they'd insisted on conducting the interview inside, but Nugent's explanation about taking an unauthorized day off sick, rather than his desire for a smoke, explained why they were here. The doors of the refrigerated van slammed shut and the engine started up.

Cantelli picked up the questioning. 'How long have you known Clive Westerbrook?'

'That's just it, I don't know him. I met him for the first time on Sunday at the angling club at Lee-on-the-Solent.'

Horton didn't know the angling club but he did know Lee-on-the-Solent, a seaside town five miles to the west of Portsmouth.

'He asked if I'd like to go out with him on Wednesday and I said OK.'

Although Cantelli showed no signs of being particularly interested in this new piece of information, Horton knew he was as equally intrigued as he was. Why had Westerbrook suddenly wanted company?

'Is Mr Westerbrook a member of the angling club?' Horton asked.

'Must be I guess.'

'You don't know?' Horton injected an air of incredulity in his tone.

Nugent shifted again and looked uncomfortable. 'I don't get down there very often these days. But he must be a member to have got in. It's only open to members.'

Unless someone signed him in, thought Horton and if that was the case then it would be in the visitors' record book, assuming they kept one.

'Why did Mr Westerbrook ask you to go fishing with him?' Cantelli resumed the questioning.

'Dunno. Maybe because we got talking at the bar and he just thought of it.'

'What else did you talk about?'

Nugent frowned as though he didn't understand the question, 'Nothing, only fishing.'

Horton held Nugent's shifting eyes. Did he know that Westerbrook had not returned home? Was there more to their relationship than Nugent claimed?

He said, 'Tell us how you fished up the container.' It was always worth going over the ground again because on the second, third or fourth time of telling witnesses could often recall something they'd earlier missed or forgotten.

'It's like I said in my statement,' Nugent answered wearily, extinguishing his cigarette with his finger and thumb and putting the stub back in the cigarette packet. 'I'd set up my line over the side of the boat—'

'Who decided where to fish?' broke in Horton.

'Clive did. Well it was his boat. I'd set up the line and was just settling down when I felt a tug on it and saw that it had got caught up in this seaweed wrapped container. I reeled it in so I could untangle it and was about to throw the container away when I saw there was something inside. Well you've got to look, haven't you? Wished I hadn't.' His brow furrowed as he recalled the gruesome moment.

'Was Mr Westerbrook with you when you opened it?'

'Yes. I called out to him and—'

'He wasn't beside you when your line got tangled up?' Horton again interjected, disguising his keenness. He'd assumed they had been in the cockpit together.

'No. He'd gone below. No, hold on, he was up the front of the boat.'

'Doing what?'

'No idea.'

'Did you hear anything before you set up your line?'

'Eh?'

'Anything out of the ordinary.' Horton didn't want to lead him into saying he heard a splash, maybe Westerbrook had thrown the container overboard.

'Don't think so,' Nugent said, puckering his brow and stamping his feet. He looked longingly towards the warmth of the building.

'Just a couple more questions, Mr Nugent. How did Mr Westerbrook act?' Horton waited for Nugent to ask why all the questions? Why not ask Clive Westerbrook direct? But he didn't.

'Like me he was horrified, gob-smacked at first, then he went very pale. I thought he was going to faint. He grabbed the radio and called the coastguard who came out and accompanied us back to port. I took the helm. Clive was in no fit state. I used to have a small boat but got rid of it after my wife left.'

Horton withdrew his mobile phone from his jacket pocket. 'Have you seen this man before?' He showed Nugent the photograph of Graham Langham.

Nugent squinted at it. 'No. I don't think so.'

'He drives a white transit van.'

'So do a lot of people.'

'His name is Graham Langham.'

Nugent looked blank. Then his eyes widened. 'Hey, you're not saying it was his hand?' he cried. 'Bloody hell. Is he dead?'

'I would think so, wouldn't you?'

He swallowed hard and left a moment's silence before saying, 'I've got to get back to work.'

Horton and Cantelli fell into step beside him. As they made their way to the front of the building a black Range Rover swept into the car park. Horton said, 'We will need to speak to you again.'

Nugent looked agitated and quickly said, 'Then make it at my flat at Lee-on-the-Solent. I don't want to risk losing my job.'

Horton followed his fearful eyes as a well-built man with short grey hair, wearing dark-rimmed rectangular glasses, early fifties, climbed out of the Range Rover. Horton recognized him from the pictures he'd been studying earlier on the walls of the reception area. It was one of the owners, Kevin Jameson.

Horton didn't promise anything. They would speak to Nugent when and where it suited them. Before Nugent could cross to the entrance Horton stalled him. Kevin Jameson glanced their way, frowned, and halted at the door. Horton said, 'Do you know where Mr Westerbrook works?'

Nugent shook his head. 'We didn't talk about work, only fishing.'

'Did he pick you up from your flat on Wednesday?'

'No, I drove to Fareham Marina.' Nugent's eyes dashed towards Jameson, who was clearly waiting for his employee, and judging by Jameson's deepening glower he wasn't too pleased at being kept hanging about.

Cantelli chipped in. 'How did you get back there yesterday after giving your statement at Portsmouth?'

'Caught the train from Portsmouth to Fareham. It's only a short walk from Fareham railway station to the marina.'

'Why didn't you return with Mr Westerbrook? You could have made your statement at Fareham police station.'

Nugent looked uncomfortable. 'Look, to be honest, I didn't trust him.'

Horton cocked an interrogative eyebrow.

Nugent flushed. 'I met him once at the angling club, he persuaded me to spend the day fishing with him, we found that hand and then he was in a right state. I didn't fancy going back up the harbour with him in his boat.'

'Was Mr Westerbrook at the marina when you arrived there to

collect your car?' Horton knew he wasn't but he was interested to hear what Nugent said. He saw Jameson dash another irritated look and pointedly glance at his watch.

'I didn't see him. His car was there though.'

Horton let him go. He watched him rush across the concourse and pull up as Jameson addressed him. He couldn't hear what they said and neither could he lip read but judging by the body language it wasn't a friendly greeting.

'The boss,' Horton said, climbing into Cantelli's car.

'Wonder if Nugent will tell him who we are.' Cantelli started the engine and turned up the heating.

'Not if it means he has to tell him why he skived off work. The fact that he met Westerbrook only once and went fishing with him is interesting.'

'If you can believe it.'

Horton nodded and stretched the seatbelt across him. 'I think more passed between them on the way back to Oyster Quays than Nugent is saying. And it's possible that Westerbrook never intended returning to Fareham and maybe Nugent knew that. But if they are involved in Langham's death then why kill him? How would they know him?'

'Through the fishing club?'

'It's way off Langham's patch. Why would he go all the way to Lee-on-the-Solent when there are angling clubs closer to where he lived?'

'To flog some fishing gear he'd nicked. If he'd stolen it from a house in Portsmouth then maybe he thought the further away he went to offload it the safer it would be.'

Cantelli had a point and a good one but Horton said, 'He wouldn't have been admitted to the angling club, unless someone signed him in, so perhaps he was trying to sell the stuff outside, but that doesn't explain why either Westerbrook or Nugent would want to hack off his hand, throw it in the sea and then fish it up and alert the coastguard.' He thought for a moment then added, 'Let's take a look at Westerbrook's car and talk to the marina manager.'

SIX

Cantelli pulled on to the Hard and parked the Ford between a blue van, belonging to a marine servicing company, and Westerbrook's black Saab. It was high tide and several boats were bobbing about in the stiff cold wind. Across the small stretch of water to the north, Horton could see the crane on the wharf and beyond it the viaduct that spanned the road on the edge of the shopping centre. He climbed out and studied the Saab. There was a bag of boiled sweets and an opened packet of biscuits on the front passenger seat, along with an empty paper coffee cup in the cup holder between the driver and passenger seat, branded with the name of a popular chain of coffee shops. There was nothing on the rear seats or in the foot wells.

Horton turned away and surveyed the area. There were several pontoons that stretched out southwards, all of which dried out at low tide. The area behind them was densely populated with modern houses and commercial buildings but this small patch fronting the old Hard had managed to retain some properties from an earlier period, such as the resplendent three-storey Georgian house behind him and a handful of what once must have been fishermen's cottages along with a brick warehouse. He wondered where Westerbrook's berth was.

They located the marina manager in a small office nearby.

'Nothing wrong I hope,' Julian Tierney said, frowning with concern as Cantelli showed his warrant card and made the introductions. Tierney was a well-built man with short dark hair, a bronzed open face, about late thirties.

'When did Clive Westerbrook go out on his boat?' Cantelli asked.

'Yesterday morning just after nine.'

It had been high tide at ten fourteen, so that tallied, and it also matched with the length of time that Westerbrook and Nugent had told Elkins they'd been fishing before discovering the hand. The tide would still have been high enough to allow Westerbrook to return to his mooring here after leaving Oyster Quays, only he hadn't, so where had he gone?

'Have you seen him since then?' asked Cantelli.

'No. He could have come in on the tide at twenty-two forty-seven and slipped out again but not even Clive is idiot enough to do that in last night's weather.'

Horton caught a hint of dislike in the manager's voice. He said, 'You don't get on with him?'

'No one does. He's always complaining about something. If it's not the mooring fees, it's the prices in the bar, the weather, the other berth holders, you name it Clive doesn't like it. I know he's not in the best of health, bad heart and all that, but I don't think he helps himself by being so negative all the time, and getting so cross and uptight, but then some people are just made that way.' He paused and eyed them curiously, his expression changing to one of concern as the penny dropped. 'Don't tell me he's had a heart attack on board his boat?'

Cantelli answered. 'We're very concerned to locate him.'

Tierney shifted and ran a hand over his hair. 'Blimey.'

'Is he married?' asked Horton.

'Divorced. And that's another thing Clive complains about, having to pay maintenance to his wife and son.'

'Do they live locally?' asked Cantelli.

'No idea. I've never seen the boy go out with him.'

'How long has he kept his boat here?' asked Horton.

'A year, but he said he was at Horsea Marina before coming here.'

That was a large marina just outside Portsmouth where Uckfield kept his motor cruiser and Catherine's father his large yacht.

'Do you know what he does for a living?'

'Some sort of financial consultant, self-employed.'

So no boss, or employees to ask where he might have gone, thought Horton.

Tierney was saying, 'Clive said he wanted somewhere for his boat so that he could get in and out of the Solent without having to fanny around going through a lock but I think the real reason he came here was the cost. Our moorings are much cheaper.'

Perhaps being a financial consultant wasn't as well paid as it once had been. Horton said, 'Did you see anyone go out with him yesterday?'

'Yes, a thin man, with a stoop, about fifty.'

Lesley Nugent. Horton asked where Westerbrook usually moored up and was given the location. He gave Tierney his card and asked him to contact him or Cantelli the moment Westerbrook showed up. They returned to the car park where only Cantelli's Ford and Westerbrook's Saab remained.

'Expensive car,' Cantelli said. 'Westerbrook must be doing well if he can afford that and a boat, despite grumbling about the cost.'

'Probably on finance.'

'He'd still have to keep up with the payments.'

Horton again tried Westerbrook's mobile with the same result, he got his automated voice mail. He didn't see any point in viewing the empty space that had been Westerbrook's mooring and besides Elkins had checked over the marina to make sure Westerbrook wasn't moored up elsewhere.

They headed back to the station. Horton knew he'd have to tell Bliss that Westerbrook hadn't been in to make his statement and they couldn't locate him, but he couldn't see why or how he could be involved in Langham's death.

Horton bought some sandwiches from the canteen while Cantelli collected his homemade ones from his desk in CID. Horton took his to the incident suite where he found Bliss installed in the spare office to the right of Uckfield's. It had originally been intended for the new DCI of the Major Crime Team, but no one had yet been appointed to the position. Horton had no doubts that Bliss had the job in her sights, which would leave a vacancy in CID. But his chance of securing that position was about as likely as him meeting the real Santa Claus. The official version for the delay was that they were still waiting on a suitable candidate, the unofficial one was that Dean was holding back in order to save money.

Bliss waved him into a seat across the excessively tidy black ash desk devoid of paperwork and boasting only a wide computer screen, keyboard, mouse and telephone. He'd never seen her dressed in anything other than her black skirt, white blouse and black suit jacket, which was currently draped on the back of her large leather chair. Her fine light brown hair as usual was scraped back off her lean face into a high ponytail and her face was devoid of make-up. He relayed what Dr Clayton had told them before adding that they'd reinterviewed Lesley Nugent to see if he could tell them more about the discovery of the hand. He claimed not to know or recognize Langham, and then Horton dropped the bombshell that Clive Westerbrook seemed to have gone AWOL.

She listened in silence with her usual frowning countenance, but surprisingly didn't accuse him of being lax in his duty by letting Westerbrook slip through his fingers. She said, 'You think it suspicious that he's taken off now after finding the hand?'

'I think he could be suffering from shock, he didn't seem too healthy when I met him,' Horton answered cautiously, and with concern. He said that Elkins and his marine unit had put a call out for him or rather his boat and that they'd check to see if they could find any connection between Westerbrook and Langham. He asked her what she'd got from Beverley Attworth on Graham Langham.

'Dennis Popham didn't know that Langham had a van. Langham claimed not to have any vehicle.'

He would.

'It's not insured, taxed, and neither does it have a current MOT certificate.'

As Horton had suspected. It wasn't surprising, Langham wouldn't be bothered about complying with the law.

'The van was last owned by a building company, who sold it for scrap to a car breakers in Havant.'

'Who then sold it on to Langham.'

'I know the company,' she said briskly.

Havant was to the east of Portsmouth and had been her patch before her promotion and appointment to Portsmouth CID.

'The owners are clean,' she declared. 'But they could have employed someone less scrupulous. I've sent PCs Seaton and Summerfield out to make enquiries.'

'Langham must have reverted to his usual trade the moment he was released. He'd never have had the money to buy the van, even if it only cost fifty pounds, he and Moira wouldn't have had that much to spare.'

Her eyes flicked to her computer screen. 'According to Popham's reports Langham attended his meetings regularly and punctually, was quiet, seemed genuinely keen to remain out of prison, did what he was told and did it without any fuss. He was practically illiterate and part of his probation plan was that he attend adult literacy classes. He'd been due to start after Christmas at the Highbury College annexe just up the road from where he lives. He was also due to continue with a voluntary community project which he began a month ago, assisting with maintaining the rose gardens and communal area around the Canoe Lake.'

Both were on the seafront.

Bliss said, 'He seemed to be doing well.'

Probably casing the area for possible burglaries thought Horton, knowing the large and expensive properties nearby. 'Anything from the prison?'

'Not yet. DC Walters is working on it. And there's nothing further on Alfie Wright.' Her eyes darted beyond Horton and she frowned. He swivelled round in his seat to see a stocky man, mid-forties, wearing a well-cut suit striding confidently through the incident suite towards them, his expression set and stern. He disappeared into Uckfield's office.

'Who's that?' asked Bliss.

'No idea.'

Bliss was obviously itching to find out. Horton knew she'd hate to miss out on anything, or anyone, who could be important to her in her career. She rose, clearly dismissing him, and entered the incident suite leaving Horton to follow. While Horton made for Walters and Cantelli, Bliss crossed to Trueman and exchanged a few words with him but as she was doing so, Uckfield's door swung open and he called Bliss and Horton into his office. Horton threw a look at Cantelli who, eating his sandwiches, shrugged an answer. He didn't know who the mysterious visitor was either but Horton was about to find out.

Uckfield curtly introduced them to the man standing to his right, then announced his guest. 'DCS Adams. National Crime Agency.'

Horton's curiosity intensified. Bliss's expression gave nothing away but Horton suspected she was, like him, mentally wracking her brains to see how NCA featured in the investigation regarding either Alfie Wright, or rather Graham Langham, which had to be the reason why Uckfield had summoned them both because Dennings wasn't here. But then Horton hadn't seen him in his office so perhaps he was out following up a lead.

Uckfield nodded them into seats around his conference table. Adams took up position next to Uckfield who asked for a report on the Langham investigation. Bliss relayed what Horton had told her while Horton continued to speculate why such a high-ranking officer from NCA was interested in a former petty crook. NCA investigated serious organized crime on a national and international level, which had never been on Langham's radar. Adams' expression remained neutral but his light brown eyes never left Bliss's face. When she'd finished he said, 'The investigation is now our remit.'

Horton flashed a questioning glance at Uckfield who returned it stoically. Bliss looked puzzled.

'May I ask why?' she asked, concerned.

Probably scared she'd cocked up or missed something vital, thought Horton uncharitably, but they hadn't because there was nothing to miss . . . except Westerbrook.

Curtly, Adams replied, 'Graham Langham was killed because he was an informer.'

Horton couldn't have been more surprised if Adams had told him that Langham had been a performing seal. He tossed Uckfield another glance. The Super was doing his best to look convinced but Horton could see he was just as dubious as him. Bliss though looked ready to believe anything Adams said even if he declared that the hand had been red and had boasted six fingers! But then she hadn't known Langham.

Horton said, 'That's not Langham's line of work, or his style.' He caught a flicker in Uckfield's eyes that told him Uckfield had expressed the same opinion.

'Prison changes people,' Adams replied sharply.

'It's never changed Langham before.'

'Well it did this time,' snapped Adams.

But Horton just couldn't believe it. Langham wasn't a grass. And why was Adams so hostile and defensive? Perhaps he suffered from dyspepsia, he certainly looked as though he did. Undaunted, Horton continued. 'So Langham, a petty crook, sought out a senior police officer in the National Crime Agency and said, please sir I'd like to become a police informant, just show me where to sign and what to do.'

'Inspector,' Bliss sharply reprimanded and eyed him with daggers drawn.

'How he became an informer is not your concern, Inspector Horton, and neither is it CID's or the Major Crime Team's. As I have already informed you, my team is taking over the Langham investigation.'

'Then you'll liaise with Moira Langham, who might go to the press about her husband's murder,' said Horton. He simply didn't believe what he was being told.

Uckfield shifted. 'We can't stop her shooting her mouth off and if the media get hold of the story I will handle it, the official line is we're exploring several lines of enquiry.'

'Without actually doing so,' added Horton.

'Not you, no,' Adams sharply reiterated. 'If any witnesses come forward, or new information comes to light during the course of your other duties, or from the Alfie Wright investigation, which is highly unlikely as they are not connected, then Detective Superintendent Uckfield will pass that on to me and my team will deal with it.'

'And the men who fished up the hand?'

'They are not involved.' Adams turned to Bliss. 'I expect everything to be handed over within the next hour. Liaise with DCI Natasha Neame.'

'Yes, sir.' Bliss rose and jerked her head at Horton to follow her.

Outside he said, 'If Langham was an informer I'll buy you a drink.' She looked taken aback for a moment before pursing her lips. He knew that spending one minute longer in each other's company than was strictly necessary was torture for them both.

Crisply, she said, 'You heard what DCS Adams said, file your reports and ask your team to do the same, then attend to our other investigations of which, I needn't remind you, there are plenty, including the petrol station robbery. I expect results.'

'Whether you'll get them though is another matter,' Horton mumbled to her disappearing stiff back. He crossed to Cantelli and Walters and picked up his discarded packet of sandwiches. 'We're relieved of duty, at least as far as Graham Langham is concerned.'

'What about . . .' Walters pointed at his computer screen to indicate he was in the middle of his research.

'I'll explain in our office.' He said nothing on the way but concentrated on eating and thinking over what he'd just heard. Only when they were in the CID operations room did he make the announcement. 'NCA are taking over the case.'

Cantelli looked startled. 'Why?'

'Langham was an informer.'

'You're kidding! Langham!' Cantelli looked as though he was about to laugh when Horton's expression stalled him. 'You're serious, aren't you?'

'DCS Adams is. But he's not going to say who Langham was informing on, or why. And neither is he going to enlighten us about why the poor blighter's hand was severed, put in that container and thrown in the sea.'

Walters said, 'Probably because he doesn't know.'

Cantelli sat back looking bemused. He ran a hand through his curly black hair. 'I can't see it. Langham is the last person in Portsmouth to become a grass. He'd rather run a double marathon than stitch someone up and he was so lazy it would hurt him to walk to the bathroom if he could pee in the kitchen sink, which, judging by what I saw earlier, he probably did. Adams must be bluffing.'

'Why would he be?' Horton asked, interested to hear what Cantelli thought.

'Because he wants us to stop asking around about Langham.'

'Which is what we've been ordered to do. Adams claims Langham converted to becoming an informer as a result of his last stretch in prison.' Horton knew there were specialist teams focusing on prison intelligence but that had always been the remit of the Intelligence Directorate; perhaps they'd passed the information on to DCS Adams in the National Crime Agency.

Cantelli was looking baffled. 'I suppose he could have been cajoled, bullied or bribed into getting involved in a big crime but when he was released he realized he was out of his depth and wanted out, only they threatened they'd harm Moira and the kids if he didn't go along with it. He got scared and . . .' Cantelli's words trailed off as he ran up against a barrier to that theory.

'Precisely,' Horton said. 'How would he know he'd need to run to Adams or anyone else in NCA? If he'd wanted to turn informer he'd be much more likely to approach me or you.'

Walters interjected. 'Unless this big time crook has told Langham that Adams is after him.'

'Possibly, but I still can't see how Langham would know where to get hold of Adams or anyone on his team which means, *if* Langham was an informer then someone from Adams' team approached him on his release from prison because they wanted information on whoever he knew inside, but even then I can't see Langham going along with it.'

Walters said, 'Maybe he thought the money would come in *handy* over Christmas.'

'Very droll.'

'Perhaps he decided to turn over a new leaf and go straight.'

Cantelli eyed Walters incredulously. 'Langham wouldn't know a leaf if he was standing in a forest.'

Horton said, 'If Adams has fabricated Langham being an informer then the most likely explanation of how Langham got caught up in a serious organized crime was he burgled the wrong house, and stole the wrong stuff. Or rather the right stuff.' He sat back and stretched his hands behind his head. 'OK, possibility number one, Langham picked on a house to burgle which was being watched by NCA. Langham discovers in it some information that is dynamite, or rather that he thought worth a great deal of money, so he confronts the person he's burgled and quotes a price for his silence. The property owner agrees. On Monday afternoon when Graham Langham waved farewell to Moira he thought he was going to collect.'

Cantelli said, 'He did, but not in the way he expected.'

Horton nodded and sat forward. 'And this robbery wouldn't have been reported because whatever Langham discovered, the owner wouldn't want it being brought out into the open and PC Plod traipsing all over his house. And Adams isn't going to tell us who has been burgled because it means revealing they are watching the premises and it could provoke this big time villain into shutting up shop.'

'Sounds feasible.'

Horton continued. 'Theory number two, Langham broke into a property and stole items from it that at first he didn't realize were valuable. Langham's fence recognized their true worth and decided to pass the information on to Adams and his team, who then approached Langham.'

Cantelli said, 'Or maybe Langham grew suspicious that he was being swindled by his fence and asked around about this potentially valuable item.'

'I can't think who he would have asked,' Horton replied. 'And he's hardly the type to look it up in the library. I doubt he even knew what the inside of a library looked like, let alone a book. And as we know from his offender manager, he was practically illiterate.'

'He could have asked someone to look it up for him and that person killed him, hoping to cash in on getting the item from the fence,' suggested Walters.

Cantelli said, 'Or the fence also told the owner of the property as well as NCA and the owner went after Langham. Maybe Moira knows what it is, which is why she's so interested in the van, perhaps she thinks this valuable cargo might still be inside it.'

Horton continued. 'Or perhaps Langham stole a large haul of drugs and had his hand chopped off to discourage anyone else from trying.' He rose with a sigh. 'Whatever it is, it's not our case. And that means locating Clive Westerbrook isn't either. We've got plenty of other work, as DCI Bliss so kindly pointed out, so we'd best get on with it.'

He entered his office, closing the door behind him. Before tackling his workload though he rang the Centre for the Study of Missing Persons and asked to speak to the senior lecturer. Several minutes later he rang off with the not so surprising news that Dr Carolyn Grantham was indeed involved in a research project and was using the centre's facilities. She came with excellent references and was very highly respected. She was genuine but then Horton hadn't doubted that, and the basis of her research was fact. But if this was a cover then everything would have checked out down to the finest detail.

He punched in her number and waited eagerly for her to answer. 'I was hoping you'd call me,' she said with obvious pleasure. 'But is it to give me good news or bad?'

'And the bad would be?' As if he didn't know.

'That you don't wish to cooperate.'

'There's nothing I can tell you.'

'Maybe that's something in itself. Look, I don't expect you to take me on trust. And I'm sorry about choosing the noisiest place on the planet to discuss it last night but if you'd give me one more shot at it I'd be grateful. Let me buy you a pizza as an apology for allowing your eardrums to be assaulted last night.'

So that was the way it was. And it suited him fine. Horton's landline was ringing. It was Gaye Clayton's number. Hastily he agreed.

'Great,' Carolyn Grantham replied enthusiastically. 'Pizza Express at Oyster Quays. Eight o'clock.'

'Fine.'

He rang off and snatched up his phone.

'I wondered if you fancied a drink tonight, Andy, there's something I'd like to discuss with you,' Gaye said brightly.

Horton stifled a silent groan and a curse. 'I can't tonight, I'm sorry. Is it concerning work?'

'Does it have to be?' she answered, then quickly added, 'It is actually. It doesn't matter, we can—'

'I'll buy you breakfast though,' he quickly interjected. Why of all nights had she suggested tonight? He couldn't get out of seeing Dr Grantham or rather he could if he really wanted to but he didn't. As though to compensate for letting Gaye down he added, 'And I haven't forgotten that I still owe you a dinner.'

'Where? Breakfast, that is?'

'The Tenth Hole, it's a café by the golf course, behind the seafront at Eastney.'

'I know it. Good choice. Their breakfast is superb. It's a date. But I'm warning you, Andy, I like the full English.'

'What else,' he said lightly and with warmth but he rang off disappointed that he wasn't seeing Gaye tonight. He glanced at his clock. He had four hours before his meeting with Carolyn, which meant he had four hours to make some inroads into his workload. He could, of course, return to his boat, shower, shave and change, maybe he should, but that would make it feel more like a date and his meal with Carolyn Grantham was anything but that he sternly told himself. It was work, albeit of a personal nature, and the sooner he dealt with it the better. Determinedly he shut out thoughts of everything and concentrated on what was in front of him on his desk.

SEVEN

The large pizza restaurant was relatively quiet. In fact, compared to where they had been the previous night it was like a monastery. Horton saw her long before he reached there. She was sitting at a table in the window overlooking the harbour. He apologized for being late.

'I was early,' she dismissed with a smile that made his pulse jump and his blood surge. There was no denying that he found her attractive. But his thoughts dashed to the petite auburn-haired woman he'd turned down tonight and he felt a wave of unease that he recognized as guilt, not that he had anything to feel guilty about, he silently chastized himself.

He asked her what she'd like to drink and ordered a glass of red wine for her and a non-alcoholic lager for himself. He assumed she was driving but now was not the time to lecture her about the hazards of drink driving. Across the water the lights of Gosport glimmered, which reminded him of why he was here. Perhaps Carolyn Grantham had chosen this place because she knew that Gosport was where he believed Jennifer had been heading on the day she disappeared.

As Carolyn consulted her menu Horton rapidly and mentally replayed his conversation with Harry Kimber, the former neighbour of his foster parents, Bernard and Eileen Litchfield. Kimber had told him in October that Bernard had served in Northern Ireland as an RAF police officer until 1979 after which time he'd joined the Hampshire Police. He'd been shot in the shoulder in 1978 while patrolling the airfield at RAF Aldergrove and he'd been sent to England to recover, or more precisely to the Royal Navy Hospital at Haslar, Gosport. Horton had no proof that Jennifer had visited Bernard or that she even knew him, or that she had gone to Gosport, except for a set of numbers inscribed on the reverse of a manila envelope bequeathed to him by a dying man, Dr Quentin Amos, who had known Jennifer and those men in the photograph from 1967, when he had been a lecturer at the London School of

Economics. Amos had told him that Jennifer had been involved with the Radical Student Alliance and the protest movement. The 1967 sit-in at the London School of Economics, the subject of that photograph, was considered to be the start of that protest movement.

The numbers, Horton believed, were the grid location of Haslar Marina, a stone's throw from the hospital. OK, so it had taken some manipulation of them to fit with his theory, and the marina hadn't existed in 1978, but the hospital had. And situated close to it further south along the shore was the heavily secured Fort Monckton, allegedly a communications training centre for MI5, and that brought him right back to Lord Richard Eames. Had Jennifer gone to meet Eames? Had he killed her?

'I'll have the Four Seasons Pizza,' Carolyn's voice interrupted his thoughts. He plumped for the American, Pepperoni, Mozzarella and Tomato.

After the waiter had taken their order, Horton said, 'I suppose you've done some research on me.'

'Of course. Joined the Hampshire Police nineteen years ago, rose fairly rapidly to Detective Inspector, now in CID after spending time on various other units including vice, drugs and the Intelligence Directorate. Accused of raping a girl while working undercover, suspended, but cleared eight months later.'

And who had given her that information. As though reading his thoughts she said, 'I got it from the media coverage. As I said the media and its reporting of crime is one of my specialist areas, usually focusing on missing persons cases but I have been known to conduct other research projects.'

OK, he'd give her that. He said, 'So I gather from *my* research.'

'And you'll probably have run my details through the Police National Computer and discovered that I have no previous convictions.'

He had done so before leaving the station. 'Doesn't mean you haven't committed a crime,' he said.

'Absolutely,' she answered brightly as their drinks arrived. 'I could be a serial killer for all you know.'

Or someone sent to check out what he'd discovered about Jennifer's disappearance. When the waiter had left she said, 'I also know that you're married with a daughter, how old?'

'Nine, and I'm divorced. The media didn't report that, can't think why,' he added facetiously. 'And you?'

'Single, no kids. There was a cohabitee but I gave him the elbow two years ago. We grew apart.'

The restaurant door swung open and a man in his late forties with close-cropped grey hair entered. He was shown to a table some distance behind them.

'Why the interest in missing persons?' Horton asked.

She sat forward and met his eyes with a calm steady gaze. They were shrewd and enquiring with a gravity in them that he hadn't quite expected. With enthusiasm she said, 'Over three hundred thousand people go missing every year, but then you probably know that. It's an incredible number. Over a hundred thousand of them are adults. Until recently there was no research into why adults choose to go missing, how they disappear, where they go and what they do, or why some of them choose to come back and others don't, and the effect on the lives of those they leave behind. The emotional and economic cost is huge and if we can understand some of the reasons behind people wanting to vanish then perhaps we can ensure we have the right processes in place to tackle it more effectively, quickly and empathetically. I'm also fascinated to see what constitutes a missing person, many don't even consider them-selves missing. Many come back after a very short time, a week or ten days. And as I said I'm keen to see how much attention the media pay to those who are missing, do they emphasize certain cases and not others, why? What gives the case an emotional pull? Does media coverage help or hinder the investigations.'

'That's a very wide area of research.'

She sat back reaching for her wine glass. 'It is but it'll all come together at some point.'

'That doesn't sound a very methodical approach for a researcher.'

'Oh, believe me I have methodology.'

He looked into her eyes. He believed her all right. He said, 'Most of those missing have mental health problems, stress, depression, financial or marital problems.' And he wondered if that applied to Westerbrook. Perhaps fishing that hand out of the sea had been the last straw for him. Jennifer though hadn't had any of those problems, or had she? How did he know? Admittedly they hadn't had much money and perhaps the strain of working nights and raising a child on her own had become too much for her, but that didn't explain why there was no employment record for her after working at the

London School of Economics, why she didn't show up on any census and neither did he, why their flat had been emptied of her possessions, why he had never been officially adopted and why Ballard had left that photograph on his boat.

'You're right,' Carolyn answered. 'I said I wouldn't ask you about your experiences but do you think Jennifer disappeared because she was depressed?'

He shrugged an answer and drank his beer. If she'd been contemplating suicide why put on her best clothes and make-up.

'What got you into this research?' he asked, not only because he was curious but because it would steer her away from asking him further questions.

'Criminology, missing persons or the media?'

'All three.'

She thought for a moment as she composed her answer. 'I've always had a fascination for what makes people tick, their personalities and motivations, hence the criminology degree and the PhD in Investigative Psychology. The media has also been an interest of mine because I grew up with it. My dad was senior crime reporter on one of the national tabloids.'

She made to continue but their pizzas arrived. Horton's mind churned over what she had said while the waiter made sure they had all they needed. Horton asked her if she wanted another drink but she shook her head. He ordered some mineral water for them both.

She said, 'Mum and Dad used to discuss the cases he reported on. He covered the Brenda Myers story. I thought why not pick up where he left off.'

Did he believe her?

She continued. 'I wanted to know more about how the media manipulate and distort a story. I saw how someone missing could be made a victim, a hero, a vandal, whatever they choose.' She cut into her pizza and took a large bite. 'I'm hooked on missing persons research.'

All this could be checked and he would check it. The waiter returned with their water and glasses. Horton poured her a drink.

'Dad's retired now, taking his pension and spending most of his time fishing, for the wet variety not juicy news stories.'

The mention of fishing brought Horton's thoughts back to Clive

Westerbrook. Where was he on this freezing cold night? Had he returned his boat to Fareham Marina by now? The restaurant door opened and a noisy crowd of six entered.

'We've got a missing person at the moment, a man,' Horton said.

'Really? Tell me.'

He did without going into details about the hand and that Westerbrook had fished it up. He simply said that Westerbrook was a yachtsman in poor health who'd had a shock and had not returned to the marina when he had said he would.

'Not a suspect then.'

Horton didn't answer but ate his pizza.

'Maybe he needs time to think things through, recover from whatever shock he's received,' she said, 'The geography of where he's gone could be important, it is with many missing people.'

'Really?' he said, interested, thinking not only of Westerbrook but of Jennifer.

'He could have gone to a place where he has happy memories, or somewhere he always feels calm when he's stressed.'

Horton thought of the Solent, it was where he always went but Westerbrook hadn't gone there, or if he had then he'd gone on somewhere else because his boat hadn't been reported as being seen. He wondered where Jennifer might have chosen to go when stressed or happy. A flash of memory returned to him. It was one he'd experienced in January when walking across the Duver, at Bembridge Harbour on the Isle of Wight. It was now a nature reserve but it had once been a golf course and he'd walked across it as a child with his mother and a man. She'd been very happy. Had they arrived there by boat? He had no recollection of that.

He brought his attention back to Carolyn who was saying, 'It's similar to how some people respond when a loved one dies. The bereaved return to the place where they were happy with their loved one as a means of trying to reconnect with them. Sometimes the bereaved will only go back once and find it's not the same, it didn't work and return home. Others will find great comfort from it and return many times. The missing person is also searching for relief from pain and anguish.'

Horton didn't know which places were special to Westerbrook, and he wasn't sure that asking Westerbrook's former wife would reveal that information either.

The waiter cleared away their plates. He asked Carolyn if she would like a dessert. She refused. 'How about coffee? At my place. I've taken a rented apartment.'

He held her eyes. They were dark, beguiling and inviting. He should say no but he found himself saying, 'Sounds good.'

While she visited the cloakroom he paid the bill, dismissing her protest that it was meant to be her treat, and trying to ignore the adrenalin that was coursing through his veins. It was just coffee, nothing more. But his body was saying something else.

Her car was parked in the underground car park where he had left his Harley. Outside the air struck chill against his face and she tucked her hand under his arm and nestled against him as though it was the most natural thing in the world, and as though she'd known him months instead of hours. His surprise swiftly turned to pleasure and roughly he dismissed his misgivings that she'd been sent to get information from him. It had been ages since he'd experienced so warm a gesture. And an eternity since he'd been this close to a woman. Her perfume sent his blood pumping and the feel of her soft body underneath her coat warmed and thrilled him.

When they reached her car she gave him her address, which he noted wasn't far from the marina where he lived. Her apartment was in the converted marine barracks overlooking the sea. He watched her climb into her car and drive off before heading for his Harley. There he put on his helmet scanning the car park and there again was the man in his late forties with short-cropped grey hair who had been in the restaurant. He was climbing into his car. It meant nothing, he told himself crossly. He was too cautious, too paranoid. He pulled away, registering another man he'd seen before with collar length fair hair in his early forties. He'd been in The Reef the previous night, talking with a group of students.

Horton reached Carolyn's apartment and waited for her to arrive. She let them into the wide vestibule saying, 'I'm on the top floor. The view is lovely but I don't think you'll see much of it tonight.'

He wasn't sure if she meant because of the weather or that they'd have other things to occupy themselves with, like drinking coffee. As she unlocked the door to her flat Horton couldn't stop his mind from wandering back to Gaye Clayton. He had a strange feeling that he was betraying her by being here, which was nonsense because there was nothing between him and Gaye. But there had been that moment not long ago when she'd stood so close to him that he'd felt intoxicated by her proximity. Hastily he pushed all thoughts of Gaye from his mind as he followed Carolyn through the narrow hall and into a large and tranquilly decorated and furnished lounge. She was right, wide windows looked out southwards across the Solent but there was nothing to see.

'I've only got the flat for another month. I'm on the move at the end of January. Another research project but this time at the Center for Studies in Criminal Justice, University of Chicago.'

'That's a shame.' He pulled off his jacket. She took it from him but didn't make any move to hang it up.

Instead she put it on the sofa beside her without taking her eyes from him. 'I'll be sorry to go. Now.'

She smelt intoxicating. He kissed her softly and gently while he pushed aside the silent nagging voice that she was using sex as a means of getting close to him. Maybe he was wrong. She responded warmly.

'Will you be here for Christmas?' he asked, pulling back, his eyes devouring her.

'No. I'm going to Scotland to stay with my parents.'

'When?'

'Not for another ten days.'

'Time enough then.'

'For what?'

'Coffee.'

'It'll keep you awake.'

'So they say.'

'Might be a good thing.'

He kissed her again long and lingeringly. She responded hungrily.

'Stay,' she said throatily.

He knew he shouldn't. Every instinct screamed at him not to. But his body was playing another tune. And why the hell shouldn't he stay? What had he to lose? This last year had taken its toll on him, he was getting paranoid about people watching him, people following him, people feeding him duff information about Jennifer. He was getting paranoid about Jennifer. So what if Carolyn had been primed to find out how much he had discovered about Jennifer's disappearance. He had told her nothing. Did it matter if Jennifer had worked for British Intelligence? So what if she'd run off with Zeus or some other lover? She was dead. He was alive, very much so, and so was the woman in his arms.

He stayed.

EIGHT

Friday

'**M**y God, Andy, you look like something the cat's dragged home.'

'Thanks.' He sipped his coffee trying to pretend he didn't have a headache, not caused by alcohol, he hadn't touched a drop, but by lack of sleep and too much thinking. Too much sex probably he thought too, uncomfortably, not because of Gaye's presence although that didn't help but because of his own emotions surrounding the night spent with Carolyn Grantham.

'Bad night?'

Her words jolted him upright. He winced inwardly. It had been anything but bad. On the contrary . . . He eyed Gaye over his coffee, as she tucked into her breakfast, he'd arrived late, but his thoughts returned to the woman whose bed he had left four hours ago and who might still be lying in it less than half a mile away. It had been four o'clock when he'd climbed out of it trying not to wake her but she'd stirred and propped herself up on one arm as she'd eyed him dressing.

'You don't have to leave.'

'I do. Work.'

'At this hour?' She pushed a hand through her tousled dark hair and he almost capitulated and climbed back into that warm, sweet-smelling bed. His body ached with longing but he steeled himself and leaned over to kiss her, wondering if he'd be strong enough to resist as her lips connected with his. She responded hungrily and his body screamed at him to stay but his instinct told him otherwise. This time his instinct won.

'I'll call you,' he'd said, pulling away.

'I've heard that one before,' she'd replied, lying back. '*I'll* call *you*. Come for dinner. I'm an excellent cook.'

'I don't doubt that for a moment.'

He had kissed her again before pulling away with a smile which had faded the moment he'd closed the door behind him and walked down the empty corridor. As he'd ridden home along the deserted promenade he couldn't shake off the impression that her smile had also faded the moment he'd left. But he had no reason to believe that. He was just being neurotic.

When he'd reached his yacht, he'd flicked on the heaters, taken a shower and had sat with a black coffee staring into nothing and trying to think of nothing, but the memory of the night had run before him in cinematic images moulding and merging together until all he could remember was the feel of her soft voluptuous body, the smell of her skin and the taste of her lips. They had spoken little and he'd divulged nothing about his background. It had been a passionate night full of longing and hunger and hers had been as rapacious as his. It didn't have to be more than that, and she had made it clear that it wasn't going to be, certainly on her part, because she was leaving for America in a few weeks. That suited him fine but even as he told himself that he knew it didn't and maybe it was that which was bugging him. But no, what also nagged at him was the fact that she'd taken the apartment for three months and only had a month left to run on the lease, so why hadn't she contacted him in November?

Irritated with himself and weary beyond measure he'd finally climbed into his bunk and closed his eyes. But it wasn't Carolyn Grantham who had occupied his thoughts but the woman before him now and that made his head ache even more.

'I had a visit from DCS Adams late yesterday afternoon,' Gaye said, cutting into her bacon. 'He told me he's taken over the case and that any information I had was to be given to him and only him.'

Horton fought to clear his befuddled brain. 'He's from the National Crime Agency.'

'So he said. He studied the hand and asked me about the kind of knife that could have severed it. I told him what I had already told you and Sergeant Cantelli.'

Horton swallowed his coffee and thought about buying another. He looked up and as he did the manageress brushed past them delivering a cooked breakfast to the couple to their right.

'Another coffee, Inspector?' she asked pleasantly, turning towards Horton.

Did he look so badly in need of it? He guessed he did. 'Thanks.'

'I'll bring it over.'

Gaye raised her eyebrows. 'Special treatment. Are you a regular?'

'I come in occasionally and our paths crossed professionally some years ago when her house was burgled.' He bit into his toasted bacon sandwich, hoping that Carolyn didn't come here for breakfast or a coffee to take out. He wished now he'd suggested somewhere else to meet Gaye. The manageress returned and placed his coffee in front of him. She gave him a warm smile before leaving. Horton saw Gaye's eyes follow her.

'Nice looking woman, good figure, about forty I'd say.'

'Probably,' Horton muttered taking the last bite of his sandwich, wondering if any of the national reporters were doorstepping Moira Langham, but only if they had got hold of the story and if Moira had told others, which she must have done by now. The press were bound to pick up on it sooner or later. But that was DCS Adams' baby not his. So what was he doing here discussing how Graham Langham could have been separated from his hand when he should be at the station wading through his other cases including the petrol station robbery?

Gaye sat back and eyed him closely. He felt a little uneasy under her curious and penetrating stare as though she might be able to read his thoughts and that she knew where he had been and what he had been doing last night. Why would it matter if she did? They weren't dating. For all he knew she could have been out with a boyfriend last night enjoying herself, just as she might have been doing in London on Wednesday night. She soon disabused him of that idea.

'As you didn't take me for a drink last night I spent the time doing some further research into knives and examining the pattern of the wound. There are a number of readily available knives that could match the weapon used or it could have been specially crafted to order.'

'Tailor-made?' he asked, feeling guilty and swallowing his coffee.

'Yes, but not necessarily for the purpose of mutilating or killing. It could have been made for hunting or horticultural work.'

'Not much of that around here.'

'Oh, I don't know, there's plenty of countryside on the Isle of Wight and over the hill beyond Portsmouth. But to get back to my research. I've whittled it down to a handful of types that are possible. And don't worry, I'll tell DCS Adams all this.'

Then why was she telling him.

'I know how curious you are,' she said reading his thoughts, 'and once you start something you like to see it through even if you're no longer on the case. Besides, I wanted someone to bounce my ideas off and try them out before I tell DCS Adams.'

He nodded, feeling flattered, and uncomfortable that she seemed to be able to read him so easily.

'Go on.'

She pushed away her empty plate and took out her phone. Lowering her voice she said, 'As I said before, the wound was inflicted with a smooth-edged curved blade. A blade that would have been at least four inches in length. So the first possibility is a Karambit knife.'

Horton looked puzzled.

She explained. 'The Karambit is of Indonesian origin and is a hand-held curved knife. It was originally used for agricultural purposes but has evolved over the years until now it is used as a weapon of self-defence.'

'And attack.'

'Yes. Today it's made of more expensive material than the original knives, which were for the peasants. It can also sometimes have a folding blade. They vary in style but they're still made in Indonesia. The Karambit knife can measure eleven inches in length and has a seven-inch curved blade.' She swivelled round her phone to show him a picture of it.

Horton thought it certainly possible.

'Then there is a Khukuri knife,' she continued, consulting her phone where she'd made notes. 'That's Nepalese and again has an inwardly curving edge. It's used both as a tool and weapon. It's also used by The Royal Gurkha Rifles and is often known as the Gurkha knife.'

'Whose motto is *Better to die than live a coward,*' Horton said, rapidly thinking. 'Adams claims that Langham was an informer. Perhaps the Gurkha motto means that the killer thought Langham a coward for grassing on them and it was better for him to die.'

'It doesn't mean the killer is a Gurkha or former Gurkha,' Gaye answered, swallowing her coffee.

'But it could be someone with knowledge and an interest in the Gurkhas.'

'Here's a picture of it. As you can see it's a large knife measuring seventeen and three quarter inches and has a twelve-inch blade. The other possibilities are a Hawkbill knife generally used for gardening and horticultural purposes because they hook thin items, such as plant stems much like a sickle, or they can be used for cutting vinyl or linoleum. They can also be used by the emergency services for getting someone out of a vehicle. It's a slashing weapon not a stabbing one so seems perfect for the purpose of slashing off the victim's hand. The Hawkbill knife varies in length but the longer ones of this type can be almost nine inches and with a four-inch blade, so again possible.'

Horton was feeling more despondent as she continued and his headache wasn't improving. The list of potential suspects was growing ever longer with each word she uttered. But he told himself it was Adams' job to sift through this lot and if Langham was a grass then Adams might know from Gaye's description certain individuals who owned such a knife.

'Then there is a boat knife and fishing knife.' But before she could show him pictures of these his mobile phone rang, drawing hostile glances from the couple in their sixties at the table to their right.

'It's Sergeant Elkins.' He rose, answering it. Gaye followed him out of the café to the veranda.

'Westerbrook's boat's been located,' Elkins announced with excitement.

'Where?'

'In the Thorney Channel.'

That puzzled Horton. It was in completely the opposite direction to Fareham Marina, and to reach it Westerbrook would need to have motored east along Southsea Bay stretching across the southern tip of Portsmouth, across the entrance to Langstone Harbour where his own boat was kept in the marina, along Hayling Bay, still heading east until he reached the entrance to Chichester Harbour. Here there were three routes he could have chosen. The first would have taken him north up the Emsworth Channel with Hayling Island on his left and Thorney Island on his right, eventually to reach the small coastal village of Emsworth. Another channel would have taken him east up to Chichester Marina, which also branched off to the small ancient coastal village of Bosham. But Westerbrook had chosen the middle, much quieter and relatively isolated, Thorney Channel, sandwiched between the coastal countryside of Chidham on its eastern flank and the rural expanse of Thorney Island on its western side. Once a Royal Air Force base Thorney Island was now home to the army and 12 Regiment Royal Artillery recruited from Lancashire and Cumbria, and known as The Lancashire and Cumbria Gunners.

'Where in the Thorney Channel,' he asked, recalling the channel. He'd sailed up it and moored there many times.

'On a buoy just past the Thorney Island Sailing Club. Someone going to their own boat moored just beyond it didn't recognize it. He found Westerbrook on board. He's dead, Andy.'

Horton took a breath and glanced at Gaye who was clearly following the conversation even given she couldn't hear Elkins' end of it. Her petite figure was almost swamped by her sailing jacket.

'Suspicious?' Horton asked Elkins.

'There's no sign of a break in, the hatch was open, and no physical evidence of it being murder. It looks as though he had a heart attack, but I'm no expert and I haven't moved the body or turned him over.'

Horton checked the time. It was just after nine, and about two and a half hours away from high tide. But he knew the channel was accessible from the pontoon by the sailing club at all states of the tide. He asked Elkins to arrange for a small boat or RIB to meet him at the pontoon. Then turning to Gaye he said, 'Are you doing anything special this morning?'

'Apart from having breakfast with you, which we've finished, and informing DCS Adams about my research into knives, which can wait, no. You've got a body.'

He swiftly relayed what Elkins had said.

'I've got my medical case in the car, shall I meet you there?'

'No, meet me at Southsea Marina. I'll leave my bike there and come with you.'

Horton returned to pay for the extra coffee but was told it was on the house. He never liked receiving freebies but he didn't have time to protest. The marina was only a couple of miles away and within minutes he'd left his Harley there and was sitting in Gaye's Mini as she negotiated the roads northwards out of the city through the tail end of the morning rush hour traffic. Horton's mind was buzzing with questions, which didn't do much for his headache, but fortunately he'd found a couple of Panadols in his jacket pocket and had swallowed them before climbing into Gaye's car. They'd soon take effect.

He called Cantelli and told him what had occurred. 'Ask Walters to dig up what he can on Westerbrook, we'll need next of kin details. And reinterview Lesley Nugent. Ask him if he has any idea why Westerbrook should be at Thorney. I'll call Bliss as soon as I've taken a look at the body, but if she asks where I am then tell her.' Horton explained that Dr Clayton was with him. He'd also have to call Uckfield if this looked like a suspicious death or rather Bliss would tell Uckfield, but maybe it was a natural death and there was nothing to investigate.

Addressing Gaye as they headed eastwards along the motorway towards Thorney he said, 'You didn't finish telling me about your research into knives.'

She passed over her phone. 'Scroll through my pictures, it's OK there's nothing embarrassing or compromising on there, anything like that I transfer to my computer or I delete,' she joked. 'One of the latest photographs will show you a boat knife.'

He flicked on it.

She said, 'You can see that a boat knife also has a curved blade but the knife is much smaller, usually about four and a half inches and the blade just over three inches. I think it's still possible it could have been used, particularly if the victim was restrained and unable to defend himself or was dead or unconscious as I said before, and the same goes for a fishing knife, which can be just over ten inches with a blade length of five and a half inches, so even more likely.'

A fishing knife fitted with Westerbrook and Nugent. And he remembered seeing one in that box on the boat when he'd first examined the hand in the container. So had Westerbrook killed Langham with or without Nugent's help, and, disturbed and sickened by what he'd done, killed himself, choosing an isolated spot to do so? Or had he been so distressed by his brutal act it had brought on a heart attack? Horton thought he was probably wrong on both counts because why draw attention to it if they had killed Langham, and that certainly didn't fit with DCS Adams' revelation.

Gaye was saying, 'As you can see there are several knives that fit the bill including butcher's knives.'

Horton dashed her a keen glance. 'What kind of butcher's knife?'

'A skinning knife for one. It's curved, and has a six-inch blade. A Victorinox Skinning Knife is used by the majority of British butchers.'

Is it indeed. So perhaps Westerbrook wasn't involved in Langham's death but Lesley Nugent was and he'd wangled a fishing trip with Westerbrook to dispose of the hand, only he cocked it up. Westerbrook saw Nugent's line hooked around the seaweed strewn container and insisted it be brought up and opened.

And *if* Westerbrook had been killed by Nugent then whether DCS Adams liked it or not Uckfield and his Major Crime Team would be involved, and that meant he would be too. He again called Cantelli and left a message on his mobile phone for him to ask Nugent his movements for Wednesday and Thursday nights.

They were stopped at the main gate to the army base as a matter of normal security procedure. Horton showed his warrant card and explained the reason for their presence. They were admitted and given directions to the slipway and pontoon. Horton already knew the way, having been here a few times, by road, as well as by water for functions at the sailing club rather than for work because, strictly speaking, this wasn't Hampshire police's patch but the jurisdiction of the Sussex police. They had crossed the county border into West Sussex. The harbours though were patrolled by the Hampshire police marine unit and that meant his presence here was perfectly legitimate and there was no need to inform Sussex.

Gaye pulled into the lane beside the church and parked in front of the slipway where a soldier met them and directed them to a waiting RIB on the end of the pontoon. The man on board, wearing casual clothes and a warm sailing jacket, introduced himself as Jeremy Dowdswell. In the channel Horton could see the police launch roped up beside Westerbrook's blue-hulled motor boat.

The wind was barrelling down the channel from the north making it bitterly cold and the sky was a deathly grey. Horton surveyed the area. He'd often picked up a buoy and stayed overnight here, enjoying the peace and tranquillity of the small natural harbour, particularly out of season. But even in the height of summer it was quieter than the crowded Solent and its adjacent harbours. And it was a desert in comparison to Portsmouth Harbour and Fareham Marina where Westerbrook should have returned after Elkins had interviewed him. There was only one small marina here and that was situated on the western side of the channel about half a mile north. Horton could see the masts of the yachts in the distance. Westerbrook probably hadn't gone into that because it was only accessible at certain states of the tide whereas this channel didn't dry out.

He turned his gaze shoreward to the single-storey building that was affiliated to the Army Sailing Association. Mounted on a long gantry close to it was a security camera, which might prove helpful. There would be other cameras positioned along the perimeter of the island, because although it was accessible to the public by a footpath, which ran around the island's boundary, it was an army establishment and members of the public not only had to press the intercom on the gate to access the footpath but had to stay strictly on it, veering off only to visit the church, next to the sailing club.

Horton addressed the RIB's pilot. He was about early forties, fit-looking, with short brown hair and wide hazel eyes in a tanned craggy face.

'Did you find the body?'

'Yes. I was on my way to my boat. That's it over there.' He pointed to a medium sized yacht a little further up the channel. 'I like to use my boat all year round, weather and work permitting, so I don't usually lay her up. This mooring,' he said as they drew level with Westerbrook's boat, 'belongs to Hugh Maltby. He's deployed in Cyprus. His boat's laid up so I thought this guy must have decided to pick up the buoy and stay overnight. No problem with that but as I was heading towards my boat I saw part of the canvas cover flapping in the wind. I called out. There was no answer or movement on board. I was concerned. It's bitterly cold and I wondered if he'd had an accident or had been taken ill so I tied up alongside, boarded it and saw he was dead. I called the police marine unit. I've met Sergeant Elkins a few times, he and his officers have been to the sailing club and given talks about crime prevention, so I had the number to hand.'

Elkins, on board Westerbrook's boat, caught the line Horton threw up to him as Dowdswell silenced the small outboard engine on the RIB.

'Do you know when he arrived?'

'No. The security cameras might show up something. I can ask the Station Commander if you can have access to them, if you need it.'

'You're in the army?'

'Yes.' He hesitated for a second then said, 'I know it's probably highly unusual as far as you're concerned, and it's too late now to save the poor man, but when you've finished I'd like to say a few words over the body before he's removed, if that's all right.'

Horton looked surprised.

Dowdswell continued. 'I'm the padre.' He smiled. 'Not what you expected, Inspector. But I'm used to that. We're not all cassocks, coffee and cake. We go on the front line and have to be fit.'

'Of course. I'm sorry.'

'No need to apologize.'

Horton said it would be fine. Elkins reached out a hand to assist Gaye, who, being used to boats and a sailor herself, climbed nimbly through the gap in the awning into the cockpit. Horton followed suit, while Dowdswell remained in the RIB. The last time Horton had been on board, on Wednesday, the blue canvas awning had been folded back to reveal the cockpit, now it was stretched over it reaching the helm, making it darker inside but protecting them from the worse of the icy wind. The boat tackle box was where he had last seen it, in the cockpit, and the filleting knife was still inside it. Could it have been used to severe Langham's hand?

Gaye stripped off her jacket and quickly donned a scene suit and gloves while Horton studied the crumpled body of Clive Westerbrook lying face down at the helm between the pilot and passenger's seat. He was wearing the same clothes as when Horton had seen him on the police launch at Oyster Quays – minus the jacket – casual dark navy trousers, trainers, and a thick navy blue jumper. The skin on the back of Westerbrook's neck and the outstretched right hand was blueish and had already begun to decay. Horton could smell the stench of the corpse over the mud, seaweed and salt of the incoming tide. Beyond where Gaye was crouching over the body, Horton could see into the cabin below. The bed was made up with a blue and green patterned sleeping bag and on it was Westerbrook's jacket. There were fishing rods in the lockers that ran along the side of the boat. On top of the work surface that covered the sink, next to the gas hob, was a plain white mug, an empty whisky glass, a bottle of whisky with only a third left in it and a bottle of tablets.

Horton's phone rang. It was Walters.

'Thought you might like to know, guv, I've just run a check on Clive Westerbrook. He's got a criminal record.'

'Has he indeed. For what?' Horton asked, keenly interested.

'Fraudulently obtaining money by deception. He applied for a mortgage advance of four hundred thousand pounds using a false name and he falsified information in order to obtain it to buy a house that he intended to resell. He got a two-year custodial sentence, served one year and was released two years ago. Nothing before then or since.'

Horton recalled that Julian Tierney, the marina manager, had said that Westerbrook was a financial consultant. And that he'd had his boat in the marina for a year, before which he'd kept a boat at Horsea Marina. Had that been before his prison sentence or since then? Westerbrook hadn't exactly come out of prison destitute.

'Contact Her Majesty's Revenue and Customs, find out what employment Westerbrook is registered for, when he last filed a tax return and whether or not he pays National Insurance. Also get on to the Financial Services Authority, find out if he's registered as a financial consultant.'

Perhaps that was why Westerbrook had been so reluctant to enter a police station and make his statement. He might have had something to hide, not connected with Langham's hand or his death, but perhaps he'd been worried they'd not only discover his criminal record but delve deeper to find he was again up to his old tricks.

Horton turned to Elkins. 'When we're finished here, drop into Horsea Marina, ask them if Westerbrook ever kept a boat there, what type and when.'

Gaye straightened up and stepped back to join them in the cockpit.

'No blunt force trauma to the back of the skull. No bullet entry wound or stab wound. And no visible signs of strangulation,' she said. 'Judging by the colour of the skin, the temperature in the cabin and outside, the body temperature and the insect life visible in the body I'd say he's been dead about thirty-five hours, possibly more.

When I get him on the slab I'll measure the potassium content of the fluid in his eyes to confirm that.'

'Which means he died at approximately nine o'clock on Wednesday night.'

Elkins looked up. 'Not long after finding that hand.'

Westerbrook had certainly not been at home on Wednesday night when Horton had paid a visit to his flat and he'd never returned to Fareham Marina.

Gaye continued. 'The position of the body indicates he was returning from the cockpit, here, to the helm, possibly with the intention of descending into the cabin. He wasn't sitting at the helm, otherwise he'd have fallen to the right. And if he'd been in the passenger seat he'd have fallen in the other direction or possibly just slumped forward.'

So perhaps he'd gone outside for a breath of fresh air. Bloody cold though, Horton thought, remembering that walk along the boardwalk with Carolyn to her car. It would have been freezing out here. There were no heaters and that sleeping bag was hardly enough to keep warm in this weather. But perhaps he'd been a hardy soul. He hadn't looked it though and according to what little Horton had learnt about him he'd had a heart condition so perhaps the cold had precipitated a heart attack. A suggestion he made to Gaye which she agreed could be highly possible.

'Cold air can be a trigger for a coronary. Someone with heart disease may not be able to compensate for their body's higher demand for oxygen when inhaling, especially if undertaking extra physical activity. Even picking up a buoy, letting down the anchor or making up the bunk could have been enough to trigger it. And drinking whisky would certainly not have helped.'

Horton recalled what Carolyn had said about missing people under stress returning to an area where they had happier memories. Perhaps Westerbrook had come here to find some kind of mental relief from what he had seen but the distress caused by that, coupled with the cold and his pre-existing heart condition had all combined to kill him. It was looking less like a suspicious death. But he'd still call in Taylor and his Scene of Crime Officers.

'Do you want me to go through his pockets?'

'Please.'

While she did Horton called Taylor and gave instructions for him and the forensic photographer, Jim Clarke, to come out. He asked Elkins to liaise with Dowdswell over admitting them to the base.

Gaye handed Horton a wallet and a set of keys and returned to search the remaining pockets, easing the body slightly but without altering its position. The wallet contained about fifty pounds, and a driver's licence, no credit cards, which wasn't surprising given Westerbrook's background, and no photographs. The keys looked like they were to Westerbrook's car and his flat. The boat keys, Horton had already noted, were in the helm. Gaye straightened up and handed Horton a mobile phone. It would be interesting to see who he had called and who had called him.

Horton asked Elkins to put the items into evidence bags.

'On the surface it doesn't look like a suspicious death,' Gaye said, stepping out of her scene suit and into her sailing jacket. 'But I'll schedule the autopsy for later today. And we'll need toxicology tests to establish that it really is whisky he drank and not whisky mixed with something that sent him into the "other world".'

Did she believe there was one? After dissecting and examining so many bodies he was curious to know her views. But that kind of conversation could wait until a more appropriate time, which he thought wouldn't be over dinner, it wasn't the kind of subject for that although it might be over a drink or two. The thought of which brought him back to Carolyn Grantham. He wondered what she was doing now and thinking. Was she recalling their night together and thinking about their next intimate dinner engagement? Or was she reporting to Lord Eames or DCS Sawyer? Well if she was it wasn't about Jennifer, because they'd not discussed her. All she could report on was his sexual prowess and he wondered what she'd say about that. There had been no complaints last night. He didn't like to think she had been faking it.

Climbing off the boat into Dowdswell's RIB Gaye said, 'Hope the headache's better although I shouldn't think this has helped.'

But it had, in fact he'd forgotten all about it. Perhaps the pills he'd taken earlier had kicked in. He watched her depart before calling Bliss. Succinctly and quickly he updated her on Westerbrook's death. 'I've got SOCO on their way.'

'I'll apprise Detective Superintendent Adams,' she said abruptly.

'Why? He said Nugent and Westerbrook had nothing to do with Langham's death.'

'He should still know, this could possibly change things,' she curtly replied before ringing off. But he knew what she was really thinking. This would give her an excuse to raise her profile with Adams.

Horton waited for SOCO and Clarke to arrive and gave them instructions to sweep the area around Westerbrook's body and the helm, and take pictures and a video of the body. The rest could be done once the boat was back in Portsmouth on the secure berth in the port. He climbed off Westerbrook's boat on to the police launch while they got to work. Elkins had already called the undertakers, and Dowdswell said he'd organize a larger boat to collect them and bring them over when Horton was ready. He returned to shore to do so.

Ripley made coffee and Horton drank his while mulling over the fact of Westerbrook's death. The air was chill with a salty icy drizzle. He didn't get any further with his thoughts, but he was very interested to see what Walters came back with.

Taylor and Tremaine weren't long. Taylor reported that they'd got several prints and hair samples from the helm and had taken scrapings from the deck, the seats and the helm.

'Any signs of blood or flesh?' asked Horton.

'No.'

Horton asked Taylor and his team to return to Portsmouth and wait at the international port for him. He told Elkins that he'd take the boat back and asked him to follow in the police launch. Jeremy Dowdswell returned and said his piece over the body and the undertakers removed it. Bliss hadn't called him back yet.

When they had all left Horton asked Elkins to check the lockers in the cockpit while he turned his attention to the helm. They'd leave the search of the cabin to SOCO. The key was already in the helm and stretching his fingers into latex gloves Horton turned it but didn't switch on the engine.

He studied the instrumentation. There was a compass and a log which gave the boat's speed and trip distance. There was also a GPS chart plotter and a Fishfinder as well as VHF radio, clock and barometer. There was half a tank of fuel in the boat, enough to get him back to Portsmouth.

Elkins appeared behind Horton. 'Fenders, mooring warps, a boat-hook, boarding ladder, four life jackets and a fire extinguisher,' he reported, peering over Horton's shoulder, adding, 'He's got some expensive equipment. Latest state of the art GPS and Fishfinder. Looks as though this guy was a serious fisherman. He must have gone out further than the Solent with that lot.'

Horton thought so too. Westerbrook must have fished in the English Channel or if he was that keen maybe he took fishing holidays abroad. Had that been alone or with buddies? In Horton's experience most fishermen went out with someone. But according to Nugent only once with him.

Horton called Cantelli and again left a message on his voicemail asking him to meet him at the quayside at the secure berth at the port in half an hour if he could. Then he lifted anchor and cast off from the buoy and, with Elkins following, took the boat out of the harbour.

NINE

Despite the circumstances, Horton enjoyed piloting the craft. The sea air helped to clear the residue of his muggy head as he motored across Hayling Bay. Within half an hour he was entering Portsmouth Harbour and another ten minutes saw him mooring up on the quayside where Cantelli was talking to Taylor, Beth Tremaine and Jim Clarke. Horton threw Cantelli the line and asked him to hold on to it, knowing that the sergeant wouldn't know how to tie it off from his elbow. Horton stilled the engine and jumped nimbly off, taking the line from Cantelli and securing it to the cleat. He nodded Taylor on to the boat and then left him and the others to it, asking them to bag up the items in the bait box and get them over to the lab.

'How did you get on with Lesley Nugent?' Horton asked, climbing into Cantelli's car.

'He wasn't at work. He phoned in sick. I spoke to Kevin Jameson. Nugent started there three months ago and has had several days off sick. I don't think he'll be working there for much longer. He doesn't work in accounts and neither does he work in order processing, he's a meat packer.'

'He seems to have an aversion to telling the truth.'

'And an aversion to meat so he told me when I finally caught up with him.'

'Eh?'

'He suffers from Carnophobia. The fear of meat.'

'You're kidding?'

'No. I looked it up. It exists all right but whether Nugent really suffers from it is another matter. I went to his flat. Had the devil of a job getting him to come to the door, but when I bellowed through the letterbox and asked him to look through the window he recognized me and let me in.'

'Why so scared?'

'He said finding the hand had given him nightmares. He chain-smoked so much that I must have had my passive smoking dose for a year. He insists that he only met Westerbrook twice, once at the angling club on Sunday lunchtime and then on Wednesday when they went fishing.'

'A lie?'

Cantelli looked doubtful. 'I'm not sure. It sounded like the truth. He says he was in the pub Wednesday night drinking to try and forget finding the hand and last night he was at home, alone. I checked with the landlord of the pub. Nugent was in there until closing time. I asked Nugent if he knew why Westerbrook would be in the Thorney Channel. He said he had no idea. He knew where I meant though, but said he'd never fished there, no point when there was the big wide Solent to choose from. When I told him that Westerbrook had been found dead I thought he was going to faint. I don't think he was faking. He asked how Westerbrook had died and I gave him the stock answer, too soon to say and all that.'

'It's looking as though Westerbrook had a heart attack. But even if he did that doesn't mean to say he's not mixed up with Langham's murder and the same applies to Nugent.' Horton relayed the gist of what Gaye had told him about the knife including the fact that she'd mentioned a Victorinox Skinning Knife used by the majority of British butchers.

Cantelli said, 'Perhaps Nugent pinched one of the refrigerated vehicles to drive the body somewhere to dump it or they used Langham's own van. Yeah, I know, why keep hold of the hand, why draw attention to it by fishing it up, and why put it in a container?'

'And what's their motive for killing Langham?' Horton frowned, perplexed. 'He couldn't have broken into either man's property, and neither of them were worth informing on, and even if they were up to something Adams would have warned us off them.'

'Not if he doesn't know about them being involved with Langham.'

Cantelli was right. Even if they discovered meat scrapings on the container it didn't mean it had come from Jamesons or that Nugent was involved.

As Cantelli made for Westerbrook's flat Horton removed Westerbrook's phone from the evidence bag and checked the address book. He found no one listed with the surname Westerbrook but there were some Christian names and one of those could be a relative. There were remarkably few people listed, about ten in total which didn't include the angling club and Westerbrook's call log was empty, which he thought unusual. Westerbrook was very efficient at deleting his messages and calls, both those he had made and received.

Soon Cantelli was pulling into a parking space opposite the flat. Horton replaced the mobile phone and retrieved the set of keys from another evidence bag. He inserted one in the outer door as Cantelli checked the post box.

'Only circulars and most of them addressed to R. Mountjoy. Could be the previous owner or tenant.'

They climbed to the second floor where they found flat sixteen and entered. The place stank of stale food, sweat and cigarettes. It clearly hadn't been aired for some time. Two doors gave off the hallway to the bathroom on the left and the bedroom on the right. Cantelli took the bedroom while Horton stepped through into the lounge. There was a small kitchenette off it.

It was very shabby. The paintwork was scuffed and dirty around the light switches. There were cobwebs in the corners and the carpet hadn't seen a vacuum cleaner for some time. There were dull pictures of country scenes in non-descript colours bought from the usual chain stores on the magnolia painted walls. There was no fire surround, only a modern electric fire up against the wall. The room was littered with newspapers, magazines and clothes thrown on to an armchair, sofa, and coffee table. As Horton crossed to a round table in front of the window he glanced at the magazines. They were a mixture on fishing and money. The newspapers were the popular daily tabloids, the last one dated Tuesday. This flat had all the hallmarks of a slovenly man and not one, he thought, who would usually be so efficient at deleting his mobile phone messages and calls on a regular basis.

In amongst the debris there was a laptop computer. He could send it to the hi-tech unit if Westerbrook's death proved suspicious and Horton thought even if he'd died from natural causes the proximity of his death to finding that hand was sufficient for him to say it was suspicious, but maybe not others. He'd take it back with them and let Walters play with it. He was good at that kind of thing, and it might provide them with some interesting background information and more contacts.

Horton picked over the paper-strewn desk. There were unpaid bills, a threatening letter from the letting agent about non-payment of rent, or rather the direct debit payment had been refused. And there were bank statements going back a couple of months.

'He's overdrawn by six hundred pounds,' Horton said as Cantelli entered. 'It could be more by now, this statement's three months old. There doesn't seem to be any personal letters or papers, and nothing that gives us his next of kin.'

'Nothing in the bedroom either just the chaos of unwashed clothes. And the sheets don't look as though they've been changed for a while. I see he kept his kitchen in the same inimitable style. Hope there are no maggots.'

Horton knew he was alluding to fishing ones rather than those that inhabited human cadavers. Cantelli began rummaging around in the drawers. He pulled a face as he opened the fridge. Horton could smell something going off from where he was standing a few paces away. He crossed to a sideboard. On it was a music system and beside that a handful of CDs. Westerbrook's musical tastes ran to Elton John, Whitney Houston and Mariah Carey. Opening the cupboard he found a box containing some fishing paraphernalia, and one with some documentation, which included a passport, and a medical card. It gave Westerbrook's GP as Dr Rostock at the North End Medical Centre. The practice would have his current next of kin listed. Perhaps he hadn't changed it since his divorce. Horton flicked through the passport. The last time he'd gone abroad had been four years ago and that had been to Turkey before he'd gone to prison. Prison made him think of Langham. Maybe that was the connection.

He said, 'Westerbrook was released from prison two years ago when Langham would have been banged up. Could they have met there?'

'I'll check when we get back.'

Horton continued his scrutiny of the cupboard. There were two bottles of whisky and one of rum, a third full, and some dusty glasses. He straightened up and looked around. There was no phone. Cantelli confirmed there hadn't been one in the bedroom either. So Westerbrook only used his mobile. Again Horton retrieved it from the plastic bag and this time flicked to the photographs on it. There was one of Westerbrook's boat and one of him with a rather large fish, and that was it. None of his son or of anyone else.

'Anything of interest in the kitchen?'

'Just a drawer full of circulars, some milk that's gone off and some mouldy bread and cheese. No sign of a bloody knife or even a curved one,' Cantelli added, tongue in cheek.

'Try ringing these numbers when we get back.' Horton handed Cantelli the evidence bag with the phone in it. He picked up the laptop computer, adding, 'Walters might be able to get something from this.' Horton left everything else where it was. There was no need to bag it up or call SOCO unless Dr Clayton discovered Westerbrook *had* been killed.

'Hope the neighbours don't think we're burglars,' Cantelli said, locking up.

'We'll soon know if blue lights come flashing after us.'

But they reached the station without incident where Horton put Westerbrook's computer in front of Walters. 'Christmas present for you. See what you can get out of it.'

Walters' eyes lit up. Horton asked if he'd got any further information on Westerbrook.

'He's not registered as a licenced financial consultant with the Financial Services Authority and he hasn't filed a tax return since he came out of prison. He's not registered as being self-employed either and there's no record of him being employed.'

Horton was puzzled. 'So what does he do for a living and one that sees him driving a new car and owning an expensive boat? The boat's an old model but it would still have set him back about fifteen, or twenty thousand pounds. There's no paperwork in the flat to show he bought that boat or car, see if you can find any record of the transactions on his computer.'

Cantelli said, 'I'll contact the Saab garage. And I'll make an appointment to see his bank manager.'

'Also get in touch with the landlord.'

Cantelli nodded.

Elkins called to say that Westerbrook had never kept a boat at Horsea Marina. So he'd lied to Julian Tierney, the marina manager at Fareham. Not that that was a crime. Maybe he'd said it to make himself appear big.

Horton gave Walters Westerbrook's medical card and asked him to contact the surgery. He made his way along the corridor to Bliss's office and as he did a text came through on his mobile. It was Carolyn. His pulse beat faster as he read it. 'Dinner tomorrow night, my place, eight thirty.' He texted back. 'Great, see you then.'

He reported to Bliss.

'So it looks like natural causes,' she said.

He admitted that was probably the case but added that there were several factors about Westerbrook that needed looking into.

'But not connected with Graham Langham,' she insisted.

He shrugged.

She said that DCS Adams was unconcerned about Westerbrook and that they could continue with their enquiries. He asked if she'd heard any news about Alfie Wright but she said he hadn't been found. Horton, heading for the canteen, thought the press in the form of Leanne Payne must be harassing Uckfield for a statement.

He intended buying sandwiches and taking them back to his office but he caught sight of PCs Seaton and Kate Summerfield and, after buying a cheese salad roll, he took it to their table.

'How did you get on at the car breakers?' he asked, biting into his roll. Bliss hadn't mentioned it. But then Langham wasn't their case and whatever information she'd gained from the two officers she'd have sent over to DCI Neame and DCS Adams, there would have been no need to tell him.

Seaton answered. 'The van was collected for scrap two months ago. The owner, Daryl Farnley, has all the correct paperwork for receiving it but not for breaking it up. He swears blind that neither he nor any of his staff recycled it and sold it on but then he would. We got a list of his staff, there are only three, one of them has a record for being drunk and disorderly, theft and violent assault. His last conviction was eight years ago, he was out in five, Wayne Gower. He used to live in Portsmouth with his common law wife and kids on the Paradise Estate. He probably knew Graham Langham and sold him the van. We reported to DCI Bliss.'

'Did you speak to Gower?'

Summerfield answered. 'He denies selling it on but he worked in a garage before his convictions, so he'd know how to recycle vehicles.'

Horton thought she was right. He returned to CID where Walters greeted him with the news that the medical centre had a Karen Tempson listed as Westerbrook's next of kin, his ex-wife, but that he hadn't tried the number they'd given him. Horton did but it was obviously an old number as the line was dead.

Cantelli reported that Langham and Westerbrook hadn't served time in the same prison. 'Langham was at Winchester prison, Westerbrook on the Isle of Wight.'

So that put paid to the theory they might have known one another while serving time.

Cantelli added, 'I couldn't speak to the manager at the Central Bank where Westerbrook has an account but I made an appointment to see him. The only problem is it's for Monday.'

Horton had guessed that might be the case.

'I contacted the garage where Westerbrook bought his car. They phoned me back to make sure I was who I claimed to be and said that Westerbrook paid cash and bought it nine months ago.'

Horton raised his eyebrows. 'Where did he get that much money?'

'He told them he'd won it.'

'And they believed him!'

'I don't think they cared either way as long as they got a sale. I've been through his phone numbers. There was a voicemail on a few of them but I didn't leave a message, and a couple of those I spoke to said they hadn't seen or spoken to Clive for some time and seemed keen to distance themselves from him. One of the numbers was his landlord and he said that Westerbrook was heavily in arrears with his rent and that he was in the process of having him evicted.'

'Well he won't have to bother now,' Horton said, somewhat cynically.

'I told him he could do nothing until we had finished with the apartment. But one of the numbers was that of Aubrey Davidson of Seaturn Marine, his business is servicing marine engines.'

'That's the van that was at the marina when we talked to the manager, Julian Tierney.' Horton recalled that it had left by the time they returned to their car.

'Yes, and he's also secretary of the Lee-on-the-Solent angling club. He wanted to know why I was calling him on Westerbrook's number so I broke the bad news. He assumed it was a heart attack. I said that we might want to speak to him. I didn't mention Lesley Nugent.'

'Call him back and ask if I can meet him at the angling club.'

'Do you want me along, only it's the twins school nativity play tonight and—'

'I wouldn't dream of depriving you,' Horton said with sincerity. He only wished he could attend Emma's school Christmas production and with a flood of guilt realized he had no idea what that was or even if she was involved in one. He felt ashamed and angry with himself for being far too wrapped up in work and his personal investigation. He'd remedy that and soon. There was no reason why he shouldn't go to Emma's private school. He wasn't barred from it or from seeing Emma there. Just because Catherine didn't want him there didn't mean he had to comply.

Cantelli said, 'We're taking Mum. It'll be the first year that Dad won't be there to see it,' he added sadly. Horton knew it was fast approaching the anniversary of Toni Cantelli's death, which had been a year ago last December. Looking more cheerful, Cantelli continued, 'Joe's a shepherd and Molly's an angel, although that might be an offence under the Trades Description Act or the United Union of Angels might object.'

Horton smiled. The twins at six were the youngest of Cantelli's brood of five and all the children as far as Horton could see and knew were good kids.

'I'm sure she'll look, act and behave angelically.'

'Until we get her home, yeah.'

Cantelli called Aubrey Davidson who said he'd be happy to see DI Horton at the angling club in about an hour, if that suited. It did perfectly. And although the meeting was earlier than Horton had anticipated he still insisted that there was no need for Cantelli to join him. He'd return to the marina and collect the Harley.

TEN

Horton didn't head straight for the angling club. He took the scenic route along the Lee-on-the-Solent seafront and pulled up opposite a modern apartment block. Several lights blazed and Christmas lights twinkled in the windows but there were none showing in the small retirement flat on the top floor of the four-storey building that had once been the home of former PC Adrian Stanley, the copper who had cursorily followed up Jennifer's disappearance. Perhaps the flat was still for sale or the new owners were out. There was nothing he could glean from being here except to recall his only conversation with Stanley which had been in April. It had been a bright cloudless day. The yachts had been racing off Cowes in the Solent. Now it was dark and cold.

Shortly after his visit Stanley had died following a massive stroke, but he'd muttered something about a brooch before dying. It was the one his late wife had been wearing on the day Stanley had been given the Queen's Gallantry Medal for Bravery in 1980 after he and another officer had gone in pursuit of armed robbers and had come under intense fire. It was also the same brooch that had once been in Jennifer's possession and which Horton had been told by DCS Sawyer had been part of a private and extremely valuable collection of jewellery stolen from a house in north Hampshire in 1977. Horton had found the report of the robbery and the list of stolen items, only there had been no mention of a brooch having been stolen.

The brooch that had been in Stanley's possession had vanished along with all photographic evidence of it. Stanley's son, Robin, couldn't remember it and Horton, only glimpsing it once in the photograph and a couple of times on his mother couldn't recall it in detail, all he had was the impression of an inky-blue stone in the centre surrounded by other stones, possibly diamonds. He hadn't asked Sawyer for a description of it, maybe he should. He wondered if Sawyer would tell him, or rather tell him the truth. He had denied his and his unit's involvement in taking the brooch and the photographic evidence of it and Horton thought that was the truth, because his suspicion of who was behind the theft fell in another direction.

He turned towards the sea. Across the Solent was Lord Eames' extensive holiday home fronting on to a private beach. Horton wondered if any of the family would be there for Christmas, Agent Harriet Eames, for example, Lord Eames' daughter whom Horton had worked with on a couple of cases. She was based at Europol in The Hague. Or perhaps Eames, like Catherine's new boyfriend, liked to spend Christmas in sunnier climes. If Eames had ordered the removal of that brooch and the photographic evidence of it then it had great significance in the case. And if his mother had worn it then how did she come to own such a valuable piece of jewellery, *if* the stones were real, it could have been paste and he could be mistaken about seeing her wearing it.

He gazed at the lights twinkling across the Solent on the small town of Cowes. The drizzling rain had passed over leaving a fresh clear early evening but there was still a stiff north-westerly wind making it bitingly cold. What had induced Clive Westerbrook to go fishing in similar weather on Wednesday? The fact he had to dispose of a body? Not so according to DCS Adams. Why had Westerbrook invited a man he had only met once to go fishing with him on a cold grey winter's day midweek, *if* they could believe Nugent's story? Well, he wasn't going to get the answers here.

He found the angling club easily and pulled up alongside a large four-wheel drive car in the otherwise deserted car park. Aubrey Davidson's he presumed. He'd obviously left his work van at home.

The club was closed but the door opened before Horton reached it and a large man whose muscles were rapidly turning to flesh greeted him warmly. His hands were broad and his handshake strong and firm. He waved aside Horton's apology for being delayed with a wide smile in a round face that was clean-shaven and offered Horton a drink, which, he said, he could fetch from behind the shuttered bar at the far end of a long rectangular room bedecked with garish Christmas decorations and a swirling-patterned brown and orange carpet. Horton declined. He got straight to the point.

'I'd like some information about Clive Westerbrook.'

'Yeah, terrible what's happened. Heart attack. Can't say I'm surprised. He'd had warnings.' Davidson's voice was as large as his build. Horton was glad the club was closed otherwise they'd have attracted an audience of curious eavesdroppers.

'You knew him well.'

'Yes, for some years.' Davidson looked slightly uneasy.

'Before his prison sentence?'

Davidson nodded his big head. His expression clouded. 'It's the gambling.' He sank heavily into the seat at one of the tables. 'That's what got him into trouble.'

Horton sat down opposite him. This new information was interesting. It explained his debts and might explain how he'd been able to buy a car for cash, and possibly his boat in the same manner. But even then, without a job and only state benefit to rely on, he must have been either a damn good gambler or very lucky to have won such huge sums of money.

'Bloody mug's game,' Davidson continued. 'I tried to tell him to chuck it in but it's an addiction, an illness, like being an alcoholic. He couldn't stop himself. Clive got sucked in real bad. It destroyed his marriage. We used to live next door to one another. He was earning a fortune as a financial consultant and bloody good at his job. He used to advise me. But he lost a lot of money and I mean a lot. He and Karen used to have one of the large houses along the seafront nearby. They had to sell it because of debts, which was when they came to live next door to me and Marilyn. Not that they were slumming it, we have a lovely house just behind the seafront here,' he quickly added. 'Clive seemed to be doing well. Then one day the bailiffs turned up on his doorstep. Clive was out, Karen was in a terrible state and that was it. She packed a case of his clothes, threw it out on the lawn, refused to let him in, changed the locks and filed for a divorce. But she had to leave the house. Clive had gambled everything away. And then there was that business of the fraud.'

'For which he got convicted.'

Davidson nodded sadly. 'That was the last I saw of him until Sunday morning when he called me and asked if he could come over to the club.'

'To see you.'

'He said he'd like to rejoin. We used to go fishing together and he was club treasurer before he went to prison.' Davidson swallowed and his eyes dropped. Horton could read the rest.

'He stole money from the club to fuel his gambling addiction.'

'He repaid every penny though,' Davidson said quickly and defensively. 'He swore he'd never do it again but I told him to step down as treasurer so as not to be tempted and to get medical and professional help. He promised he would, through Gamblers Anonymous. The next I hear is that he's been sent to prison for mortgage fraud. Then he rang me like I said on Sunday morning. I was surprised to hear from him but I wasn't going to turn my back on him. He arrived just before midday. I signed him in, we exchanged a few words but I didn't get much time to talk to him because Ed, who was due to be behind the bar, called in sick and I had to help out. And now Clive's dead.'

'How did he seem on Sunday?'

'OK.' Davidson answered vaguely.

'But?' probed Horton.

Davidson frowned as he considered his response. 'More uptight than he used to be, I'd say. Edgy, like, but perhaps prison had made him like that.'

Horton wasn't sure if that was hindsight talking or rather Davidson was saying that because he was expected to say something.

Davidson continued. 'He told me he'd returned to his financial investment business.'

That was a lie then. Maybe Westerbrook said it to save face.

'Clive said he'd bought a boat. He wanted to relax more, doctor's orders because of his heart problem. And he wanted to put the past behind him, get back into circulation, meet more people. He thought fishing would help him.'

'Does his ex-wife still live here?'

'No, married a Welshman and moved to Porthcawl. I can give you her number if you'd like it. My wife is still in touch with her. Does she know about Clive yet?'

'Only if your wife has contacted her. We don't have a current contact number for her.'

'I haven't told Marilyn yet.'

'Could you ask her not to contact Karen until we do? I'll arrange for an officer from the local police to call round and break the news.'

'I don't think you'll find she'll be heartbroken but there's a boy, though Clive hasn't seen him since Karen threw him out six years ago. He was seven then so he probably doesn't know or remember much about his dad.'

Horton was going to make damn sure that never happened with him and Emma.

'Do you know why Clive would be moored up in the Thorney Channel in Chichester Harbour?'

Davidson shook his head. 'Is that where he was found?'

'Yes. I wondered if it had any particular significance for him.'

'Not that I know of. It's not one of the places he would regularly have fished either.'

'Did he have a boat before he was convicted for fraud?'

'Yes. A large motor cruiser. It got repossessed about the same time as the bailiffs moved in on his house. Clive used to keep it at Haslar Marina, Gosport.'

Why hadn't Westerbrook told Tierney that instead of saying Horsea Marina? 'How long did he stay in the club on Sunday?'

Davidson screwed up his malleable face as he tried to remember. 'Must have been about an hour or just longer. Yes, he came over to the bar, said he had to go, that was about one fifteen. Said he'd call me.'

'Did you see him talking to anyone?'

'Les Nugent. Les has been a member for over ten years.'

'So he and Clive know one another.'

'Probably. Les has had his ups and downs, but he's always enjoyed his fishing.'

'What kind of ups and downs?' asked Horton interested, wondering why Nugent had lied about not knowing Westerbrook.

'The usual,' Davidson answered with a hint of regret in his deep booming voice. 'Divorce. His wife ran off with a sales rep. No kids. Les went to pieces, had some kind of breakdown and lost his job. He was the accounts manager at Smedleys, the builders' merchants, doing very well until Vera left him. He was out of work for a long time before getting that job at Jamesons.'

'What does Mr Nugent do at Jamesons?' Horton asked casually, disguising his interest.

'Works in accounts, like he did at Smedleys.'

Not according to Nugent and Kevin Jameson. But maybe Nugent had lied to Davidson because he was ashamed that he'd been forced to take a job as a meat packer because it was all he could get. But the fact that Nugent had worked in accounts and Westerbrook in finance made Horton wonder if they had been involved in or had been planning some kind of financial or accounting fraud together.

'We'll need someone to formally identify the body. We could ask Clive's former wife but is there a relative who lives nearer who might be able to do it.'

'Clive's brother emigrated to Canada years ago. And I don't think Karen will want to do it. It's a long way for her to come, and like I say she cut off all ties with Clive years ago. I'll do it if it helps.'

'That's very good of you. Thanks. Would tomorrow morning eleven a.m. be OK?'

'Fine.'

'Would you like a car to take you?'

'No, I'll go in my own. I take it the mortuary is at the hospital? I've never been there before.'

Horton said it was and that he'd meet him there. Davidson relayed Karen Tempson's telephone number and address and showed Horton out.

Outside Horton rang Walters and gave him the details and asked him to arrange for a local police officer to call round. Then he headed back for the station by which time Walters confirmed that Westerbrook had indeed been a gambler.

'His internet browsing history is full of gambling websites.'

Horton addressed Cantelli. 'Does Nugent gamble?'

'If he does he's not winning.'

'Does anyone?'

'No,' Cantelli firmly agreed. 'His flat is small and squalid. But if the three of them, Langham, Westerbrook and Nugent, have large gambling debts that gives us a link and a motive. Maybe Langham was silenced and his hand planted on Westerbrook's boat as a warning to him and Nugent that if they didn't pay up they'd end up the same way.'

Horton considered this. 'I can't see where Langham would get enough money to gamble with but if he *was* gambling then he wasn't doing it online, unless he was using Moira's phone or she lied about him owning one. I'd say he was more of a betting office gambler.'

'Nugent too,' agreed Cantelli. 'I didn't see a computer in his flat but then I didn't search it and, like you say, he could have been using his phone to access the gambling websites. But if they were all into gambling then I can think of one man in this city who doesn't like being owed money.'

'Larry Egmont.'

Cantelli nodded. 'He owns betting shops, amusement arcades, and casinos.'

And one of those casinos was situated near the civic centre, not far from the law courts, where Cantelli had parked on Thursday when they'd talked to Ewan Stringer. There was nothing on Larry Egmont. He'd never been arrested or convicted but perhaps that was because he was clever. If his casino was being used as a front for criminal activity and money laundering then it would be a reason for DCS Adams and the National Crime Agency's interest. Horton swiftly considered Larry Egmont. He'd inherited the business from his late father-in-law George Warner who had come on the scene in 1961 as soon as the law had permitted betting shops and casinos. Many casinos had quickly become a cover for criminal activity. Warner's had been no exception. And the one along South Parade opposite the pier, where Jennifer had worked, had certainly entertained some.

He picked up on Cantelli's theory, 'Perhaps Langham was about to inform on Egmont about some illegal activity in his casinos. Something he overheard or learnt about while in prison. Egmont gets wind of it and abducts, tortures and kills Langham and gets one of his boys to leave the hand on Westerbrook's boat as a calling card, a warning that if he doesn't pay his debts the same could happen to him.'

Walters looked up. 'Perhaps Egmont got Nugent and Westerbrook to kill Langham and dispose of him in return for writing off their debts.'

'But why report finding the hand?'

Cantelli answered. 'Only one of them, say Westerbrook, was to do the job and Nugent inadvertently fished up that hand.'

'But why would Westerbrook want someone to go fishing with him? Much simpler to dispose of the body parts when alone. And why draw attention to the hand?'

'Maybe Nugent's the prime mover in this,' Cantelli suggested. 'He could have given Egmont, or one of his boys, access to Jamesons at night where the deed was done and then he was told to dispose of the body parts but to make sure that the hand was found on Westerbrook's boat as a warning to him.'

But Horton frowned. It still didn't add up because why go to all that trouble? How would Egmont or Nugent know that Westerbrook would go to the angling club on Sunday?

Cantelli added, 'Westerbrook could have been money laundering for Egmont, and he used some of that money to buy the boat and car in cash. I don't think Egmont would have been very pleased about that. Maybe he'd only recently discovered it and the fact that Langham was going to inform on him.'

'If Westerbrook was running scared then why not take off for France or the Channel Islands, not the Thorney Channel.'

'Didn't have his passport on him.'

Cantelli was correct. But Horton said, 'He could have headed east to Brighton or west along the coast to Dorset and on to the West Country or Wales.' He could even have put in at Porthcawl. In fact, thought Horton, he could have travelled around the British Isles, stopping off along the way at many places, and avoided being traced.

Horton addressed Walters. 'Is there a list of his contacts on his computer?'

'They could be in his email address book but I can't access that, it's password protected. I bet his password is written down though, somewhere in his flat. I could take a look around it on Monday, guv, see if I can find it, or we could approach his hosting company. We'd need a warrant for that.'

And they'd probably only get that if Westerbrook's death was suspicious. Horton was convinced it was. Maybe not directly but certainly indirectly. It might not be connected to Langham though. There were, however, too many questions that needed answering and too many lies for him to feel comfortable about putting this down to natural causes.

'Do it tomorrow,' Horton instructed.

'But it's Saturday.'

'So?'

Walters sighed heavily.

Cantelli said, 'I'll get in touch with the army at Thorney and obtain the CCTV footage. It might give us some idea when Westerbrook arrived there.'

Horton agreed but he hesitated. He had no qualms about making Walters work over the weekend but he did in tearing Cantelli away from his wife and children. Not that Barney complained and neither did his wife Charlotte, unlike Catherine who had never come to terms with the unsocial hours his job demanded. She'd accused him of using them as an excuse to get out of family gatherings and engagements connected with her work as marketing executive for her father's marine manufacturing company. She'd actually been correct, not that he'd ever admitted to it.

This wasn't officially a suspicious death so he had no need to authorize overtime, and Bliss certainly wouldn't. Neither Walters nor Cantelli were duty CID at the weekend. He was, but Cantelli said, 'It'll get me out of Christmas shopping.' Horton smiled his thanks and made for his office hoping that Gaye would have some news for him soon. She rang just before six forty-five as Horton was in the middle of answering a tedious email from Bliss about the recent spate of thefts on business premises. Why didn't the bloody woman just speak to him about them?

'Clive Westerbrook died of a massive coronary,' Gaye announced on the telephone.

Natural causes then. There was nothing to investigate. He felt slightly disappointed. 'Brought on by shock or overexertion?' he asked.

'I can't say, except that it was only a matter of time before it happened. His arteries are so clogged I'm surprised the blood pumped through them for as long as it did. His liver was none too healthy either. I think you'll find that the toxicology tests will reveal he consumed a large amount of alcohol before his death. I'm not sure how many of his heart tablets he took but those and the alcohol, combined with the freezing conditions and his already poor health were certainly enough to finish him off. There were no stomach contents and lividity was well established. His body hadn't been moved. He died sometime between nine p.m. and midnight Wednesday night.'

Not long after finding the hand then.

'There is something else though,' Gaye said.

Horton's ears pricked up.

'Although there is no evidence of bruises on the skin I found what appears to be bruising in the deep tissues around the abdomen and the kidneys and on the face.'

Concerned, Horton said, 'Are you saying he was beaten up?'

'The facial bruises could have been caused by the fall.'

'But not those to the abdomen and kidneys.'

'No. *If* they are there. It's difficult to tell immediately after death, they could be just post-mortem changes. Deep bruises often need between twelve and twenty-four hours to become apparent and some may never do so,' she explained. 'I'll examine them and the rest of the body tomorrow using ultraviolet light in case there are other bruises not immediately visible.'

'When would these bruises have been inflicted?'

'Difficult to say but probably not long before he died.'

If he'd taken a beating it didn't mean it was connected with Langham's death. Horton said he'd appreciate any information she could give him.

He rang off after informing her that Westerbrook's body would be formerly identified tomorrow morning at eleven. Then he packed up, left his Harley at the station, and headed on foot for the centre of the city. There was someone he wanted to see and he hoped to find him in one of the town's public houses.

ELEVEN

There was no sign of Billy Jago in the first pub, a run-down poky affair on the edge of the shopping precinct. Horton left without buying a drink and without asking if anyone had seen Jago because that would have been tantamount to announcing to the underworld of Portsmouth that Jago was an informer. Not that those in the pub knew he was a police officer, or hopefully they didn't, but news of someone asking after the slight man with bad teeth, thinning black greasy hair and a crinkled face was enough to raise suspicion. Strictly speaking Billy Jago wasn't a police informer, at least not a registered one. Bliss didn't know about him and Horton had no intention of telling her or letting her discover the fact. By-the-book Bliss would never approve even if Jago revealed Langham's killer, which Horton thought was unlikely but he could always live in hope.

He set off through the busy shopping precinct bedecked with Christmas lights and with Christmas music blaring out from every orifice. The Salvation Army were making a valiant attempt to compete with their traditional Christmas carols by the fountain. He put some money in their tin, earned himself a smile, thank you and God Bless from the cheerful sixty-year-old man and made for the next possible haunt of Jago. It was even more decrepit than the last pub with flaky plaster, scuffed paintwork, filthy windows and dirty blinds. It was also one of a dying breed. The clientele looked to be the same, he thought, surveying the gloomy interior which no amount of Christmas decorations could brighten. There wasn't a man under seventy, and no female in sight unless you counted the brassy blonde of about sixty behind the bar. The decorations looked to be about the same age.

He remembered this place as a boy. Not that he'd ever been inside then, and he didn't think his mother had been either, leastways he'd never waited for her outside like some of his fellow schoolmates had done with their parents. But he recalled seeing the dockyard workers coming in here and the smell of the beer in the hot summer when the doors were wide open. He'd been called here many times as a young uniformed copper over trouble between the then very tough regulars and the gays who had made it fashionable for a while. But those days had gone. The nearby polytechnic had become a university and had expanded phenomenally since then and the students demanded cheap booze, music and food and the chain pubs had taken over. The smoking ban had put the final nail in the coffin for pubs like this. They were dinosaurs soon to become extinct and clearly Jago wouldn't be seen dead in one. Horton didn't stop to buy a drink.

On his third attempt, in a more fashionable bar, close to the Guildhall and civic square, frequented by office workers and students, Horton struck lucky. Jago gave only a flicker of recognition as he pumped the one armed bandit machine in the corner by the gents.

Horton crossed to the bar and ordered a non-alcoholic beer which he drank making a show of looking at his watch as though he was only killing time before going on somewhere. He saw Jago leave and gave him five minutes before he drained his bottle and did the same. Zipping up his jacket he struck out towards the square under the railway bridge knowing that he'd find Jago at the war memorial on his right.

'I can't stop long, Mr Horton,' Jago said, sniffing and pulling a cigarette packet from his shabby fleece jacket. His shifty eyes scanned the civic square in front of him. Horton followed his gaze. People, mainly office workers, were hurrying home or to the bars further along the road towards the university buildings. Horton made to turn when he caught sight of a familiar figure striding across the square. His breath caught in his throat. It was Carolyn. She seemed completely oblivious of the cold. Her short black winter coat was open to reveal a clinging, short woollen red dress, black tights, and medium heeled boots. She was hatless and looked radiant. He thought of the previous night spent with her and the evening and possibly night to come tomorrow and his heart hammered against his chest, fire coursed through his veins and he ached with longing and desire. He watched as she raised her hand and her dark features lit up. A broad smile crossed her beautiful face and for an instant Horton thought it was directed at him before reality rushed in. She wasn't looking at him but ahead. He stiffened as he watched her embrace a man. It was no half-hearted kiss, but a long, lingering and passionate one, something she was very good at he thought with bitterness. He felt a furious flood of envy, which was swiftly consumed by anger, not because of her deceit, but because he'd been foolish enough to let his loins rule his head. He cursed his stupidity as he watched her tuck her hand under the man's arm and snuggle up to him in exactly the same manner she'd done with him last night and she turned back towards the bars in Guildhall Walk.

He'd been an idiot to think the swiftness of their relationship had been the result of a mutual attraction. Even his instinct had been flashing bloody great blue lights at him that it might be some kind of trap but he'd ignored it. Christ, he should have learned by now, but, like an idiot teenager, he'd fallen for it. He'd been feeling lonely and dejected and he had been ripe for the plucking. He'd almost let his guard down. But the trauma of his upbringing had saved him from taking the final step and from making a complete fool of himself by betraying his emotions, and confiding his research findings.

He'd suspected there had been more to her desire to dine and sleep with him and he'd been correct. And that was what had so troubled him in the early hours of this morning. In his heart of hearts he knew it was a trap. And tomorrow night she was banking on getting what she wanted from him during and after that intimate dinner for two in her rented apartment. Was it possible it was bugged? Shit, he hoped not. Not that any recordings could be used in any way to threaten him but the experience of that false rape allegation made by Lucy Richardson – and all he'd done on that occasion had been to have a drink with her in a hotel reception – sent an icy chill through his veins.

By now she would have reported to Eames that he'd accepted the invitation and tomorrow night someone would be listening into their conversation. Why was Eames so keen to discover what he knew about Jennifer? What was it that was dynamite? Was Eames keen to know what Antony Dormand had said about Jennifer being involved or informing on the IRA?

'Can we hurry this up, Mr Horton?' Jago's whining voice broke through Horton's thoughts.

He pushed them aside but not before he had registered that the man Carolyn had been with was the same one he'd seen on their first encounter in The Reef and who he'd seen in the car park at Oyster Quays last night. In his early forties, slender, with slightly too long fair hair. On the first occasion he'd been talking to a group of students and last night heading for his car. One of Eames' men? Possibly.

Curtly, he said, 'Graham Langham.'

'Yeah, what about him?' Jago pulled on his cigarette.

'He's had an accident. A fatal one seeing as his hand has been separated from his body.'

'Christ! Who would do that?' Jago's bloodshot eyes widened with surprise.

'That's what I'm asking you.'

'It don't sound like anyone I know.'

And Jago knew some very tough villains. He thought Jago was probably telling the truth. 'Who did Langham associate with?'

'No one. He was a loner, a one-man job. Unless you count the lads in The Crown but he didn't do no jobs with them. He was in there last Sunday trying to flog some stuff.'

'What stuff?' asked Horton, keenly interested in this new lead.

'A couple of kiddies bikes, a lawnmower.'

'This time of year!'

'Reduced price ready for the spring he said.'

'Who bought them?'

'No idea.'

But Horton could see that Jago knew very well who had purchased the stolen goods but wasn't going to say. It certainly wasn't the stuff that a big villain would have had nicked from his home, a theory that he'd discussed previously with Cantelli and Walters to explain DCS Adams' claim.

'Have you ever had word that Langham was a police informer?'

Jago looked so shocked that he almost swallowed his cigarette. Then his face creased up in thought. 'Could be why he had his hand chopped off,' he ventured hesitantly. 'Hope whoever did it don't know I help you out from time to time Mr Horton.' Jago's eyes darted nervously around him.

'The kind of information you give me Billy is hardly enough to warrant mutilation.'

'You never can tell what upsets folk. Some nasty bastards would cut your head off if you looks at them the wrong way.'

True. 'Is Larry Egmont one of those?'

Jago thought for a moment before replying. 'Maybe. If you get on the wrong side of him but Graham Langham wasn't a gambler.'

'How do you know?'

'I've never seen him in any betting shops. And he wasn't the type to get into Egmont's casino.'

'He could have been betting online.'

'Maybe.'

'Have you ever been inside the casino?'

'Nah. Egmont's choosy about who he lets become a member.'

'I wouldn't have thought he'd worry just as long as he could take their money.'

'They gotta have it in the first place.'

'Point taken. Do you know a man called Clive Westerbrook?'

Jago shook his head.

'Have you seen this man before?'

Horton showed Jago the photograph of Westerbrook he'd taken from his driving licence.

Again Jago shook his head. He removed his cigarette and pinched it out with his finger and thumb and stuck it back in the packet. Horton wasn't sure if that was out of respect for where they were or because he wanted to save the last piece for later.

'It's bleeding freezing out here and I've got nothing more to tell you, Mr Horton.'

Horton eyed him steadily. It was probably the truth. He asked if he had heard of a man called Lesley Nugent but Jago said he hadn't. Horton gave him twenty pounds and let him go. Horton made no attempt to follow, not in order to give Jago time to get away but because he was hesitating over whether to check out the bars along Guildhall Walk to see if Carolyn and her lover were in one of them. If he found her what would she do he wondered? Introduce him as a colleague? A friend?

He headed that way, scanning the road for any sign of them. There were only a few smokers outside the bars, shivering in the cold north-westerly wind. And no one lingering outside Larry Egmont's casino. Horton stopped and eyed it. He recalled the statements that had been taken from George Warner and a member of staff, Irene Ebury, after Jennifer had failed to show for work. PC Stanley hadn't bothered talking to anyone else at the Southsea casino or if he had, and had transcribed the statements, they had vanished from the case file. Warner had simply said that Jennifer had been a good worker, attractive and popular. Irene Ebury had suggested Jennifer had had a lover who had let her down because she'd been dejected for a while and then just before she vanished she had brightened up and had hinted that she was destined for a better life. According to Irene Ebury, Jennifer had kept singing the song made famous by Marilyn Monroe, 'Diamonds Are a Girl's Best Friend'. In the course of a recent investigation, the one that had sparked Horton's research, he'd discovered that Jennifer had known a diamond thief called Peter Croxton. Horton had assumed that Jennifer had been in love with him and planning to run off with him, except he'd learned from another villain and confederate of Croxton that she hadn't. That villain and Croxton were both dead. But perhaps the diamonds weren't part of that haul, or one allegedly stolen from the house in North Hampshire, perhaps they were a brooch given to Jennifer by a boyfriend.

Horton crossed the busy dual carriageway leaving the thought where it was, at the back of his mind, and eyed the bar ahead of him wondering if Carolyn and the man she'd embraced were inside it. It was a popular haunt with the students and Horton knew how Carolyn seemed to like them. As he reached it though, he hesitated and before he could make up his mind whether or not to enter it two men emerged, both of whom he recognized.

'I didn't know this was your kind of place, Tim,' Horton greeted the Chief Crown Prosecutor affably. 'Or yours, Ewan.' Stringer smiled but he looked uneasy.

Shearer answered. 'The demographic is a bit on the young side but on a Friday, after work, a few us from the courts head here to unwind. Not that I'd drink and drive,' he added hastily.

'Never thought you would.'

'And I'm on foot,' Stringer added. 'Are you on duty, Inspector?'

'No, just heading home.' It was better than saying I was following a woman I fancied and made love to last night, who's with another man.

Shearer asked if there was any further news on Alfie Wright.

'Not that I'm aware of. He's still missing. Have you heard anything from him?' Horton addressed Stringer.

'No.'

But Stringer looked increasingly ill at ease. There was something he was holding back. Horton had sensed it yesterday after he and Cantelli had spoken to him, now he knew it. He held Stringer's troubled eyes. Would he confide what it was? Horton hoped so but Stringer pulled himself up and his gaze swivelled to Shearer. 'I'll see you on Sunday, Tim.' He walked away in the direction of the civic centre a rather dejected figure thought Horton.

'Ewan and I are going sailing,' Shearer explained, looking after him with a worried frown.

'You own a boat? Or is it Ewan's?'

'Mine. I've kept one here in Portsmouth for some time even when I was living in London. It's at Horsea Marina, where I'm currently renting a house, so very convenient.' He smiled but it quickly faded. 'He feels he's failed, Andy, not the police but Alfie Wright.'

'I shouldn't think Alfie's conscience is troubling him for one second so Ewan's shouldn't.'

'Probably not but I'm concerned that we've let a dangerous man walk away and if he reoffends and someone gets hurt or killed it'll be on our conscience. And that's what I've stressed to Ewan. Is it possible that Graham Langham's death is connected with Alfie Wright?'

'I don't know. I'm not on either investigation. But personally I don't think so. Ewan knows something about where Alfie's gone, doesn't he?'

Shearer nodded. 'He wouldn't tell me, but he is very worried that Alfie could be connected with Langham.' Shearer shifted before adding, 'I don't like to betray a confidence but I don't think I'd be doing my job if I didn't tell you, although I have stressed to Ewan it's important that he tells the police what he knows. He's checked Alfie's records and discovered that Alfie and Graham Langham shared the same offender manager, Dennis Popham, but as it was at completely different times I told Ewan I thought it unlikely their paths would have crossed that way. I urged him to talk to Uckfield but the superintendent is not the most approachable of police officers. If Ewan doesn't speak to Uckfield I'll see what I can get out of him on Sunday while we're at sea, it's a good place for exchanging confidences,' he added with a wry smile and Horton wondered if that was what Westerbrook and Nugent had done. Maybe after they had Nugent had wanted to distance himself from Westerbrook, which was why he had been in such a hurry to get away from him and the boat. It could also explain why Nugent was so scared. Perhaps Westerbrook had confessed what he was involved in with Egmont or some other villain, or perhaps he'd tried to enrol Nugent in his scheme.

Shearer continued. 'Ewan's a very conscientious man, Andy. He takes his work seriously but he gets a pittance for what he does. He could be making four times as much, probably even more, with his Master's degree in criminology.'

Horton's mind flicked to Carolyn Grantham, that was the subject of her degree.

'Ewan trained for the Bar but he chose to divert into forensic mental health in order to help others, so try not to be too tough on him and tell Detective Superintendent Uckfield that.'

'I'll try but it'll probably have about as much effect as me telling that lot in there that alcohol is bad for them.'

Shearer smiled and took his farewells. Horton looked up at the bar and thought what the hell. He made to head back to the station to collect his Harley then changed his mind. He'd walk home. He needed some air to clear his head.

At the D-Day museum and Southsea Castle on the seafront he broke into a gentle jog, his mind running in the background like a computer programme, his troubled thoughts keeping pace with his pounding feet. He was probably reading far too much into what he had witnessed between Carolyn and that man. He should forget it. He should forget her, but he couldn't, not until he knew why she was really here. And what about Jago's snippet of information? Tomorrow he'd follow it up. It probably had no connection with Langham's death but it might help clear a few robberies off the books, no harm in that, he told himself as he reached the boat, because petty theft was not the remit of DCS Adams. And having justified that to himself, Horton took a hot shower, made himself something to eat and went to bed trying desperately to put both Langham and Carolyn Grantham from his mind.

TWELVE

Saturday

The moment he entered the station early the next morning Horton caught the buzz of excitement. Uckfield's car, along with Dennings' and Trueman's, was already in the car park. He wondered if the rest of Langham's body had been found but revised that opinion because there had been no sign of DCS Adams' car or any other vehicle he didn't recognize. He was about to head for the incident suite when the door to one of the interview rooms opened and a beaming Uckfield stepped out. Horton immediately guessed the reason for Uckfield's good temper. 'You've got Alfie Wright.'

'The shifty bastard was picked up this morning just before six.'

'Where?'

'On a canal boat just outside Devizes.'

'How did you locate him?' As if Horton couldn't guess. Stringer's conscience had troubled him. After speaking to Tim Shearer he'd plucked up the courage to come in. Uckfield confirmed it.

'Ewan Stringer came in yesterday evening to tell us that Alfie had mentioned a woman he'd got close to. Alfie had said he might go straight and kick the booze if he could be with her. He was spinning Stringer a line of course and the dozy git believed it.'

'Some people see the good in everyone.'

'They wouldn't if they did our job.'

No, thought Horton.

Uckfield scratched his backside. 'Stringer said he didn't like to break a confidence but he'd thought it over, wrestled with his conscience and all that sort of twaddle and decided it would be better if Alfie could be found and get help for his illness. I said the best help he could get was being banged up. I don't think Stringer went a bundle on that but tough shit. He said he was worried that Alfie might have had something to do with Graham Langham's death and he didn't want that on his conscience. The woman's called Barbara Everton. Alfie shacked up with her for a few days the last time he came out. She's some kind of new age hippy, into witchcraft, druids, worshipping at Stonehenge and all that cobblers. She was easy to trace, says she makes and sells jewellery but claims benefit and is probably on the game. The Wiltshire Police and Dennings staged a nice little dawn raid this morning and found Alfie all snuggled up nice and cosy in her arms.'

Dawn didn't break in December until now thought Horton but why let that small fact get in the way of a good arrest.

'Any news on Langham?'

'If there is I haven't been told it.' Uckfield declared. Then he lowered his voice, 'But I'll tell you this, Andy, Adams has got it wrong and it won't be the first time. He couldn't find his way out of a paper bag even if someone ripped it open for him. He only made Chief Superintendent because no other bugger wanted him in their department. And if he finds Langham's body parts before the fish have finished with them then I'll hang up my handcuffs. Now I'm getting some breakfast,' and he strutted off down the corridor towards the canteen. Horton decided against joining him. He had other matters to attend to.

CID was deserted, as he'd expected. Bliss had thankfully seen no need to have her weekend disturbed. Cantelli was going from home to the army base to view the CCTV tapes and Walters was going to Westerbrook's flat to see if he could unearth a password to give them access to his emails. Horton wondered if they were both wasting their time but there were those bruises and the unexplained fact that Westerbrook had somehow managed to obtain lots of cash since coming out of prison, despite not having a job.

Horton rang Elkins who told him that Westerbrook's boat was still secured at the ferry port. Horton thought he'd take another look over it and check the log, which might give him some idea of how far Westerbrook had travelled after he'd left Oyster Quays on Wednesday, before showing up dead at Thorney.

Glancing at the clock he rang Moira Langham. He waited impatiently for her to answer, hoping that Adams hadn't put a trace on her phone. He had toyed with the idea of calling on her personally but Adams might be having her watched in case anyone showed up to check her husband hadn't passed on to her any information that could point the finger at the criminals he and his team were allegedly after.

'What do you want? Have you found him?' she said grumpily as though half asleep, after he had announced himself and apologized for calling her so early.

He said they had no news and asked if Graham had gone out at night last weekend.

There was silence. For a moment he thought she'd cut him off, but then there came a sniff before she said, 'Yeah, on Saturday and Sunday night, so what?'

'What time did he return home on Saturday?' Horton knew where he was on Sunday, Jago had told him, in The Crown trying to flog his stolen goods.

'Late. Why?'

'Do you know where he went?'

'No.'

'But he did go out on a job on Saturday night.'

'How should I know?' she said surlily.

But she did know. He could hear it in her voice. 'Is that why you're worried about us finding the van because there'll be stolen goods inside.'

'If there is it's nothing to do with me,' she said quickly and defensively.

'I didn't say it was, Moira.'

'And you can't nick the bugger now, can you? So sod off.'

The line went dead. What had he expected? What he'd more or less got. Maybe Moira had been hoping they'd find the van without them discovering the contents had been stolen so she could sell them. Or perhaps she was hoping to give her children the bicycles as

Christmas presents. They didn't need the lawnmower for their square of concrete back yard but Horton wondered if the rest of Graham Langham's mutilated body was in that van. It would be a grisly find if that were so.

Moira didn't know about any lock-up, or so she had said, but perhaps Langham had left home on Monday afternoon and met his killer there and his remains were inside the van in the lock-up. That would account for it not being found yet. If Langham did have a lock-up then it would be located close to where he lived. Had DCS Adams already considered this? Had he already asked uniformed officers to check it out or was he keeping it quiet so as not to alarm the crook he was after.

Horton rang through to Sergeant Warren and asked him if his officers had been briefed to check out garages in the centre of the city around the Paradise Estate.

'No, should we?'

'Yes, but keep it low key. Get them to ask around for sightings of a white van—'

'Bloody hundreds I should think.'

'This one belongs to Graham Langham.'

'We're already looking for that.'

'I know but it's possible Langham has a lock-up close to his flat. If he does and one of your officers locates it tell me, no one else, OK?'

'Whatever you say, Inspector.'

Warren was a grumpy old git but he usually did as he was told. Next Horton called Walters on his mobile.

'Are you at Westerbrook's flat?'

'Just arrived, guv.'

'Well don't spin it out.' Horton knew Walters. He'd happily stay there all morning if he could get away with it. 'When you're done there get in touch with the city CCTV control office and get hold of any video footage around the Paradise Estate for the weekend prior to Langham's hand showing up and for the following Monday, the day he disappeared.'

'DCS Adams might have them.'

'You'll soon know if he has. But if he hasn't study them for any sign of Langham's white van, particularly if it turned into any of the roads where the lock-up garages are.'

'Thought we weren't on that investigation.'

'We're not.'

Horton rang off and turned his attention to the list of burglaries that had occurred in Portsmouth last Saturday night. There had been five but none of the stolen items matched those Jago had mentioned which Langham had been trying to sell. Langham rarely went off his patch but Horton decided to look a bit further afield than the city for reported thefts. He ran through the list of robberies in the surrounding area of Waterlooville to the north of the city. There had been several opportunist burglaries, more than usual except for in the summer when people foolishly left their doors and windows open. This time of the year the thieves were after Christmas presents, all neatly gift wrapped and stashed under the Christmas tree. And with curtains open to show off the Christmas lights it was a welcome sight to many crooks and crackheads who viewed it as an invitation to help themselves. Langham's theft of bicycles and a lawnmower though suggested that he had been engaged in his usual MO, stealing from garages and sheds. He was essentially an outdoor thief, he rarely broke in and entered properties unless the chance presented itself.

He drew a blank in the outlying regions and turned to Fareham where he sat up keenly interested and devoured what was on his computer screen. Four properties had been burgled last Saturday. The stolen items included two boys' bicycles, two lawnmowers, garden implements, a gas fire in a box, a case of toys and some fitness equipment, all stashed away in garages and sheds. This had Langham stamped all over it and what was more the properties targeted were all in Green Parade which faced the marina where Westerbrook moored his boat.

Excited, Horton picked up his phone and rang Fareham police station hoping to get the duty CID officer. A weary-sounding DS Reynolds answered the phone to him.

After announcing himself Horton said, 'Gary, do you know anything about the robberies in Green Parade, last Saturday?'

'Only what's on file.'

Horton had only read a summary of the stolen items. For now he was anxious to short-cut reading the full report. 'Any reports of a white van seen in the vicinity?'

'Yes. Why? Have you got the scumbag who did it and he's owned up?' Reynolds' voice lifted.

'If it's who I think it is he won't be owning up. He's dead.' Horton told him. 'What was seen by your witnesses?'

'Just a dirty white van parked outside a couple of the houses. No signage on it and no one got the registration number. They didn't take much notice of it. They assumed it was a workman connected with someone living in the street.'

'Have you got any video footage from the area?'

'Some. There are cameras at the nearby wharf and on the approach road but I haven't had the chance to run through them yet. There's only me and DC Whittle and he went sick on Wednesday.'

'We'll do it. Can you send them over?'

'With pleasure.'

'Any fingerprints?'

'A crime scene officer went out. I haven't chased the fingerprint bureau yet and they haven't got back to me.'

'I'll call them. I'll let you know if a dirty white van shows up.'

Horton immediately rang through to the fingerprint bureau. He quoted the crime numbers to Jane Astley and asked if she and her team had a match on any prints. Not yet was the answer.

'Can you fast track them and if it helps they could match Graham Langham's.'

Horton doubted if Langham had bothered to wear gloves while committing his crime, or if he had, Horton was damn sure he'd have taken them off for some reason even if it was just to pick his nose or scratch his arse and then he'd forget to put them back on. Jane said she'd call him as soon as she had anything.

Horton printed off the summaries of the reports on the burglaries and stuffed them in the pocket of his jacket. He grabbed his helmet and headed out of the station. Within twenty minutes he was pulling up in Green Parade, where the robberies had taken place. This area was to the south of the Hard where he and Cantelli had been on Thursday. A narrow alleyway led off to his left, northwards, past the old warehouse and into the small square that formed the Hard. Horton stared across the stretch of recreational green at the boats moored up on pontoons in Wallington River which fed into Salterns Lake and then into the upper reaches of Portsmouth Harbour, and out into the Solent. Across the narrow stretch of water he could see the greens and bunkers of Cams Hill Golf Club. There didn't appear to be any golfers on it. Horton couldn't say he blamed them in the damp chilly morning.

From here he could see the empty space that was Westerbrook's mooring. Two people were walking their dogs on the green and another was following the footpath that hugged the shore. He climbed off the Harley and turned to view the houses behind him, they were a mix of terraced and semi-detached properties. One of them had been badly affected by fire. The top floor had been severely damaged, which was where the fire must have started. Horton shivered as he recalled his own experiences of being trapped inside a burning building. The upstairs windows were boarded up, the brickwork blackened but the roof was intact which meant the firefighters had arrived before the fire had got too strong a hold. He hoped the occupants had got out safely.

He pulled out the reports of the robberies and read that they had taken place between four thirty and eight thirty a week ago, on Saturday, when it had been dark. Two of the garage doors had been forced open, the third, the owner admitted, had been open to begin with. The lock had been faulty and he'd been too busy to have it fixed.

Horton began walking along the road eyeing the houses that had been burgled. He was certain this was Langham's work. He must have spent some time studying which garages and sheds to target, perhaps seeing the owners leave or noting the houses that were in darkness denoting that the occupants were out. Langham would have simply walked up the driveways and helped himself to the contents of the garages. Or he'd opened the rickety side gates, entered the gardens, forced the flimsy padlocks on the sheds and carried and wheeled out the stuff as though he was being paid to do so. Langham had been a cocky bastard with a quick enough mind and a ready tongue to wrangle his way out of many awkward situations, except the last, Horton thought sanguinely.

But Horton couldn't see that any of these houses belonged to the Mr Big that Adams was allegedly after and who Langham might have been informing on. He gazed up at the fire-damaged house. Something niggled at him. The fire could have no connection with Graham Langham, why should it, but he was curious to know when it had occurred. He found himself reaching for his phone and calling Maitland, the Fire Investigation Officer. Horton apologized for disturbing him at a weekend.

'Have you got a moment to talk about the house fire in Fareham?' Horton asked.

'I've got several. You mean the fire in Green Parade and the fatality. Leonard Borland, aged sixty-six.'

Horton felt sorry for the poor man and his family. 'Anyone else inside at the time?'

'No, he lived alone.'

'When did it happen?'

'It was reported at six fifty-three, Tuesday, by a couple who were returning from work and saw the smoke. The fire service arrived three minutes later. Mr Borland had fallen against an electric fire in one of the upstairs bedrooms. He could have stumbled on it or been taken ill and fell on it but whatever happened he made no attempt to fight off the flames or try and escape from them so he could have suffered a major stroke, aneurism or heart attack. I haven't got the results of the post-mortem yet. The bedroom door was shut but a window was open, which fuelled the fire, that and Mr Borland himself lying on top of the electric fire.'

Horton shuddered at the image Maitland had conjured up. The fire had been three days after Langham had been here on his robbing spree and the day before his hand had been fished up. The times for it having anything to do with Langham or with Westerbrook's death were wrong but there was the common factor of the *location*, and that nagged away at him.

Maitland said, 'Do you think it was suspicious?'

'Probably not.' It couldn't be.

Maitland said, 'Well, let me know if you want to take a look at it.'

Horton said he would but that he doubted it would be necessary. Nevertheless he rang the mortuary and Dr Clayton.

'I'm examining the bruises later this afternoon,' she said.

'I'm not ringing about that. I'm enquiring about another body. A Leonard Borland, he died in a house fire on Tuesday evening. His body might already have been released to the undertaker.' There was a pause while she obviously looked up the record on the computer. He wasn't sure why he was following this up. It was probably as Maitland had said a tragic accident. But that pricking sensation between his shoulder blades told him he couldn't leave it unchecked.

'No. He's not been done yet,' Gaye answered. 'There's a backlog. This latest flu epidemic and the cold weather are causing a log jam in the mortuary. Would you like me to take a look at him?'

She was busy. It would be a waste of her time but he said, 'Please.'

'I'll make a preliminary examination but a full autopsy will have to wait until tomorrow if it's urgent or Monday.'

'Monday will be fine. Is there a next of kin noted on your records?'

'A daughter. Sandra Trenchard. Lives in Boston. Massachusetts that is, not Boston Lincolnshire.'

That could explain why she wasn't jumping up and down demanding the autopsy to be held immediately and for her father's body to be released. It would take her a while to get a flight. And for all he knew she might not care for her father, she might be ill or she could have decided to hold off her visit and the funeral until after Christmas. He'd doubt the undertakers could arrange a funeral before then even if the autopsy had been conducted.

Gaye said she'd try and have something for him by the time he accompanied Aubrey Davidson for the formal identification of Westerbrook's body.

As Horton wasn't far from Lee-on-the Solent he decided to go in search of Lesley Nugent. He wanted to probe Nugent to find out if Westerbrook had shared any confidences with him while out fishing, but there was no answer to Horton's repeated knocks on his flat door. Horton peered through both the letter box and the window but could see no sign of life. As he was leaving a woman came out of the flat below.

'If you're after Les he went out about an hour ago.'

'Any idea where I might find him?'

She shrugged. 'The pub or the betting shop I expect.'

It was too early for the pub so Horton tried the local betting shop, mentally noting that Nugent was a gambler. He didn't find him but he was told by the betting office clerk that Nugent enjoyed a flutter on a regular basis but not with very high stakes, and he rarely won.

Horton made for the mortuary where he met Davidson in the small waiting area outside the viewing room. Davidson was grim-faced. He pulled himself up and nodded at Horton to indicate that he was ready for the ordeal ahead. Taking a deep breath he stepped inside the small chill room and a mortuary attendant lifted the cover on the corpse. There was a slight tensing of Davidson's body, a moment's stunned silence, then shakily, he said, 'Yes, that's Clive Westerbrook. Poor bugger.'

They left the room. 'Never thought I'd be doing that,' Davidson said, taking a handkerchief from his pocket and wiping his perspiring brow. He was trying not to show that it had disturbed him more than he'd thought it would.

Horton offered him refreshment but Davidson shook his head. He said he'd like some air though. They stepped outside. Horton said, 'Did you service the engine on his boat?'

'Yes.'

'Did he ever say who he had bought it from?'

'No. He'd had it about a year.'

Which tied in with what Tierney had told them.

'So you go to Fareham Marina frequently.'

'I go to a lot of marinas,' Davidson said puzzled, clearly wondering what Horton was driving at.

'Were you at Fareham Marina last Saturday, late afternoon early evening?' Perhaps Davidson had seen Langham or his van.

But he shook his head. 'No. I was fishing during the day and then opened up the club for the evening.'

'You own a boat?'

'Yes, a motorboat. I keep it at Gosport Marina.'

Horton thanked him and watched him leave before heading back into the mortuary.

He found Gaye bending over what remained of Leonard Borland lying on the mortuary slab. Horton's stomach churned and he steeled himself to study the charred remains. The body was lying face down. It was a gruesome sight. He only hoped the poor man had been unconscious or dead when he'd fallen on that electric fire.

'I'm sorry if I've wasted your time,' he began but she cut in.

'You haven't. See here,' she pointed to the back of the skull. Horton couldn't see much except blackened bone and flesh. 'He's been struck forcibly, more than once, there is a massive contusion.'

Horton's blood ran cold. His mind raced with thoughts, coincidence that Borland had been brutally attacked in the same area that Langham had burgled and Westerbrook had kept his boat? Maybe but until he knew more he wasn't going to make a judgement.

'Could he have struck his head against something when falling?' Horton asked, wondering why it hadn't been picked up before. But then the body had probably been removed from the room by the firefighters and shipped straight here by the undertakers. The back log in the mortuary, and it not being flagged up as suspicious, had delayed matters.

'Not unless he staggered about, twisted and turned and then fell face down over that fire, and not by the pattern of that wound,' she answered with conviction. 'There is one forcible impact and then others around the area where the victim was repeatedly struck.'

Horton tensed with anger. 'Did he fall on the fire?'

'Maybe.' She looked up from the corpse and eyed him steadily and soberly. 'Or maybe he was placed on it in the hope it would cover up the attack.'

'It nearly did.'

There was a moment's silence.

'I'll do a full autopsy. I've called Tom, he's on his way in.'

There were other mortuary attendants but Horton knew that Gaye always liked to work with Tom who had a penchant for whistling songs from Rodgers and Hammerstein musicals. He asked if she had Borland's personal effects or if they were at the station or with the undertaker.

'They're here.'

While she went to retrieve them Horton called Maitland. 'Can you meet me at Leonard Borland's house in fifteen minutes?'

'His death is suspicious?'

'As hell.'

THIRTEEN

'It's safe to go in, but you'd better put this on anyway.' Maitland handed Horton the hard hat he'd retrieved from the back of his fire investigation van parked outside the burnt house.

They entered by the front door. The downstairs was smoke-damaged but not burnt. The house smelt of damp and death. Horton shivered as they climbed the stairs. His own fate could so easily have been the same as Leonard Borland's. Twice he'd been caught in fire in the course of his investigations. It was unfortunately an all too common method used by villains to try and hide their crimes and confuse the scene, and its use was increasing, but it was usually ineffective, as Gaye Clayton had proved. As he came out on to the landing, Horton couldn't help wondering if another pathologist might have missed that blow to Borland's head or put it down to a fall. Gaye couldn't give him precise details of the weapon used but she'd said it could have been a poker, a golf club, walking stick or a heavy duty torch. He didn't expect to find whatever it had been in the house but he'd look anyway.

The charred remains of the door to the front bedroom lay around them on the floor. Reading Horton's thoughts Maitland said, 'The door had been burnt through and the fire had just started to get a hold on the landing when the firefighters arrived.'

They stepped inside. Horton's feet crunched on the plaster that had fallen from the ceiling. The room felt chill and clawing and there was the lingering stench of roast flesh. Even though it was only an hour after midday the room was dim because the windows were boarded up and there was only a limited amount of light coming through from the landing. It was enough to see by but Maitland switched on his powerful torch. In its beam Horton saw the twisted remains of the small three-bar electric fire that had claimed Borland's life, unless Dr Clayton found the victim had died from those blows to his head. The electric fire was in front of what was left of a table and chair positioned in the bay window.

Maitland said, 'The house is centrally heated and there's a radiator in this room.' Horton could see its blackened metal underneath the bay window. 'But when I checked the boiler clock in the kitchen it wasn't set to come on until seven p.m. and the fire started at six fifty-three. It took hold quickly given the material in this room, wooden table, wooden chair, bookcase, carpet.'

Horton eyed what was left of the bookcase and its contents, some of which had crumpled in a heap on the floor. The plaster from the walls and ceiling had fallen on some of them. The old fire place had been boarded up and there was no grate, iron or otherwise, and no mantelpiece for Borland to have fallen against and struck his head on, but then he hadn't, someone had ruthlessly and cold-bloodedly killed him. Neither was there a bed, dressing table or chest of drawers.

He said, 'It looks as though Mr Borland used this room as a study. Strange having the window open when he was using an electric fire to heat the room and didn't put the central heating on. Why not close the window and keep the heat contained.'

Maitland shrugged. 'Maybe he just liked a bit of fresh air.'

'Maybe someone else opened that window after striking him on the back of the head and dragging his body to position it over the fire.'

'So that's what Dr Clayton found.'

'Yes. Massive blows to the back of the skull.' Horton saw Maitland's eyes travel the room. 'Precisely,' Horton added. 'Nothing to have caused that violent trauma to the skull and I said blows, plural.' Borland's death was murder, or manslaughter at the least, and that meant this would be Uckfield's baby unless there was a link with Langham and then DCS Adams would assume control and that was the reason why Horton hadn't yet called this in. He wanted to view the scene first because if Adams took charge then he'd certainly be excluded from any subsequent investigation.

Horton continued to study the room, envisaging what might have occurred here. 'Mr Borland comes in, shuts the door behind him, switches on the electric fire and sits at his table in the window to do what?'

'Read a book, write a letter? There was no computer—'

'It could have been taken by his assailant.'

Maitland nodded. 'But there were binoculars.' Maitland pointed to their blackened and buckled remains on the floor.

Interesting. But maybe Borland just liked looking at the scenery. Horton couldn't see outside because of the boarded up windows but he knew that from here Borland would have had a clear view of the boats on the pontoons. He'd also be able to focus on anyone sailing or motoring up or down Wallington River, into Salterns Lake and then into Portsmouth Harbour. And on the opposite side of the river there was the golf course. Perhaps Borland's interest had been focused on the golfers or on others using the bunkers for another form of recreational activity. Perhaps Leonard Borland had been a peeping Tom and a blackmailer and whoever he was blackmailing had killed him.

'Was there any evidence of a break-in?'

'No. And the back door was locked.'

'It could have been locked by the assailant himself when he left. Where were Borland's house keys?'

'In the kitchen, on the work surface.'

'Perhaps Borland kept a spare back door key outside under a mat or flower pot. The assailant knew it was there, let himself in and then calmly let himself out again replacing the key as he went. He'd have enough time to get away before anyone noticed the smoke.' And where had he gone? Had he climbed into a car and driven off, or simply walked away? Had he entered the marina and gone on board a boat? Teams of officers would be deployed here to ask questions and take statements. They needed to know when Leonard Borland had last been seen alive.

Maitland's voice pierced Horton's eager thoughts. 'Maybe Leonard Borland willingly let someone in, showed him upstairs and when his back was turned he was attacked.'

'That means it would be someone he knew and someone he trusted.' Or someone he was blackmailing. A golfer perhaps who'd come armed with a club.

Maitland said, 'Or it could be a con merchant who got violent when Borland wouldn't tell him where he kept his savings.'

Possibly. 'Do we know anything about his background?'

Maitland shook his head.

'Let's take a look around. You do the back bedroom and bathroom. I'll take the other front bedroom.'

It was small with a single bed, unmade, a wardrobe and chest of drawers, both empty and smoke damaged. The window was also boarded up and the walls were blackened by smoke, and plaster had come off the walls and ceiling just as it had on the stairs as Horton descended them. The front room overlooking the green, footpath and then the pontoons was untouched by the fire except for a layer of ash over everything. It was where Borland must have spent his time when he wasn't looking through his binoculars upstairs. There was a fairly new television, a music centre, comfortable sofa and two chairs. There were also family photographs on the walls and on the mantelpiece. Some were of a woman in her thirties with three young children, the daughter and grandchildren in Boston, Horton presumed. There were several of a couple, a lean, tall man with a sun-tanned smiling face, intelligent and kindly grey eyes, whom he assumed was Leonard Borland and presumably his late wife beside him, because if they had been estranged then Horton didn't think there would have been any photographs of her or of them as a couple.

He'd expected a larger set man with a solemn expression or one who had looked shrewd rather than friendly, he didn't know why. He took the most recent picture from its frame and slipped it into his notebook wondering when Mrs Borland had died. They would be able to get all that information from the daughter, or possibly a neighbour.

He met Maitland in the hall who said, 'There are only his clothes in the back bedroom and a photograph of him and his wife beside his bed along with a thriller. And only the usual toiletries in the bathroom.'

'No golf clubs?'

'No.'

Horton asked Maitland to check out the kitchen while he entered the back room. It had once been used as a dining room. In it was a round oak table and four matching chairs all darkened by the smoke. In the alcove to the right of the fireplace was a dresser displaying crockery and cupboards below it. The cupboards revealed six blue folders neatly inscribed. Borland had been a methodical man.

Horton spread the folders out on the dining room table. They were marked, correspondence, bills, insurance, guarantees, pensions, personal. Horton turned to the latter. It revealed Borland's birth and marriage certificate and his wife's death certificate. She had died two years ago of an aneurism. He turned his attention to the file labelled 'pensions'. A few minutes later Maitland entered.

'Nothing in the kitchen except the usual.'

'According to this,' Horton said, indicating the piece of paper in his hand, 'Leonard Borland was in the civil service for forty years. He retired at the age of fifty-eight after achieving the grade of Senior Executive Officer. He worked for the Department for Work and Pensions.' That certainly didn't throw any light on why he had been killed. And it didn't sound like a blackmailer. He took his phone from his jacket pocket. 'I'll call this in. Do you have any photographs of the body in situ?'

'No. The fire fighters pulled the poor beggar out in the hope he might still be alive.'

That was standard practice. He asked Maitland to check the contents of the garage and garden shed while he rang Uckfield. 'We have a suspicious death, Steve.' Horton quickly brought him up to speed.

Uckfield listened in silence until Horton had finished, then Uckfield said, 'Could be a coincidence that Langham was in the area, and he was there three days before the fire, it could also be chance that Westerbrook kept his boat there.'

'That still doesn't alter the fact that Leonard Borland was viciously assaulted before being left to die in a fire.'

'Seal it off, get SOCO in. Trueman will get the incident suite up and running.'

'I'll bag up the files and bring them back with me.' Horton said. 'Maitland will send over the photographs of the fire scene and his full report.'

Maitland returned. 'Just the usual stuff in the garage, old tools, bits of furniture he no longer wanted in the house and a fairly new car. Garden implements, pots and compost bags in the shed. No golf clubs, walking stick or torch.'

Horton left Maitland to brief SOCO and the uniformed officers when they arrived and went to speak to the neighbours. There was no answer at the property the other side of the shared driveway but at the adjoining house he found himself facing a neatly dressed slight woman in her early seventies, with soft white waved hair. Horton introduced himself, showed his warrant card and told her she was at liberty to contact the local police station to check his credentials but seeing the police patrol car arrive she declined and showed him in.

'It's awful what happened to poor Leonard and him such a careful man,' she said, waving Horton into the rear room, which judging by its comfortable furniture and the television was the one she lived in, while preserving, Horton guessed, the front room overlooking the road and marina as her 'best room' in the old tradition of the British working and middle classes. 'I can't think how he could have set fire to the house.'

'How well did you know him, Mrs . . .?'

'Samson. Margaret. Very well, both him and Jean, his late wife.

Nice couple. They were good neighbours, which counts for a lot these days. Not sure who I'm going to get in there next,' she said worriedly, gesturing him into one of the three comfortable chairs in the room. 'You read and hear so much about difficult neighbours. People aren't as respectful as they once were. Oh, I've been lucky, nice professional couple the other side of me. Out at work all day, hardly see them except sometimes at weekends when they're in the garden in the summer or washing their cars. They've each got one, new models too. It makes you wonder—'

But Horton didn't want to wonder not unless it concerned Borland. 'Did Mr Borland have any hobbies or interests,' he quickly asked, stemming the flow.

'He liked his garden. And he used to go birdwatching.'

'He told you that?'

'He'd go out with binoculars,' she declared as if that sealed the matter.

'Did he say where?'

'No.'

'Or what kind of birds he'd seen?'

'No,' she eyed him, slightly puzzled.

He gave her what he hoped was a reassuring smile. 'I just wondered if he took any books with him, to help him identify the birds and perhaps he showed you these when you got chatting.'

'No, nothing like that. We never talked about birds, just the weather, the local news, that sort of thing.'

And that to Horton didn't sound like a keen ornithologist. The binoculars and his walks were used for another purpose.

'Did he have a boat?' he asked.

'Good gracious no,' she declared, smiling at Horton as if he was mad, her tone conveying that it was beyond the realms of fantasy for anyone like her and her neighbours to own such a luxury.

'So he didn't go fishing?'

'No,' she firmly answered, which backed up the fact that neither he nor Maitland had found any fishing equipment in the house, garage or garden.

'I understand he was retired,' Horton said.

'Yes. He used to work in the civil service like my late husband. He died two years ago. He'd had dementia for years. I nursed him right to the end. He had a series of mini-strokes then pneumonia finally took him off. Leonard had a good pension like my Jim. And only the one child. Sandra. She went to live in America. Pity really, because neither Leonard nor Jean got to see their grandchildren as often as they would have liked, although they did go to America not long after Leonard retired and again before Jean was taken.'

Picking up something she said earlier, Horton asked her what she had meant by Leonard Borland being 'careful'.

'Well he wasn't one to do things in a hurry, or on impulse. Jean used to say it drove her mad sometimes. It took him ages to make a decision. He'd research everything, go to the library, read books, write it down, weigh up all the pros and cons. And he had to have everything just right in the house, boiler checked, doors properly equipped with locks.'

But no alarm system, Horton had noted, so perhaps not so careful after all. 'Apart from the walking with the binoculars and his garden do you know how else he spent his time?'

'Like most retired people living alone, cleaning, shopping, cooking, changing his library books.'

Horton smiled. 'When did you last see Mr Borland?'

'Monday morning.'

So Langham hadn't killed him on Saturday but Horton hadn't thought that for longer than a nanosecond.

'I was wiping down the front windows, it's the condensation, it builds up in this cold weather, when I saw him walk past. I rapped on the window and waved. He waved back and smiled. And to think—'

'Did he have the binoculars with him?'

'No. He was smartly dressed, suit and overcoat. Though he was never a slovenly man, always neatly turned out.'

'But he didn't usually wear a suit?'

She looked puzzled as though she didn't understand the question and she probably didn't. 'Well not since he retired,' she said. 'Only when he was going somewhere special.'

'Such as?'

Again she threw him a confused look. Clearly she didn't know. So where was he going, wondered Horton. Not that it was relevant. And why hadn't he taken his car. Horton asked if he often went out leaving the car behind.

'Yes. Well, it's so expensive these days to run a car and to park it. And Leonard gets, got,' she corrected with a sorrowful expression, 'his free bus pass and discount on the trains. It's not worth taking the car into Fareham when you can walk it from here or hop on a bus, unless he was doing a big shop, then it's always handy to have a car.'

So maybe he was just staying local but not going to shop, or, as she suggested, perhaps he had been taking public transport somewhere. 'Did you see him return?'

'No.'

'And you didn't see him at all on Tuesday?'

'No.'

'Do you know if Mr Borland had any visitors on Tuesday afternoon or evening, anyone who might have parked a car on his driveway or who you saw approach his house?' He didn't hold out much hope of her having seen anyone because she lived at the rear of the house and not the front.

'He might have done. I don't know. I was out in the afternoon and early evening. Good job too because if I'd have seen that fire it would have frightened me to death. I came home to find firemen all over the place with hoses and three fire engines outside the house, it almost gave me a heart attack.'

Horton wasn't sure about that. He thought Margaret Samson was made of stronger stuff.

'The firemen assured me the fire was out and that my house was safe. I asked about Leonard and that's when they told me they'd found him dead. He must have had a heart attack and knocked over or fell on a fire. He didn't smoke I know that. Such a terrible way to go.' She shook her head sorrowfully.

He rose. She looked momentarily disappointed. Perhaps she didn't get many visitors. As she showed him to the door Horton told her that there would be a police presence for some time as they were investigating the circumstances surrounding Mr Borland's death and that an officer would call on her again to take her statement. She didn't seem surprised or curious but accepted it as a matter of course.

The SOCO van had arrived but there was no sign of Taylor and Tremaine or Maitland which meant they were inside the house. The area had been cordoned off and a uniformed officer stood outside. The activity was beginning to attract the interest of passers-by. Soon the local press would be here. Uckfield would probably set up a mobile incident room on the green opposite and would delegate officers to conduct a house-to-house. Horton crossed the road and made his way through the narrow footpath to the Hard where he found Julian Tierney in the marina office.

Tierney spoke first. 'I hear that Mr Westerbrook's been found dead, heart attack.'

'Who told you?'

'Aubrey Davidson. He was here a moment ago. Just left.'

'He came specifically to tell you?' Horton asked, thinking Davidson must have headed here from the mortuary.

But Tierney shook his head. 'No. Said he had a boat to check on. Told me he had to identify the body, quite shook him up.'

Horton showed Tierney the photograph of Graham Langham and asked if he'd ever seen him at the marina or in the area. Tierney said he hadn't. Horton then showed him the photograph of Leonard Borland and asked the same question.

'Yes, I've seen him around the marina and passed the time of day with him now and again. Pleasant enough chap.'

'Can you remember the last time you saw him?'

'A couple of weeks ago, I think. Aubrey will tell you.'

'They know one another?' Horton asked, interested.

'Well they were chatting together by Aubrey's van. Why? Who is he?'

Horton told him but didn't mention the fact that Borland had been viciously assaulted just that he had died in the fire in the house opposite the pontoons.

Tierney looked solemn. 'Poor soul.'

Thanking him, Horton wondered if Uckfield would want to check if any berth holders had been on their boats at the time of the fire and witnessed anything suspicious. But it had been late and dark when the fire had begun, so that was unlikely.

He headed back to Borland's house where Maitland told him Taylor had been able to lift some prints from the back door, the bannister and under the fire. 'They've also found blood by the table under the plasterwork. Oh, and Trueman rang to say that DI Dennings is on his way over.'

That, thought Horton, was his cue to leave.

FOURTEEN

Horton headed back to the secure berth at the port and Westerbrook's boat. He unzipped the canvas awning and climbed on board leaving the awning open. It flapped in the chilly stiff wind that drove icicles of rain into the cockpit. Horton called Walters and asked how he had got on at Westerbrook's flat.

'I found two passwords written on a piece of paper, stuffed at the back of a kitchen drawer.'

'Careless.'

'Yeah. But they're not to his email account. They're to two gambling websites. I've been studying his account. He gambles like there's no tomorrow.'

'There isn't for him.'

'Well he's gambled away thousands of pounds over the last year.'

'How many thousands?'

'Over fifteen grand and there could be other accounts. He could have gambled in private syndicates, and we know they'll bet on a fly crawling up a wall. He might also have used street bookies and gambled at casinos.'

Which made Horton think of Larry Egmont. He said, 'Only in the last year?'

'That's all that's on here. He might have used another computer before this.'

Horton recalled that Walters had said Westerbrook had been released from prison two years ago after receiving a custodial sentence of two years, and had served one year. So had he kept free of gambling for a year, or had he, as Walters said, used another computer or visited a betting shop?

'Find out the conditions of his release. Have you got the CCTV footage for the Paradise Estate?'

'What there is, yes.'

So DCS Adams hadn't been interested in that. Horton told Walters to take a look through it and the CCTV footage that DS Reynolds had sent over from Fareham for sightings of Langham's van.

'Is Cantelli back?'

'Just.

'Put him on.'

The boat rocked as a ferry made its way into dock. Horton felt cold and damp.

'There's no sign of Westerbrook's boat coming into the channel on the army's CCTV footage,' Cantelli reported. 'And nothing around that area while he was moored up there until Dowdswell shows up before reporting it.'

So the cameras had missed him. 'Not good for security,' Horton voiced.

'I was assured they would have picked up anyone attempting to land or who posed a threat.'

'Yeah?'

'So they said.'

Horton brought Cantelli up to speed with the news of Borland's death and that he believed Langham had been robbing houses in the area three days before the fire. He hoped the fingerprint team would be able to confirm that soon. He asked Cantelli to assist Walters and warned him that they might be called in tomorrow, Sunday, to help with the Borland investigation, something he hadn't told Walters. Cantelli could break the news to him.

Horton turned to the helm and extracting the boat keys from the evidence bag he'd brought with him he inserted one in the ignition. He focused his attention on the instrumentation. Studying it he saw that Westerbrook had set the log and the GPS on Wednesday morning when he had gone fishing with Nugent. The GPS had taken them to the area where Elkins had said they'd fished and where they said they'd found Langham's hand. The log also tallied with them returning to Oyster Quays. After that, according to the log, Westerbrook, or rather his boat, was still at Oyster Quays. He hadn't reset the log after leaving Oyster Quays last Wednesday so there was no record of knowing how many nautical miles he had travelled before reaching his final destination in the Thorney Channel. And neither had he set a course for Thorney Island or anywhere else using his GPS after that ill-fated fishing trip. He might have kept a manual log but neither he nor Elkins had found it when they had looked earlier. So wherever Westerbrook had travelled before ending up at Thorney, if anywhere, he hadn't wanted any record of it.

Horton turned his attention to past trips plotted into the GPS. There were several dating back two months, two to France and many out in the Solent. He'd also fished off Sandown Bay on the Isle of Wight, and on the eastern side of the island not far from Ventnor, and off Selsey where he'd been with Nugent, and along Hayling Bay. Horton returned the keys to the evidence bag. His eyes swept the deck before climbing off the boat, his mind turning over what he could see here and what both Davidson and Walters had told him about Westerbrook's gambling habits. His phone rang just as he was about to climb on the Harley. Eagerly he answered it seeing it was Jane from the fingerprint team.

'We have a match on the fingerprints from two of those robberies in Fareham. Just as you said, Inspector, they're Graham Langham's.'

Horton thanked her warmly and hurried back to the station. It was a long time since he'd last eaten, breakfast in fact, but he didn't stop to grab a sandwich, he made for the incident suite. It wasn't fully mobilized yet. Horton knew they were waiting for Gaye's report. He glanced at the clock, the earliest they could expect anything would be in about an hour's time. Tomorrow the investigation would step up a few gears but the death having occurred four days ago meant the trail was already cool if not cold. And Sunday was not the best day to get any progress on an investigation, although the house-to-house might give them more occupants than they'd find during the week.

Horton put the files he'd taken from Borland's house in front of Trueman. Uckfield, looking up from his desk, saw him and left his office. Trueman confirmed that Marsden was overseeing a house-to-house and Dennings was still at the scene. Trueman had already placed the photographs taken after the fire and those taken by Clarke in the last couple of hours on the crime board.

'I take it the fire victim *is* Leonard Borland?' Horton said, studying them.

'Yes. Although a formal ID and fingerprints are impossible given the fire, his dental records were accessed shortly after he was taken to the mortuary and they matched. I ran Borland's details through the computer. He had no convictions.'

Horton hadn't expected him to have any. He relayed the news about Langham's prints being found at two of the properties that were robbed on Saturday night. 'We also have a witness who says Leonard Borland was alive and well on Monday morning.'

'And so was Langham according to his missis,' rejoined Uckfield. 'He could have returned to Borland's house Monday evening, killed him, stolen from him and then taken off.'

'Where?'

'How the hell do I know?' Uckfield said grumpily. 'But whoever he went with chopped his ruddy hand off and probably threw the rest of him to the fish.'

'But he couldn't have set the fire on Tuesday evening because he didn't return home Monday night or Tuesday.'

'Moira could be lying.'

That was possible. Horton said, 'Langham was alive on Sunday night. I have a sighting of him in The Crown, trying to flog some of the stolen goods.'

'Who says?'

'A reliable source.'

Uckfield scoffed but didn't press him.

Horton asked if his team was needed tomorrow to assist with the Borland investigation. There was a chance that Uckfield would want them on the house-to-house or in the mobile incident suite but Uckfield said he was using officers from Fareham. He stomped off to his office where Horton saw him lift the phone, no doubt to update DCS Adams about Graham Langham's illegal activities, but whether Uckfield would tell Adams about the fire and Borland's death, Horton didn't know. He hadn't told him that Cantelli and Walters were looking through the CCTV tapes from the Paradise Estate. If they found something then he would.

They'd found nothing but Walters had checked on Westerbrook's prison record. 'The condition of his release was that he attend Gamblers Anonymous. I haven't checked whether he did, his offender manager can confirm that. He'd have been on probation for a year after his release.'

'Call the probation service on Monday. And do the rounds of the bookies close to where both Westerbrook and Langham lived. Show their photographs around. Find out if they've been in, when and how frequently. You might as well both get off home, there's nothing much more can be done tonight and Uckfield doesn't need us tomorrow.'

Horton was pleased for Cantelli, who would get to spend the day with his family. He didn't know how Walters spent his Sundays when not working and he didn't bother to ask. Neither did he know what Bliss did with herself during her spare time, when she wasn't studying for her next promotion exam. He didn't even know if she had a partner. She'd never mentioned anyone with the exception of a woman called Eunice Swallows, who ran a private investigation agency, and Horton knew from a case in October, which had brought him into contact with the formidable Ms Swallows, that she and Bliss had dined out together. And talking of dinner he reached for his mobile phone and called Carolyn. She answered almost immediately.

'I might not be able to make tonight,' he said, the memory of her kissing that man swimming before his eyes. 'Something's come up at work.'

There was a moment's silence. Was she thinking he was giving her the elbow?

'That's a shame,' she answered lightly, but Horton thought he detected a hint of disappointment in her voice. Perhaps he only hoped there was. She said, 'I can turn dinner into supper. You might be ravenous by the time you finish work.'

He was now.

'And if you can't make supper then come for a drink or just turn up when you can. It doesn't matter how late.' She left a pause before adding. 'They must let you home at some time.'

'Thanks.' She was very keen to see him. He should be flattered and he would have been if he hadn't witnessed her with that man. Maybe he'd ask her about him and get her reaction. It would be interesting to see.

It was six forty-five. Horton rose and peered out of his window. Uckfield, Dennings and Trueman's cars were all still there. He had another two hours to kill. And a stomach to feed as he was going to skip Carolyn's dinner and supper. He made for the canteen and bought cottage pie, vegetables, chips, and a large mug of black coffee and found a vacant table. He'd barely begun to eat though when Uckfield entered carrying a piece of paper. The Super made straight for his table nodding at a blonde woman in her early thirties behind the counter. Horton saw her smile and nod back. Uckfield's latest conquest, wondered Horton, shovelling in a forkful of chips.

Uckfield plonked himself down opposite. 'Got the results of the autopsy.' He didn't ask if it would put Horton off his food, Uckfield wasn't that sensitive. But before Uckfield could begin the blonde woman, who Horton knew as Alison, put a large cup of coffee and bacon sandwich in front of Uckfield. She'd only been working there three weeks.

'Thanks, love.'

She beamed at Uckfield before walking off. Nice figure beneath that tight, short overall. Good legs. Uckfield's type but then most women with make-up and a good figure under forty were. The fact that Uckfield was married to the former chief constable's daughter and had two daughters didn't stop him.

Uckfield slurped his coffee before reading from the paper in front of him.

'Soot deposits below the level of the larynx indicate Leonard Borland was alive when the fire started. There is also evidence of soot in the oesophagus and the stomach, and carbon monoxide in the blood.' Uckfield picked up his bacon sandwich but didn't bite into it. 'The cause of death is as a result of the fire but he was struck several times beforehand with a heavy round-shaped implement, possibly a club or a heavy duty torch, and with considerable force. The victim is six foot one . . .' Uckfield took a bite.

With his mouth full, he continued. 'Dr Clayton says the assailant could have been as tall or taller than Borland but judging by the angle of the blows she believes the victim was struck while he was leaning over—'

'To consult his notes, photographs or computer,' interjected Horton, eating his meal, adding, 'none of which were found in that room.'

Uckfield nodded, and chewing, said, 'The pattern of burns on the body confirm he was dragged and positioned over the fire.'

'Bastard,' Horton said softly.

'Not Langham,' said Uckfield with conviction.

'No,' Horton concurred, they both knew he wasn't capable of that. He pushed away his empty plate and took a swig of coffee. 'But it could be the same person who chopped off his hand. What does Adams have to say about it?'

Uckfield mopped up some sauce on his plate and pushed the remainder of his sandwich in his mouth. He chewed and swallowed before answering. 'Never heard of Borland, doesn't figure in his investigation and the fact that Langham was in the area thieving on

Saturday night has no bearing whatsoever on their investigation. I asked who Langham was supposed to have been informing on but Adams went all tight-lipped and prissy-arsed. I don't think he's got a bloody clue what's going on.' Uckfield sat back. 'Come to that neither have I.'

'Westerbrook's boat is moored opposite Borland's house and he found Langham's hand.'

'Coincidence.'

'You believe that about as much as I do.'

Uckfield sat forward. 'Yeah, OK then, what *is* going on?'

'That's what we need to find out but somehow I can't help thinking that all three, Westerbrook, Langham and Borland, are connected. We might not be able to investigate Langham but we can certainly investigate Borland's death and try and discover why Westerbrook's body was bruised and why he was beaten up before suffering a heart attack.'

Uckfield sniffed loudly.

Horton continued. 'Westerbrook was a heavy gambler and a former crook. Walters has discovered he gambled away at least fifteen thousand pounds in the last year and he has a boat and a car both paid for in cash, so where did he get the money? He has no relatives to leave him any, and no job and although he might have won large sums gambling he's lost even more. So who is financing him and why?'

Uckfield frowned and looked thoughtful. 'Someone he met while serving time in prison?'

'Possibly.'

'I'll get Trueman looking into that. I'll also get the hi-tech unit working on Westerbrook's computer and a team going over his boat, car and flat.'

Horton told Uckfield that Cantelli had an appointment with Westerbrook's bank on Monday and that Walters was going to do the rounds of the bookmakers. Horton glanced at his watch. 'I'm going to talk to Larry Egmont. I want to know if Westerbrook was a member of his casino.'

'You think Egmont might be behind this?'

Horton shrugged. There was nothing on Egmont. He'd never been implicated or suspected in anything illegal but, the only son of a shipwright and laundress, he was known to be tough and the men he employed tougher. He'd married George Warner's only child, his daughter, and had taken the betting business to new heights. He was an astute businessman and was rumoured never to miss a Saturday night in his Portsmouth casino, unless he was on holiday. He was also extremely clever and shrewd, which meant he was cunning enough not to have been caught.

Uckfield hauled himself up. 'I'll keep Dennings working on the Borland murder investigation. The mobile incident unit will be in situ on the green in front of Borland's house tomorrow morning. Marsden will oversee that. His team have so far drawn a blank on the house-to-house.'

Horton rose and picked up his tray.

Uckfield continued, 'We'll get a list of berth holders and run them through the computer.'

Falling into step beside Uckfield, Horton said, 'I'll talk to Aubrey Davidson. The marina manager says he saw Borland talking to Davidson in the car park a week or so ago but he couldn't remember exactly when. Davidson might throw some light on what Borland was interested in, but whatever it was I don't think it was bird-watching, the feathered variety that is,' Horton added as Uckfield flashed a smile at Alison behind the counter.

'Do you think Borland was observing Westerbrook?'

'It's a theory, but if he was, what could he have seen that could have aroused his suspicions? Westerbrook was just a man taking out fishing rods, beer and a bait box and bringing back fish.'

'Maybe that wasn't all he was bringing back.'

Horton thought the same but they both knew that if it was drugs then Borland would never have spotted it. The drugs would have been concealed in either the bait box, a cool bag or inside the fishing rods. But it could have been a more visible cargo and Horton said as much to Uckfield.

'Illegal immigrants you mean,' Uckfield said, pausing at the bottom of the stairs.

'Or girls for sex trafficking. And both would fall under the remit of DCS Adams.'

'Yeah, but he doesn't know about it otherwise he'd have had us out of the area and off the investigation quicker than a rat up a drainpipe.'

'Perhaps Larry Egmont is too clever for him.'

'Perhaps he's not involved and Borland was beaten about the head and killed by some lowlife con man.'

Horton would see what Egmont had to say for himself. He just hoped that Egmont was still a creature of habit and that he'd find him at the casino.

FIFTEEN

Horton showed his warrant card to the glamorous blonde receptionist who said she would inquire if Mr Egmont was available. Horton had been pleased to see Egmont's Bentley Continental parked in its space at the rear. She disappeared through a door to the right marked 'Private', leaving Horton to gaze around the plush deep red and gold vestibule of the casino.

It had been about three years since he'd last interviewed Egmont here. Then it had been in connection with a robbery on one of his female clients as she'd left the casino. Since then the place had been refurbished. The cloakroom was on his left, the reception desk to his right and ahead in front of the obscure glass double doors with shiny brass handles that led into the casino was a wide man dressed in evening attire with a radio mic plugged in his ear and a steely suspicious eye plugged on Horton.

Horton returned the stare with equanimity before turning his attention to the framed photographs, which hadn't been here before. They were of the casinos that Egmont owned along the South Coast and of his staff. Horton scanned them idly noting the staff shots went back to 1961 and the first casino opposite the pier in Southsea. Then there was a jump to 1965, 1968, 1972, 1975 and 1978. Horton froze and stared at the last picture, but a voice hailed him and he turned to see the receptionist, who was asking him to follow her. He did so, a little reluctantly, while his thoughts stayed with that photograph. He'd barely had time to register the group of people – gaming managers, croupiers and staff – smiling into camera, but he'd certainly registered the year. Was his mother one of those smiling people? She'd been employed as casual labour, which meant she was unlikely to be in a staff photograph, but even if she wasn't in that picture could she possibly be in other photographs taken at the time?

He shelved the thought as he followed the receptionist's shapely body and long legs down a corridor, up thickly carpeted stairs and along another corridor until she halted outside a door at the far end overlooking the rear of the building. All was deathly silent. Horton noted, with approval, the security cameras on the ceilings. This place carried a lot of money and was a target for thieves, except that Egmont would probably have his boys cut off their hands if he caught them. But Langham would never have dared to rob here. And he'd never have got beyond the front or rear door, both of which were heavily alarmed.

A voice bid them enter and the girl ushered Horton in with a smile.

Larry Egmont was in his early forties. Fit, tanned, dark-haired, and dressed in an expensive dinner suit he rose from behind his desk with a smile, stretching out a hand. His grip was vice-like and the brown eyes studying Horton were cool, intelligent and curious.

Horton showed his warrant card, not expecting Egmont to remember him but he waved it away, obviously doing so. Remembering people was Egmont's business. He gestured Horton into one of two cream leather armchairs in the contemporarily decorated spacious room, which was in complete contrast to what Horton had seen so far. There was a cream-coloured carpet, cream walls with some stunning modern, primary-coloured paintings on them, and a large cream leather sofa positioned around a low, light-wood coffee table that matched a sideboard, with drinks on it, and Egmont's large desk on which was a telephone, computer and television monitor. There was another wide plasma screen on the far wall. It was switched off. Horton suspected it would show Egmont the various images from around the casino rather than the latest episode of a popular TV programme.

'Drink?'

'No thanks.'

Egmont sat and Horton followed suit.

'How can I help you, Inspector? I trust there's no trouble.'

Egmont looked anything but anxious but then that was no less than Horton expected. They were alone but Horton got the impression they were being watched. Probably behind a concealed camera.

'I'd like to know if Clive Westerbrook or Graham Langham were customers here, and before you claim customer confidentiality they're both dead.'

Egmont raised his dark eyebrows then shrugged. 'I don't know the names but I'll check.' He rose and crossed to his desk. Punching into his computer, after a short while he looked up and said, 'No.' He returned to his seat and Horton withdrew the photographs of Westerbrook and Langham.

'Have you seen either of these men before?'

Egmont studied them. 'I haven't but my staff might have. Do you want me to ask them?'

'Please. I'll email these over to you or I can run some off and get them dropped in.'

'No, email will be fine. What have they done apart from ending up dead? I take it their deaths are suspicious otherwise you wouldn't be here.'

Horton certainly wasn't going to divulge their suspicions or any facts of the case. He said, 'We know that Clive Westerbrook gambled heavily. Does he owe you money?'

'No.'

Horton eyed the shrewd man in front of him.

Egmont added, 'I can assure you, Inspector, if he owed me money I'd remember the name and the face.'

And that Horton knew was the truth but perhaps Westerbrook's debt wasn't officially on the books because his gambling wasn't official. There was little more Horton could ask but he ran Borland's name past Egmont to see what his reaction was and got a blank look for his pains.

'He lived at Fareham opposite the pontoons in the marina. He died in a house fire on Tuesday evening,' Horton pressed, studying closely Egmont's expression. Again blank.

Horton rose. 'If you come across any information about Graham Langham or Clive Westerbrook, or if any of your staff recognize either man, could you let me know.'

Egmont took the card Horton handed him. 'Always happy to cooperate with the police.'

Horton held his stare. Was there something mocking about it and behind his words? He said, 'Do you have a boat, Mr Egmont?'

Egmont looked surprised at the question. 'Yes.'

'Where do you keep it?'

He looked amused. 'At the end of my garden.'

Of course. He should have guessed that Egmont could afford a property with its own mooring.

'Which is where?'

'Bosham.'

A small village in West Sussex to the west of Chichester and which fronted on to Chichester Harbour. Easy enough for Egmont to motor his boat from there into the Thorney Channel. But if Egmont was involved with Westerbrook's death then Horton sincerely doubted he'd get his own hands dirty.

Horton had a few more questions for Egmont but they weren't about Langham or Westerbrook. As he reached the door he halted. 'Those photographs on the wall downstairs, where did they come from?'

'You mean the ones of the old casinos,' Egmont said, surprised.

'Yes.'

'Someone gave them to us. He used to work for George when he had the casino in Southsea in the 1970s. I think he's got a website dedicated to it. Some people are rather sad in that way.' Egmont smiled. Horton returned it but he was cursing himself for not checking it out.

'Do you have his name?'

'Not off the top of my head but I can ask my secretary on Monday. She'll know, or you can probably find him by surfing the Net.'

And Horton would. He was escorted to reception by a big man of the same ilk as the one standing on the door to the gaming rooms. Horton hadn't seen Egmont summon the man so he must have been monitoring the conversation by security camera. He eyed Horton steadily and unsmilingly. Yes, he could have killed Langham and beaten up Westerbrook or if not him then his mate downstairs.

In reception Horton turned to the man escorting him and said, 'One moment.' He knew that Egmont was still watching him on that screen in his office and probably wondering what the pictures from the 1970s had to do with his investigation. Was Egmont worried? Probably not. The Egmonts of the world didn't need to worry.

Horton studied the photograph from 1978 closely, his heart racing a little faster. There were twelve men in the picture, wearing white shirts and bow ties, four with moustaches and two with beards. The women, ten of them, were dressed in evening wear, six in long black evening dresses with a sweetheart neck. They were the girls on the gaming tables which was where Jennifer had worked, but none of these or the other women in the photograph was Jennifer. He noted that the picture had been taken in September 1978, two months before Jennifer had disappeared. Perhaps it was her evening off or she was ill that day. Perhaps the man who had donated this copy to the casino had other pictures from that time and with Jennifer in them. He might even remember her and the men she'd been friendly with. Or perhaps Jennifer had made sure not to be available for any photo call, official or unofficial, because if what he'd been told was true, and that Jennifer had been working for British Intelligence, then she would have been certain not to be photographed, just as Eileen Litchfield, his foster mother, had made sure not to have any photographs of herself or of him taken. He wondered if John Guilbert had managed to get hold of the photographs of the Ducale twins, Eileen and her brother Andrew, from Violet Ducale. He would have called him though if he had.

Horton stepped out into what had become a remarkably mild night after the brief cold snap. The area was getting busy with early revellers. It was nine forty-five. He swung the Harley towards the seafront and a few minutes later was pressing the bell of Carolyn's apartment.

'You made it! Great!' she said, answering the intercom, she'd have seen him on her CCTV system.

She sounded genuinely pleased and as she buzzed him in and he climbed the stairs to her apartment he wondered if he'd imagined her embracing that slender, fair-haired man. He hadn't though.

There was a slight delay before she opened the door to him, smiling. His pulse skipped a beat and his loins stirred as he gazed at her radiant face and smelt her soft sensual perfume. When she wrapped her arms around him and kissed him lingeringly and seductively he knew this was going to be a hell of a lot tougher than he'd reckoned. Did it matter if she liked to have two men on the go? They'd hardly agreed a mutually exclusive relationship and declared undying love for each other. He could simply take what was on offer and enjoy it, without confiding anything. But as he pulled away from her he knew that wasn't his style.

He thought she looked disconcerted but if so she quickly recovered. 'Drink?'

'Coke.'

'I forgot, you don't, why not?'

He followed her into the lounge. 'Don't like the taste,' he said, pulling off his leather jacket. It wasn't the truth but he saw no reason to tell her that. And perhaps she could guess why, after all she had researched his background. It didn't take a leap of faith to work out that during his suspension he'd taken to drinking heavily before coming to his senses and since then he'd stayed off the booze.

'Coke it is.'

While she fetched it he crossed to the window. She hadn't drawn the curtains. He gazed across the black Solent. An occasional glimmer of a fretful moon turned streaks of the sea silver before the scudding cloud plunged it back into darkness. He could see the pinpricks of lights from a passing ship on the horizon and those of the houses straddling the hilly roads of the town of Ryde on the Isle of Wight beyond the Solent. He was transported back to another apartment in a tower block where he'd sat and watched the ships sail out of Portsmouth Harbour and had dreamt of travelling on them to lands he'd only read about in books. He'd never managed that and maybe there was still that deep urge inside him to take off. But that would mean leaving Emma and he didn't want to do that. Catherine's words about his boat being unsuitable for their daughter to sleep on drifted into his thoughts. Maybe it was time to get an apartment and if so then one like this, where he had the wide open space of the ever-changing sea to gaze on and ease his troubled thoughts. He started slightly at the touch of a hand on his arm and turned to take his drink from Carolyn.

'You look solemn and tired.' Her expression softened. He almost capitulated then.

'It's been a long day.'

'Want to talk about it?'

'Not really.'

'Want something to eat?'

'Not really.' He was tired and his heart felt heavy. He studied Carolyn Grantham's dark attractive face and remembered how good it felt to hold her. He could do that again. He could abandon himself to making love to her. Forget Westerbrook and Langham. But they weren't the focus of his weariness. It was memories of his childhood and his mother, her laughing face, her arms wrapped around him, her softness, her perfume and her kisses. Her worried face, her crying, and then her smiles, false now he guessed and his heart and hands ached with longing and the pain of rejection. He so desperately wanted to forget his tormented childhood and although he could for a while with Carolyn Grantham he knew it wouldn't be enough. It would never be enough, not with her, just as it had never been with Catherine. Maybe not with anyone. But especially not with Carolyn because he didn't trust her.

She sensed and probably saw in his expression his doubts, and maybe she even sensed a hardness in him. 'You've come to a decision,' she said, taking the seat opposite him rather than next to him. 'About Jennifer?'

'There's nothing to tell you about Jennifer because I don't know anything about what happened to her, and raking up how I felt then and how I feel now doesn't achieve anything. It's the past. I've moved on.'

'Have you?'

'Yes,' he answered firmly and forced a smile which he hoped to her seemed genuine. 'I can't help you, Carolyn.'

'Don't you want to know what happened to her?' she asked, eyeing him steadily.

'It won't change things.'

'It might change the way you remember her.'

He knew that. It had already. 'It won't change what happened though.'

'No.' She sipped her drink. In the silence that followed Horton heard only the clock on the mantelpiece ticking.

'You believe she's dead, don't you?'

'Yes,' he replied with conviction.

'Accident or suicide?'

Why didn't she say murder? Because she was waiting for him to suggest it? He shrugged. 'Does it matter?'

'For a police officer I'd say it does. Why don't you get the case reopened?'

'Because I'm afraid of what I might learn.'

She eyed him, surprised and curious. 'You believe then that there is *something* to learn.'

'There's *always* something to learn.'

She frowned. 'But if her death was suspicious then someone has gone unpunished.'

'That's often the way. Even if I found out who had killed her, *if* someone did, getting evidence of that to take it to court and secure a conviction would be practically impossible, so why waste the time.'

'But you do have some ideas.' She pressed. Was she too eager? Too pushy? Time for him to test it.

'There are always ideas. There are also rumours, suppositions and theories, some of them ludicrous such as Jennifer could have been involved with someone in the IRA in 1978 which was why she vanished.'

'My God!' She looked startled.

If it was an act it was a damn good one.

'How do you know this?'

'I don't *know* it. It was just something someone said. Maybe they overheard her talking to this person about the Troubles and assumed it was her boyfriend.'

'She ran off with him?'

'Or was killed by him or because of him or because of what she knew.'

'About a bombing campaign.'

'Possibly. There were a whole series of bombs here on the mainland and in Northern Ireland at that time and after she vanished.'

'You could dig a bit deeper, apply to see the records in the National Archives.'

'I could but what would it achieve?'

'Closure,' she said quietly.

He smiled wryly. 'I doubt it. And I doubt I'll ever get that. It's over, Carolyn.' He held her gaze. Did she know what he meant? Her expression never wavered. She studied him sympathetically. He was weary and lonely. He wanted so much to trust, to confide, not to be alone. He remembered Thursday night. Taking a mental breath he continued, 'It's time to move on. My marriage is over, but I have a young daughter and a job, I won't say career because that's probably stalled, and besides I'm not sure if I want to go any higher. I might even come to the conclusion that I don't want the job.'

He thought she looked shocked. 'What would you do?'

His eyes travelled to the window. 'Sail.' He'd considered not long ago about taking up yacht racing, he might reconsider that, it depended to a certain extent on Emma.

She rose and sat down beside him. God, she was so very hard to resist.

'I understand,' she said softly and she looked as though she did, but that picture of her embracing that man meant all this was a lie.

'Do you?' he said, trying to squeeze the harshness from his voice.

'I've spoken to a lot of people who still have the yawning ache of desertion inside them. I've seen what it can do.'

He looked into her dark brown eyes and was certain that what she said was genuine. He felt himself drawn to her warmth, her softness and her scent. He kissed her, longingly, and she responded. It would be so easy to forget. So easy to make love to her. Too easy. He pulled away.

'Tomorrow's a long day,' he said, his voice, even to his ears, sounding taut with emotion.

She eyed him with surprise before she forced a smile from her lips that never touched her deep brown eyes and withdrew herself gracefully. 'Of course.'

He rose and picked up his jacket. 'I'm sorry for spoiling your evening. I shouldn't have come. I'm just out of sorts.'

Looking concerned she said, 'It's OK. Another time. You'll call me?'

He forced a smile. 'Yes.'

She let him out but his smile faded as the door closed on him and his frown deepened as he ran down the stairs. He started up the Harley and headed slowly out of the estate and along the seafront, but when he reached the end of the promenade instead of turning right for his boat he continued until he came to a left-hand turning and soon he was pulling into a side street. Locking the Harley he ran swiftly to the rear of her apartment, where he waited in the shadows. He didn't have long. A car drew up and parked in the allotted space for visitors. A man climbed out and made for the building. The outside door buzzed to let him in without him having to call the number. She was waiting for him. Horton took a breath and made for his Harley. It was the same man he'd seen her with in the civic square.

He rode home with even more questions to add to those already crowding his throbbing head. Who was that man? Was he from Eames and the intelligence services or was he working for someone else who was keen to discover what he had unearthed about Jennifer, or rather what he believed about her disappearance? Why would Carolyn assist whoever it was though? Perhaps that man was just her lover and she was on the level regarding her research project. Finding herself rejected and alone she'd called her boyfriend and he'd come running.

Horton unlocked the boat, turned on the engine and let it run, warming up the boat. Retrieving his phone he called up the internet and very quickly found the website that Egmont had been alluding to earlier. On it was the same photograph that was on the casino wall and there were others taken of the outside of the casino and the surrounding nightclubs dating from the 1960s and 1970s. Horton studied them all closely but Jennifer wasn't in any of the photographs. The website was run by a man called Melvin Cooper. The name didn't register with him. It certainly hadn't been on the missing person report and that meant Stanley hadn't obtained a statement from him, so perhaps he hadn't known Jennifer. Or perhaps the statement had been destroyed or accidentally omitted.

Horton rang through to the station and asked the duty sergeant to run the name through the computer and get an address for him. He also relayed the vehicle registration number of Carolyn's boyfriend and requested an address. Sergeant Stride said he'd call him back.

Impatiently Horton waited, lying on his bunk, listening to the wind moaning through the rigging. His mind ran through several scenarios. If Eames had sent Carolyn to find out what he'd been told by Antony Dormand and what he'd discovered about Jennifer's disappearance then perhaps it was because Eames was getting scared he knew too much or was getting too close to the truth. If, as he had thought earlier, his conversation with Carolyn had been recorded, then he'd planted the seed that he knew about the possible IRA connection, and had dismissed it. What would Eames do next? How would Eames stop him if he thought he was getting too close to the truth? Would he try to discredit him in the same way he'd been framed and discredited by Lucy Richardson and those false allegations of rape? Was that Carolyn's purpose in this? Or would something else occur in the course of his job that would throw his honesty into question? Or perhaps he'd meet with an accident? Would Eames go that far? Horton knew he would. After all, four of the men out of those six in the photograph had met with accidents of one kind or another. And again he mentally ran through the catalogue of their deaths: Timothy Wilson had been killed in a motorbike accident, James Royston had died of a heroin overdose, Zachary Benham had died in a fire that had raged through the ward of a psychiatric hospital and Rory Mortimer had been killed by Antony Dormand.

Where was Antony Dormand now? Had he thrown himself overboard from the small boat Horton had watched the dark night swallow up in October? No body had been recovered. Or had Dormand made it to another boat ready to take him to the continent?

Horton turned his mind to Sawyer and his quest to find Zeus, the master criminal. Horton couldn't see Sawyer using Carolyn to obtain information from him about Jennifer's disappearance, not unless Carolyn was a copper. Horton stiffened as the idea took root. He'd wondered if she worked for the intelligence services so why not consider her to be a police officer working under cover for Sawyer and Intelligence Directorate. The case was still active and Sawyer was pursuing it. Perhaps the man Horton had seen Carolyn with was also a cop.

His phone rang. It was Stride with the news that the vehicle was registered in the name of Dr Rufus Anstey whose address was Chichester, a small Cathedral city in the neighbouring county of West Sussex, some twenty miles east of Portsmouth. He also relayed that there were several Melvin Coopers. Horton asked if any of them lived in Portsmouth.

'Yes, one, just off Clive Road. Aged fifty-seven.'

That sounded like the right man. Stride gave him the address.

Tomorrow he'd conduct some research on Dr Rufus Anstey. And tomorrow he hoped to find Melvin Cooper at home. Whether he'd obtain another piece of the fragmented and sparse jigsaw that would give him the answer to Jennifer's disappearance was another matter entirely.

SIXTEEN

Sunday

'Yes, I remember Jennifer Horton,' Melvin Cooper said, taking Horton by surprise, he'd been so used to denials and disappointments that he could hardly believe what he was hearing.

Horton eyed the dishevelled man who had opened the door of the narrow terraced house to him. He was wearing a navy-blue heavy towelling dressing gown over a pair of paisley pyjamas and rundown slippers on his bare feet. Horton had aroused him from his Sunday morning lie-in. He'd apologized for the early timing of his call and with a flash of his warrant card said he was making enquiries about a woman who had worked at George Warner's casino on the seafront in 1978, a Jennifer Horton, and from viewing Mr Cooper's website, and seeing he was something of an expert, Horton hoped that he could help.

Cooper had been flattered as Horton had intended and had invited him inside making no comment about the similarity in name, maybe because he'd forgotten Horton's already, people often did immediately on introduction and especially if followed up quickly by a question. Even if Cooper made the connection Horton was ready to say, 'no relation', there were other Hortons in the UK, his name wasn't unique, unless he'd get more from Cooper by telling the truth, but he'd reserve judgement on that until he could hear what the man had to say. He'd also made no mention of Jennifer having gone missing.

'Perhaps you could tell me what you remember of her?' asked Horton as he was shown into a tiny kitchen at the rear of the house made even smaller by the amount of clutter in it. But he wasn't here to pass judgement on the décor or the cleaning habits of Melvin Cooper. Horton refused the offer of a tea or coffee and remained standing, mainly because there was nowhere to sit. Cooper flicked on the kettle and threw a tea bag into a large mug. He bore very little resemblance to the man Horton had seen in the photograph on the casino wall and on the website. The long wavy dark hair and moustache had gone, along with the laughing brown eyes and wide smile. Now his hair was short, thinning and grey and his eyes hollowed out in a lean face grown sharper over the years, along with an expression that had grown wearier.

'The punters loved her. Nice figure, blue eyes and long blonde hair. A real looker.'

Horton felt choked as he listened to the description of his mother and one in such glowing terms. For so long too many people had spoken of her as a slut.

'Any particular punter?'

Cooper shrugged. 'We weren't allowed to fraternize with the customers. George Warner was a bit of a tyrant. Even though we're all smiling in that picture that's because we were told to or else. You did what George wanted or you were out.'

Horton wondered if Melvin Cooper had tried it on with Jennifer. 'Did she speak of her background?'

'Might have done. I don't remember and you don't always listen. It was a long time ago.'

He looked wistful and Horton reckoned Cooper spent more hours looking back to a time when he thought he had been happy than looking forward to a time when he knew he wouldn't be. Horton wasn't getting very far.

'Did she mention having any children?' He held his breath as he waited for the answer.

Cooper looked taken aback for a moment then said with conviction, 'She couldn't have done. Not in those days with that job, working until the early hours of the morning, and no husband. George didn't employ married women and if you lived with someone and weren't married that was frowned upon then, bloody hard to believe now.' He poured the hot water on to his tea bag.

His words bore out the flimsy content of the statements Stanley had taken. Neither Warner nor Irene Ebury had claimed to know of a child, and perhaps Jennifer had kept silent about his existence for fear of losing her job.

'Jennifer's not in the picture, why?'

Cooper squeezed out the tea bag with his fingers, and left it on the side of the scratched and stained sink along with the others that had dried and shrivelled up. 'Probably her night off,' he said, sloshing some milk in the mug and heaping in four spoons of sugar. He picked it up and gestured Horton to follow him into a musty-smelling, cramped living room. 'Or she could have been off sick.' Cooper sat down and Horton perched on the faded seat opposite.

'Do you have any other photographs from those days?'

'Only what's on the website.'

'Would anyone else who worked there at that time have any?'

'I doubt it. We weren't allowed to take cameras into the casino. There are only the official pictures like that one, and they're all on the website, apart from the pictures of the casino from the outside and I scanned those in from the local newspaper.'

Pity, but Cooper's words rang true. It was a different story these days with photographs being taken in casinos and everywhere else. But the idea made him think of Westerbrook's death and Horton wondered if it was worth Walters' time, or someone in the hi-tech unit, trawling the internet and social network sites to see if Westerbrook appeared in anyone's photographs taken inside Egmont's casinos. It would be a mammoth task though and probably not worth it.

Cooper slurped his tea and eyed Horton curiously. 'Why are you trying to trace her?' But before Horton could reply, Cooper answered his own question. 'Don't tell me a punter from those days has remembered her in his will and left her a fortune. Lucky old thing.'

Horton just smiled, leaving Cooper to believe that. It was a nice idea and one that hadn't occurred to Horton but he'd run with it. Not that the police would investigate such an occurrence, that would more likely be the province of a private detective employed by executors of the will, but he wasn't going to quibble.

Cooper said, 'Wish someone would leave me a fortune. I lost my job three years ago and I'm buggered if I can get another one. I've tried everything but when you get past fifty you might as well be dead as far as some employers are concerned. I can tell you that despite what you read in the newspapers *nobody* wants to employ an older man.'

And Lesley Nugent would probably agree, thought Horton. He too had struggled to get that job at the meat wholesalers and according to Davidson had previously worked in accounts. Horton wondered if liking a flutter had led Nugent to dipping into those accounts.

'Can you remember anyone working at the casino who was particularly close to or friendly with Jennifer?' Horton didn't hold out much hope of him coming up with a name unless it was Irene Ebury and she was dead.

Cooper's lined forehead creased in the act of trying to remember. 'Susan Nash was pretty friendly with Jennifer.'

Horton's hopes rose. They soared when Cooper added, 'I've got her contact details, she emailed me after seeing the website. Would you like them?'

'Please.'

Cooper rose. 'I'll get them.'

'Thanks.'

Horton heard him climb the stairs. He rose and crossed to the rain-spattered and dust-laden window. There was no one in the street or in a waiting car. And there had been no sign of anyone watching his boat or following him. He wondered if Rufus Anstey had spent the night with Carolyn. His stomach knotted at the thought which he quickly pushed aside to concentrate on Susan Nash. There was no mention of her in the police file. Horton wondered if Stanley had questioned her.

'Here they are.'

Horton spun round and took the paper Cooper was holding. He was disappointed to see that Susan Nash lived near Abbotsbury, the other side of Weymouth, about eighty miles to the west of Portsmouth so he couldn't call on her immediately. But there was an email address and a telephone number.

'Do you know her maiden name?' he asked, folding the paper into his pocket.

'Kemble.'

That definitely didn't ring any bells.

At the door Horton asked him if the police had ever contacted him about the whereabouts of Jennifer. Melvin Cooper shook his head. Horton added, 'Has anyone spoken to you about her either recently or over the years?'

'No.'

Horton thought that was the truth. Outside he made a slow job of returning to his Harley, surveying the area casually as though he was looking for a house number. As he climbed on his Harley he glanced up at Cooper's house. Cooper was standing in front of the window with his back to Horton. He was on his mobile phone. Was he calling Susan Nash to tell her to expect a call from him? Maybe. Horton was very keen to speak to Susan Nash and wondered if he should head to Abbotsbury now. As it was Sunday there was a good chance of finding her at home, and it being Sunday he didn't think that much would happen with regard to the investigations into Borland or Westerbrook's death. Besides he wasn't working on either today. It wouldn't take him long to reach the Dorset village on the Harley. But he made south for the seafront instead of heading north out of the city. He'd call her first. It would be a wasted journey if she was on holiday or out for the day visiting friends or relations.

He pulled over just past the pier. Silencing the engine, he removed his helmet and gazed out to sea. He could see a handful of yachts in the Solent and a couple of motorboats heading out past the Bembridge Lifeboat Station around the Isle of Wight, they were probably fishing boats like Westerbrook's. There were now some gaps in the heavy grey clouds that occasionally brought a glimmer of winter light to the silver grey sea. He reached for his mobile phone and as his eyes alighted on the Wightlink ferries crossing just past Spitbank Fort something nagged at the back of his mind. He felt it was connected with Westerbrook but he couldn't think what it was. Maybe it would come to him later.

He tried the number Cooper had given him and was pleased when Susan Nash answered promptly. Horton quickly explained who he was, saying that he was trying to trace the whereabouts of Jennifer Horton, wondering if she would pick up on his name but just as Cooper hadn't, neither did she. He said that Melvin Cooper had given him her details and that the last known information they had on Jennifer was that she'd worked at the casino until the end of November 1978.

'You're going back some time,' she said pleasantly.

'Can you remember if she said why she left and if she gave any indication of where she was going?'

'No, because I had no idea she was intending to leave. When she didn't show up for work I thought she must be sick. The next I heard was that a policeman had come asking if anyone knew where she was.'

'Did the police speak to you?'

'No. They spoke to a girl I worked with though, Irene. She told me this police officer had asked her and Mr Warner questions, just routine the officer said. I thought Jennifer had just got fed up working into the early hours of the morning but I always wondered if she left to be with her boyfriend.'

'There was someone then?' Horton asked, wishing he had now spoken to Susan Nash face-to-face.

'Not that I knew for definite but she changed so much after that funny turn that I could see she was in love.'

Horton's heart was hammering. 'Tell me about it. It might help us to trace her,' he quickly added, trying not to sound too keen.

'She's not in trouble is she?' Susan Nash asked anxiously, obviously picking up something in his tone.

'No. It's nothing like that,' he hastily reassured her, hoping she'd believe him and that she wouldn't press him. If she did he'd resort to the line that Cooper had assumed. 'She'd been unwell?' he prompted, making an effort to keep his voice neutral.

There was a moment's brief silence before she answered. 'It wasn't long before she left. She was at the gaming tables and she went deathly pale as though she'd seen a ghost. She froze while taking bets. I was serving drinks and I looked across at her and asked if she was alright. I thought she was going to faint. She just left the table. Mr Warner was furious. We all thought she'd get the sack and she would have done if Mr Warner hadn't been crazy about her. But she wasn't interested in him. He was married for starters and that was no go as far as Jennifer was concerned, although others weren't so fussy. I got the feeling she'd been caught out in a relationship with a married man before, which had gone sour, and Jennifer said she wasn't going to be one of George Warner's long line of conquests.'

'But she returned to the tables.'

'Yes, about half an hour later. Mr Warner called her into his office and tore into her but because he fancied her he couldn't stay cross with her for long.'

Horton wondered if Warner had been the man with the flash car he'd seen outside the flat a couple of times talking to his mother. 'Do you know who she saw to make her react like that?'

'No, and she never said, although there wasn't much time to talk about it because this was only about a week or a few days before she left. I think she saw someone she thought she would never see again. Perhaps because he'd thrown her over or told her he was going abroad to live and then there he was back in her life and she picked up with him again and that's why she left.'

But there was something more, nagging at the back of Horton's mind. Susan Nash's words reeled around his head: *she went deathly pale as though she'd seen a ghost* not someone who had thrown her over but someone she believed to be dead. There was little more that Susan Nash said she could tell him about Jennifer's disappearance but Horton thought there was a great deal more about Jennifer as a person, although he'd learned throughout his investigation that Jennifer, like Eileen Litchfield, had been a very private woman. Was that because Jennifer was engaged by the intelligence services? Or perhaps in hiding from them.

Horton thanked her and rang off. He'd speak to her again but next time it would be face-to-face.

He stared at the sea, his mind spinning. Whoever Jennifer had seen in that casino had been someone from her past, someone she had known in London. One of those six men in the photograph or the man who had taken the picture who Horton suspected had been Edward Ballard. But he wasn't dead although Jennifer might have believed him to be so. Before he could progress his thought further his mobile rang. It was Uckfield.

'We have a match on the fingerprints at Borland's house,' Uckfield keenly relayed. 'The prints on the back door and the bannister are Graham Langham's. Langham was in that house, when though is something the prints can't tell us. The set of prints under the electric fire are not so clear but they're working on it.'

'I'd lay money he didn't set that fire.' Horton insisted. 'Or that he dragged Borland's body over it.'

'Perhaps he assaulted Borland on Monday night and left his body in that room for someone else to drag and place over that fire. He chickened out at the last moment and was killed because he failed to go through with it, and because he knew too much?'

'About what though?'

'How the hell do I know?' Uckfield growled bad-temperedly.

'It leaves Borland lying there unconscious or dead for a long time.'

'Yeah, but that's not impossible.'

'Perhaps Langham saw who attacked Borland and was killed because of it.' Horton relayed what he'd got from Larry Egmont last night, which was nothing, and asked Uckfield if someone could email the photographs of Westerbrook and Langham to Egmont for circulating to his staff. Horton said he'd interview Aubrey Davidson. It being Sunday he thought there was a good chance of finding him at the angling club.

It was just after eleven fifteen when he pulled in beside Davidson's car. The car park was relatively full and the club house door was open. He found Davidson behind the bar beside a well-built brunette in her late forties showing an expanse of cleavage, a few rolls of fat around her midriff which the tight black sleeveless T-shirt did nothing to hide, and a lot of gold jewellery around her neck and on her fingers.

'It's all right, Inspector, we're not serving alcohol until midday,' Davidson hastily said. 'Just coffee and teas.'

Horton asked if he could have a word in private.

'Won't be long, love,' Davidson jovially addressed the woman but Horton thought he caught a hint of concern in his voice. A glance passed between them before Davidson led Horton into a storeroom behind the bar. He wondered if Davidson would lower his usual booming voice when the questions became more personal.

'Do you know a Mr Leonard Borland?' he launched in right away.

Davidson looked a little taken aback by the question. 'No. I can't say I do.'

'You were seen talking to him in Fareham Marina car park.'

'I talk to a lot of people. I don't know anyone by that name.'

'Then perhaps you recognize him.' Horton showed Davidson the photograph of Borland.

'He looks vaguely familiar. I might have seen him around but I don't remember talking to him.'

Was he lying or was Tierney lying or were they both mistaken? Did it matter because Borland had been alive and well until Monday, at least when Mrs Samson claimed to have seen him.

'He lived opposite Fareham Marina. He died in a fire on Tuesday evening.'

Davidson looked shocked. 'I know the house. I mean I saw it. Dreadful.'

'He lived alone. We're trying to find out who saw him and when.'

'I'm sorry but I can't help you.'

'Were you at the marina a week ago last Saturday late afternoon and evening?' Horton had already asked him that question but he thought it worth asking again.

'No.' Davidson shifted uneasily. 'Why do you want to know?'

'There was a series of robberies in some of the properties there, we're looking for witnesses.'

'I was fishing in the morning then I came here. I left about three thirty when we closed.'

'And after that?'

Davidson fidgeted and a thin film of sweat had broken out on his brow. He was clearly uneasy. His big hands didn't seem to know what to do with themselves and he turned to straighten up some beer bottles, saying in a much lower voice than was his normal manner. 'I went home. Well, not straight away,' he added, 'I had some jobs to do.'

'Where?'

'On some boats, of course. Look, why are you questioning me. I had nothing to do with any robberies.'

'In Fareham Marina?' asked Horton eyeing him carefully, not sure why Davidson was so nervous.

Davidson rubbed a hand across his brow. 'No, at Gosport Marina.'

It was clearly a lie. Horton decided to push it. 'I'll need the names of the boat owners.'

Davidson looked horrified. 'And make them wonder if I'm crooked, not bloody likely.'

'We just need to eliminate you from our inquiries,' Horton said smoothly.

'Into what? I've nothing to do with any robberies or with that poor man perishing in a fire.'

'Do you know a man called Graham Langham?' Horton pressed.

'No.'

Horton eyed him steadily. 'Where were you Tuesday between five p.m. and seven p.m.?'

'At home. Look, I don't have to answer your questions.' He made to leave but Horton stopped him with his next question.

'And your wife can confirm this?'

'Of course she bloody can.'

And that, thought Horton, was at last the truth. 'Good, then perhaps we can start again, your movements for the Saturday before last?'

Davidson took a deep breath, pulled himself up and held Horton's steady gaze. After a moment his big shoulders slumped. He looked nervously over his shoulder towards the bar. Horton recalled the glance between Davidson and the woman behind the bar. 'You were with someone,' he said.

Davidson nodded. Lowering his voice he said, 'This mustn't come out. My wife will kill me.' His big face flushed. 'I was with Janet, she's the woman you've just seen. I told Marilyn, my wife, that I had some paperwork to sort out here at the club and that I'd stay on until it opened Saturday evening and have a drink. Marilyn doesn't come here. She's not keen on fishing and she likes to be at home with the kids, even though the two eldest are seventeen and fifteen. I've got three girls. The youngest is ten.'

'Saturday, Mr Davidson.'

Davidson sighed heavily. 'We went to Janet's house, it's not far. She's divorced. I came back here at about eight thirty, had a couple of drinks and got home just after ten. You won't have to talk to Marilyn, will you?' he asked, alarmed.

'I need to check it with Janet and someone who can confirm you were in the bar.' He didn't really need to because he didn't believe Davidson had anything to do with Langham or Borland's deaths and he didn't think he had beaten up Westerbrook but he'd check anyway.

'They'll think I'm up to something,' Davidson said miserably.

'Aren't you?'

'No! Yes. I'll ask Janet to come in. And you can speak to Ed, he's the other barman. He was working last Saturday. But don't say anything to him about me and Janet, he doesn't know. No one does.'

Horton thought the whole bloody club probably knew. He had one more question to ask, just to make absolutely certain he could rule out Davidson. 'And your movements for Monday night?'

Davidson looked as though he was about to lie then obviously thought better of it. 'With Janet at her place and then I went home, got in about ten thirty. I told my wife I had to finish off the paperwork here.'

And Horton thought that lie must be wearing a bit thin with Mrs Davidson. Perhaps she was the unsuspecting sort, or perhaps she didn't really care. He stayed long enough to speak to Janet and Ed separately who both confirmed what Davidson had said. Janet looked worried and Horton could see her rapidly revising her opinion of her boyfriend, trying to work out what he'd done to warrant police questioning, while Ed seemed to take it for granted that it was just routine. Horton asked them both if they knew Clive Westerbrook. Ed said he didn't but Janet remembered him not only from his visit last Sunday but from when he'd previously been a member.

'Always fancied himself. Nicely spoken but a bit on the big-headed side. Thought he could spin me a line and I'd fall for it.'

She'd fallen for Davidson's though.

'How many times has he been in the club recently?'

'Just last Sunday. We're only open at weekends. I saw him talking to Les Nugent and then he left.'

'Has Mr Nugent been in since then?'

'No.'

'Did they know one another?'

'Must have done.'

That didn't mean they had.

Horton left. Davidson was in the clear but he wondered why Tierney had said he'd seen him talking to Borland, when he hadn't been. He'd return and ask him. But on the seafront he pulled over. It was lunchtime and he was hungry. He bought some fish and chips and took them down on to the beach hoping that food and the fresh salty air blowing off the sea would help clear his muggy head. There was so much crowding it. Carolyn Grantham's appearance and research, and her boyfriend Rufus Anstey. Then there was what Melvin Cooper and Susan Nash had told him. Susan's statement tied in with what Irene Ebury had said about Jennifer being down and then happy.

Then there was this investigation. Why had a man perished in a fire after being violently assaulted? Why hadn't Westerbrook returned to Fareham Marina after fishing out that hand? Had he been too scared to? Was there someone waiting for him at the marina who had threatened to do the same to him? Had Westerbrook known that the fire that had killed Borland was murder and arson? Again something niggled away at the back of Horton's mind.

He sat on the stones and ate slowly while watching the handful of yachts sailing off Cowes. He thought of Westerbrook's boat at the port. Uckfield had said the forensic team was going over it. He recalled his search of the boat at Thorney. Elkins had commented on Westerbrook having very expensive state-of-the-art navigation equipment, and that he must have been a very keen fisherman. But was he? One photograph of Westerbrook with a fish was all Horton had found on his mobile phone. Nobody listed on his mobile phone had gone fishing with him and he had only renewed contact with the angling club last Sunday. So, was he really that keen? Maybe his trips in the Solent, across to France and to the Isle of Wight weren't to reel in the wet fish variety but to pick up a very different kind of fish, the kind that he'd already discussed with Uckfield, humans, with the possibility that it could also still be drugs, except as he'd expressed earlier Borland wouldn't have been able to see evidence of that, unless . . . Horton paused in the act of eating. Unless he'd seen through his binoculars or maybe even overheard and witnessed something taking place either on the pontoon or on the Hard when Westerbrook had returned to his car.

Horton's thoughts quickened as he recollected the routes that had been on Westerbrook's GPS: France, the Solent, the English Channel, and a bay on the east coast of the Isle of Wight. Horton knew it well. He'd sailed close to it on his previous yacht and on Catherine's father's yacht when he'd taken the tender into the bay with Emma on board and they'd played on the isolated sandy beach and hunted for fossils in the cliff side. They'd climbed to the top where a track led to the road. There were no houses. It was remote.

He finished his chips, screwed the paper into a ball and tossed it in the bin. Perhaps that bay was a good place to fish. But if it was then Westerbrook hadn't been there on Monday night because the date that was on the chart plotter was three weeks ago. But perhaps he just hadn't bothered to re-enter it because he knew how to navigate into it.

They needed a sighting of Westerbrook for Monday and Tuesday when Borland had been alive. Perhaps someone in Westerbrook's apartment block had seen him. Uckfield could get officers over there or Horton could call in and detail a unit to start knocking on doors but the thought of that bay nagged away at him. He stared across to the Isle of Wight and the elusive thought that had niggled at the back of his mind earlier crystallized. It was possible that Westerbrook had put in there on Monday night to ostensibly drop off a valuable cargo. Was it also possible that Graham Langham had been told to meet him there in his white van? Langham had gone in the hope of being cut in on the deal. Instead he'd been cut out of it. Was his van still there? Only one way to find out. Horton headed for Portsmouth and the Wightlink ferry terminal.

SEVENTEEN

Forty minutes later Horton was outside the ferry booking office calling the marine unit hoping that Elkins was on duty. He was. He asked Elkins to meet him at the port and headed there on the Harley knowing that he should call Uckfield and tell him that Langham's van *had* crossed on the Wightlink ferry on Monday night and that it *hadn't* returned. But Uckfield would probably tell him that uniform could check it out, and they could and most probably should, it was a much better use of manpower but the police RIB would get him over to that cove and back within the hour, even accounting for a check around the area, and an hour wasn't going to delay anything.

Elkins and Ripley were waiting for him. As Horton donned his life jacket he quickly told Elkins what he was hoping to find above a secluded cove on the east coast of the island. Ripley opened up. They sped across the Solent, the noise of the engine and the movement of the RIB prohibiting further conversation. Within fifteen minutes they were rounding the Bembridge peninsula and another five took them across Sandown Bay. Ten minutes later Ripley was easing the craft into the deserted cove. It was high tide, just as it had been on Monday night and therefore the cove was highly accessible by RIB or a flat-bottomed boat, such as Westerbrook's.

Horton jumped out and asked Elkins to follow him and to bring the bolt cutters. 'Hope you're up for a climb?'

Elkins eyed the cliff face dubiously. On the way up the twisting narrow path Horton relayed more information.

'Langham was booked on the six p.m. ferry from Portsmouth to Fishbourne, due to return on the ten o'clock sailing. He paid cash, which someone probably gave him.'

'Westerbrook?'

'If he did then someone gave Westerbrook the money. I think Langham was told to come here to pick up a consignment, possibly illegal immigrants or girls being brought in to be exploited in the sex trade, which on this occasion was a lie to get him here. Whatever the cargo, Langham didn't care because he thought he'd hit the big time.'

'And once here he was killed.'

Horton nodded. 'His van could have been driven away by the killer and dumped somewhere but my bet is it's still where Graham was told to leave it and instead he was taken away and dumped.'

'Or he could be in the back of it minus his hand, and other body parts,' Elkins said, breathing heavily from the climb.

'We'll soon find out,' Horton said gravely. He continued, 'I think that his hand was put on Westerbrook's boat without Westerbrook's knowledge as a means of scaring him that the same would happen to him if he didn't keep his mouth shut. Westerbrook didn't discover it until Wednesday while out fishing and tried to ditch it but Nugent inadvertently reeled it in.' It made sense except Horton wondered why Westerbrook had asked Nugent to go fishing with him.

Elkins wiped the sweat from his forehead as they reached the top. The grass and shrubs gave on to a rough track and Horton set out along it walking briskly as Elkins tried to keep pace. They hadn't gone far though when Horton spotted the van. It was parked behind some tall shrubs just off the track. He swiftly crossed to it and peered through the driver's window. The inside was strewn with old parking tickets, petrol receipts, sweet wrappers, fag packets, drink cans and old tabloid newspapers. It was a mess. There was no blood and no sign of Langham.

'No other vehicle tracks,' Elkins said, stretching his fingers into latex gloves.

Horton did the same. 'Ready?'

Elkins nodded.

Horton tried the rear door. It was unlocked. 'We won't need those,' he indicated the bolt cutters. He took a deep breath and glanced at Elkins who did the same and nodded. Horton steeled himself to meet the mutilated body of Graham Langham. He threw open the door and let out a sigh of relief. He heard Elkins exhale. It was empty. Or rather there was no sign of Graham Langham or any of his body parts, only rusty garden implements and a lawn mower, presumably the one he'd stolen on Saturday evening and hadn't been able to sell on Sunday night.

Horton gazed around the secluded area with its shrubs, hollows and trees. Perhaps Langham's body was lying somewhere close by in the undergrowth. Or perhaps he'd been killed and transported elsewhere. But the path he and Elkins had climbed was fairly steep. Westerbrook, with his bad health, would have been in a worse state than Elkins had been when he'd reached the top if he had climbed up it on Monday night and if he had then Horton didn't think he'd have had the breath to kill Langham, let alone transport his body back down the cliff to the bay and his boat. In fact the climb would probably have killed him. But Langham could have voluntarily descended the cliff to the bay to meet at the agreed rendezvous believing he was going to benefit from it financially, then he had been killed, his hand amputated, his body bundled into a boat and dumped in the English Channel. Without the rest of his body they had no idea how he'd been killed, he could have been shot, stabbed, throttled or beaten to death, but Gaye Clayton's words about the kind of knife possibly used to cut off his hand came back to Horton. It could have been used to slash Langham's throat first. He tensed and stared out at the cold grey sea.

Elkins' voice broke through Horton's thoughts. 'If Langham was butchered on Westerbrook's boat then Westerbrook must have spent some time cleaning it. I didn't see any blood.'

Neither had Horton either the first time he'd been on board last Wednesday or yesterday. He rang Uckfield. Before explaining where he was and what he'd found he asked him what Adams had said about Langham's fingerprints being in Borland's house.

'Claims they must have got there when he burgled him on Saturday. And before you say how do we know he did, how do we know he didn't. There's no one to tell us what if anything was nicked from that house.'

'Then you'd better tell Adams I've found Langham's van.'

'Where?' asked Uckfield eagerly.

Horton swiftly told him and gave him the news that it was minus Langham's body.

'I'll call DCI Birch and get him to organize a search of the area and for the van to be taken away and forensically examined.'

Birch, head of the island's CID, wasn't going to be very pleased to find him on his patch, thought Horton. Their enmity went back several years when Birch had hounded a mentally ill man – who Horton believed innocent of committing a vicious assault – into committing suicide. Birch hadn't liked it when Horton had been proved correct and had got the real offender and given Birch a piece of his mind.

Horton said, 'I'd like to return to Portsmouth with Elkins and break the news to Moira, *if* I have DCS Adams' permission,' he added with heavy sarcasm.

'OK, but do it quickly.'

Which meant before Uckfield told Adams they'd located the van, and if Adams complained, Horton knew Uckfield would backtrack and claim he'd never given Horton permission to interview Moira, or he'd say that he must have misheard him.

Horton waited until the first uniformed officers arrived and gave them instructions to seal off the area and await DCI Birch. There was only about an hour left until sunset and unless Birch called for lights to be set up Horton knew the search would have to wait until the morning.

With Elkins he headed back to the RIB. An hour later Horton was knocking on Moira's door.

'We'll talk outside,' she said, grabbing a packet of cigarettes and her coat, leaving the three boys sitting in front of the television. She looked paler, thinner and was clearly more agitated than on his previous visit.

They stood in the small courtyard as the traffic on the main road ground past them. Sundays were rapidly becoming one of the busiest shopping days of the week, particularly in the run up to Christmas. In half an hour though the shops would be shut, the dark was already descending and it was only just on three thirty.

'We've found Graham's van,' Horton announced solemnly.

Her head came up and her eyes narrowed. 'Where?'

'The Isle of Wight.'

She eyed him, surprised. 'What the bleeding hell was he doing there?'

'I thought you might be able to tell me that.'

She lit her cigarette. 'I have no idea. Where is he?'

'He wasn't in the van. Moira, he's not coming back,' Horton added gently.

She exhaled and her eyes held his for a moment before dropping. She shuffled her feet as though cold, drew on her cigarette and then looked back up at him. 'Will they make it official, that he's dead. Only I've read if there's no body you have to hang around and wait years until you can get a widow's pension. Well, what am I supposed to do,' she declared angrily. 'I've got three kids to feed and they can't live on fresh air, not that there's much of that around here.' And she coughed as though to prove it. 'I've only got the kids benefit to live on and that's bugger all. There's no food in the house and that tight-arsed copper told me that if I thought of selling the story to the newspapers then whoever got Graham might come after me and the kids.'

'Which tight-arsed copper?' Horton asked, wondering for a moment if she meant Bliss.

'I don't remember his name, dark hair with sharp evil eyes.'

So not Bliss but Adams. The description didn't quite fit but it was him all right.

'What did he tell you about Graham?'

'Said he was a grass. I laughed in his face and the tart that was with him.'

Adams must have come here with DCI Natasha Neame. Not that Horton knew what she looked like but a 'tart' was any woman Moira didn't like or trust, and that was most of them.

'Did he say what Graham was meant to have grassed about?'

'No. Just that he'd met some nasty bastards in the nick who had contacts and he didn't want anything to happen to me or the kids.'

So Adams had put the fear of God into her. Maybe he genuinely believed she was at risk if Langham had grassed up a big time villain but Horton thought it more probable that Adams had been checking to see if Graham had told his wife anything. Horton wondered if her flat was under surveillance, if so Adams would have seen him arrive. He'd soon know if it was.

But Moira also had a point about her financial situation. Whatever benefits Graham Langham had been receiving would stop. Horton didn't know if she would be entitled to a widow's pension, but clearly she would need help whether or not Graham was found dead or declared dead. Graham hadn't been much, but it was going to be tough for her and the kids and he didn't want any of them stealing to help make ends meet.

He said, 'Graham went out on a job on Saturday night. We have evidence, Moira, that he stole from some properties in Fareham.'

'Yeah, well you can't nick him for that, can you?' she sniped.

'How did he seem when he returned?'

She shrugged and drew on her cigarette.

'It might help us to find his body and speed up that widow's pension.'

She looked at him distrustfully but then seemed to see sense in what he said. 'He was hyper. Came banging into the flat, making a noise and singing. I bawled at him to shut up or he'd wake the kids.'

And her bawling wouldn't have helped matters but maybe the children were immune to it.

She said, 'I thought he'd been drinking. He acted like it but he didn't smell of drink. He said we'd be in the money, no more worries. I said what the hell was he on about, told me to wait and see. I said, oh yeah, I've heard that before, what you done, won the bleedin' lottery? He said better than that.'

He'd seen or heard something then as Horton had suspected. 'And on Monday when he went out did he say anything about being in the money? Please Moira it's important you tell me.'

She sighed. 'He said he'd be out all night but that when he came back we'd be OK, only the bugger never did come back. What did you find in the van?' she asked, slightly nervously.

'Some tools and a lawnmower.'

She looked relieved and drew on her cigarette. 'When can I have the van back?'

'When we've finished with it.'

'Hope that's before Christmas. I need the money.'

She wouldn't get much for it, a couple of hundred pounds if she was lucky but then to Moira that was a small fortune. He took out his wallet and plucked out some notes.

'I ain't no grass,' she cried, recoiling as though it was poison he was offering her, but he could see her eyeing the money keenly.

'It's for food for you and the kids. To help tide you over and I'll get someone from the Citizens Advice Bureau to contact you tomorrow morning, they'll be able to help you with vouchers for the food bank and with applying for any additional benefits.'

She hesitated for a moment then her thin hand snaked out and she grasped it. She didn't thank him.

Horton headed for the station hoping she wouldn't spend the money on booze and fags. He immediately made for Uckfield's office and told him that Adams had visited Moira and relayed what Moira had said about Langham being hyper and his theory that he'd gone to the island to meet someone he'd seen and spoken to the night he'd illegally entered Borland's house.

Uckfield agreed to get a team into Westerbrook's apartment block to try and determine if anyone saw Westerbrook on Saturday and the Monday and Tuesday before his fishing trip. The search around Langham's van hadn't discovered his body but it would resume in the morning and the van had been taken to the forensic workshop in Shanklin.

Horton returned to his office where he turned his attention to Carolyn's mystery boyfriend, Dr Rufus Anstey. He ran his details through the computer. He was clean, no criminal convictions. Then he entered his name in an internet search engine and discovered he was a lecturer at the university. Horton clicked on the university's website and was soon reading that Anstey was a senior lecturer in history, at the School of Social, Historical and Literary Studies, specializing in the British Empire, national identities abroad, social and cultural history, the occult, magical beliefs and myths, witchcraft, the supernatural, superstition, and science fiction. It seemed an awful lot to specialize in and it didn't sound as though he was one of Eames' men but then you never could tell.

The photograph of Anstey on the university website matched with the man he'd seen. Perhaps he should tell Anstey that his girlfriend had slept with him, and see what reaction he got? Perhaps Anstey was under the illusion that Carolyn only had eyes for him. Or perhaps their relationship was an open one. Whatever it was, Horton wasn't interested in being second fiddle or sharing her with anyone else. Maybe some men could handle casual sex. He wasn't one of them. His mobile phone rang and he saw with excitement that it was John Guilbert.

'I've got three photographs from Violet Ducale,' he announced.

Horton's heart leapt into his throat.

'They're of the twins taken in their teens. I'll scan them and email them to your phone but it'll have to be tomorrow. I'm tied up with a case tonight.'

Horton curbed his impatience with difficulty. He was grateful to
Guilbert for his help and said as much. He had to ring off because
his office phone was ringing and Horton could see from the display
that it was Uckfield. It was a summons to his office.

Uckfield wasn't alone. He nodded Horton into a seat around the
boardroom table. Along with Uckfield was DI Dennings, DCS
Adams and a woman whom Horton assumed was the 'tart' Moira
had mentioned though she looked anything but. She was a brunette
with an oval perfectly made-up face and clear complexion, about
late thirties, dressed smartly in black trousers and a black top with
a casual red jacket hanging over the back of her chair. She wore a
wedding ring and small opal ear studs. Horton thought of Bliss who
would have eyed her up as the competition. Bliss would be highly
hacked off tomorrow when she learned so much had happened on
her weekend off.

Uckfield introduced the woman as DCI Natasha Neame.

Adams addressed Horton, 'What did Moira tell you?'

Horton didn't look at Uckfield. He didn't think the Super had
told him about his visit there. It was as he had suspected, Moira's
place was under surveillance.

'*She* didn't tell me anything. I told her that we'd located her
husband's van.'

'How did you know where to find it?' Adams' tone was light but
his eyes held suspicion and his lips were set firmly.

'I didn't *know*. I just put some of the information I'd been told
together and thought it was possible.'

Neame spoke, 'What information?'

They think I'm involved. But in what he wondered? Not mutilation and murder, surely? Possibly smuggling. Crisply he began to
count off. 'One, everything centres around Fareham Marina:
Langham, Westerbrook, Nugent and Borland. Two, why had Graham
told Moira they were going to be hitting the big time?'

'So she did tell you something,' Adams almost sneered.

'The first time Sergeant Cantelli and I visited her, she said he
was in good spirits.' He wasn't going to reveal she'd repeated it
and embellished on it, not until he knew where this was heading.
'Three, we know that Westerbrook is a heavy gambler and that he
has lost a great deal of money that has come from somewhere. Four,
since coming out of prison he's managed to buy a car and a boat

with cash and his boat is equipped with the latest state-of-the-art and very expensive navigational equipment. Five, he's supposed to be a keen fisherman but there's no evidence to back that up except one photograph of him with a fish. Six, his boat trips include several to France and across the Solent and to the Isle of Wight. And seven, Borland used binoculars not only in that front bedroom where he died but he also took them out with him. He witnessed something and I believe it was Westerbrook bringing in illegal immigrants or girls for the sex trade. Langham also saw this or overheard someone talking about it, possibly Borland and Westerbrook, and wanted a cut. Knowing Langham like I do he thought he could muscle in. He was asked to meet Westerbrook and possibly his accomplice or rather someone working with Westerbrook at the rendezvous point, which was plotted on Westerbrook's GPS, that cove on the Isle of Wight. When I knew that Langham had taken his van over I was even more convinced I'd find it there.'

Adams didn't look very happy about all this but that was his problem. Horton said, 'You didn't suspect Westerbrook of being involved with Langham but he is.'

Adams' expression remained stoical but there was, Horton thought, a glimmer of unease in his eyes and tightness of anger about his mouth.

'We thought it best to let Langham run. We didn't know it would lead to his death or that Westerbrook would die of a heart attack.'

Bullshit thought Horton. Adams had had no idea.

'And it's not people trafficking, it's drugs.' Adams added crisply.

'And you know who's behind it?' Horton asked, surprised that it was drugs.

'Jacob Crowe.'

Horton wracked his brains trying to place him but couldn't. Neither could Uckfield and Dennings judging by their expressions.

Adams continued. 'Crowe is a drug dealer, who we believe still holds the reins from inside. He was arrested and convicted five years ago. We broke his drug routes but he wouldn't name his confederates and we don't know where the money he obtained, and probably still receives from his illegal activities, is stashed. He got fourteen years, and he'll be released next year having served six if he keeps his nose clean, and he has until now, at least on the inside.'

Neame took it up. 'Crowe was in Winchester Prison for three years when Langham was serving time there. Then Crowe was transferred to the Isle of Wight prison where Westerbrook was serving time. Westerbrook was a Category C prisoner so did his time in the lower security wing while Crowe was and still is in Category B with higher security but it's a training prison, we think they came across one another.'

So when had that idea occurred to them, wondered Horton? Possibly only two hours ago when Uckfield had informed Adams about finding Langham's van and Uckfield had told them Westerbrook must be involved. Horton was still convinced they'd had no idea of that before then but if Crowe was the brains behind this then it would explain where Westerbrook's money had come from.

Adams said, 'It's possible that Crowe told Westerbrook he'd have a lucrative business lined up for him when he came out, if he did as he was told. All Crowe had to do was give his girlfriend, who visits him regularly, Westerbrook's name and Crowe's contacts on the outside would easily find him. Westerbrook went along with it because of his heavy gambling debts.'

But that didn't explain why Westerbrook had only been given the money for the car and boat a year ago and not immediately or soon after his release. Perhaps Crowe had wanted one of his minions to suss Westerbrook out first, make sure he was sound before coughing up.

Adams said, 'Crowe also recruited Graham Langham when he was in Winchester.'

'Crowe's been very busy,' Horton said sarcastically.

Adams narrowed his eyes. 'When Langham was released he decided to inform.'

'But he didn't tell you about Westerbrook or the drugs?'

'No.'

So what had he told them, wondered Horton? Judging by the expression on Uckfield's craggy features he was thinking the same. Horton said, 'Why would a big time villain like Crowe enlist the services of a petty crook like Langham never mind confide in him.'

Adams ignored the question. 'Langham decided to play it both ways, he wanted to inform but it appears he's been working with the drug runners. Despite what you think you know of Langham he was tied up in this and he killed Leonard Borland. His fingerprints are under the electric fire. The fingerprint bureau has confirmed it.'

Horton didn't bother to hide his surprise. He was convinced that Langham couldn't have dragged Borland's body and placed it on that fire. 'The timing's wrong. The fire was started on Tuesday just before six fifty-three and Langham was already dead then.'

Neame said, 'How do we know that? Dr Clayton can't confirm exactly when that hand was amputated.'

'His van was on the six o'clock sailing to the Isle of Wight on Monday and it never returned.'

'*He* might have done. By boat, Westerbrook's boat,' Adams answered crisply.

'Then where was he all day Tuesday after clubbing Leonard Borland on the back of the head before shoving his body over that electric fire?'

'Langham spent the day with Westerbrook.'

Horton still couldn't buy it. 'But why would Langham return to Fareham Marina with Westerbrook, leave his van on the Isle of Wight and hang around all Tuesday before killing Borland?'

Tersely Adams said, 'Because he was told to. Just as he was instructed to kill Leonard Borland who, as you say, Inspector, had probably witnessed what was happening at the marina.'

Adams was trying to make it fit but it didn't. 'Firstly I don't believe Langham is a killer, secondly he wouldn't meekly stay on board Westerbrook's boat all day, he'd use the opportunity for more thieving—'

'Not if he didn't have his van,' Neame said.

'And thirdly,' Horton continued, ignoring her, 'How did Langham get away after supposedly pushing Borland over that fire.'

Dennings answered. 'He went back on board Westerbrook's boat where he was killed. Nugent could be involved. He works in a butcher's, he obtains the knife. Between them they kill and dismember Langham but the hand gets left behind. When they go fishing the next day they find the hand still on the boat. They aim to throw it over the side then one of them thinks if they stuff it in a container and pretend to find it we won't think it's them and the fingerprints found in Borland's house will prove that Langham is the killer. Westerbrook loses his nerve though, and he goes on the run by boat.'

'Not to where he ended up,' Horton interjected. 'That leads nowhere.'

Ignoring him Dennings continued. 'He tells his contact he wants out, and gets beaten up for his pains and suffers a heart attack. Nugent gets scared and goes on the run.'

'No, I don't buy it.'

Crisply Adams said, 'Whether you do or not, Inspector, is of no consequence. When we find Nugent, who has gone missing, we'll ask him. As far as CID are concerned, Inspector, this investigation is no longer your remit. DCI Bliss will be informed of that tomorrow morning. You are not to see Moira Langham again or interview anyone connected with the case, and neither are any of your officers. The Major Crime Team will work with my team on gathering the evidence and locating Nugent.' Adams nodded his dismissal.

So that was it, thought Horton, they had it all figured out. He returned to his office to collect his helmet and jacket. It all fitted if you stretched a few points here and there, but there were still many questions that needed asking and perhaps between them the Major Crime Team and Adams' lot would find the answers. Trueman would collate all the statements and conduct further research, and maybe Nugent, when he was apprehended, would fill in the blanks. Horton heard a car start up and looked out of his office window. Adams and Neame were leaving. Time he was too.

EIGHTEEN

Monday

'Do you believe all that?' Cantelli said the next morning, 'Thought not,' he added, reading Horton's expression. But some new ideas had occurred to Horton during his restless night. He'd woken early, keen to put them to Uckfield, only to find that Uckfield was in a meeting and wouldn't be available until mid-morning. Horton asked Trueman about the validity of Langham's fingerprints under the electric fire.

'They're smudged but there was enough to get one clear print.'

Dennings had entered and grumpily said, 'Thought you were no longer involved in our investigation.'

'I'm not.' Horton had replied. He'd met Cantelli in the corridor and, as they headed towards the CID operations room, he'd told him about his interview with Davidson, finding Langham's van and his interview with Moira, ending with his summons to Uckfield's office and DCS Adams' theory.

Horton continued. 'Discounting all that stuff about Langham being an informer and both him and Westerbrook being linked to Jacob Crowe, let's go back to Borland's death. Margaret Samson told me that Borland was a very cautious man. I can't see him confronting Westerbrook or Nugent if he believed they were involved in smuggling. And neither can I see him letting either of them into his house, unless Trueman discovers that he knew one of them. And I don't see Borland as a blackmailer.'

'We could look into his bank accounts.'

'Not our case, which means you're relieved of talking to Westerbrook's bank manager. You'd better let Trueman know though, in case he wants to send someone from his team.' Horton sat back. 'We know that Langham was inside that house because his finger-prints are in the hall and on the bannister but Borland wouldn't have admitted him and I don't think Borland would have been duped into allowing Langham inside. Knowing Langham's form I think that when he was robbing that area on Saturday he discovered the back door of Borland's house was unlocked. The house must have been in darkness, otherwise Langham would never have entered it. Langham thought the occupant was out. He crept in and up those stairs thinking he could help himself. He entered the front bedroom and startled Borland who was in the dark looking through his binoculars. Borland swung round, Langham picked up the nearest thing to hand, a heavy-duty torch, and struck him. You're looking sceptical, Barney.'

'Because the Langham I knew wouldn't have lashed out, he'd have panicked and fled.'

'I agree. And if anyone was going to do the striking it would have been Borland hitting Langham.'

'And Langham would never have returned to that house. He'd simply get out and scarper back to Portsmouth with whatever he'd managed to steal in the back of his van.'

'So even if he did strike Borland, just say he did,' Horton added when Cantelli looked about to protest, 'he wouldn't have gone back on Tuesday evening and put his body over that electric fire.'

'No.'

'Not even if he'd returned home and, worried about what he'd done, felt he had to check. So he returned Tuesday and seeing Borland dead thought he'd cover up his crime?' Horton knew he hadn't but he was keen to test all this out on Cantelli.

'No,' Cantelli firmly replied. 'He'd have stayed well away. Besides Moira didn't say that Graham was worried or irritable, and even though she might have lied to us I don't think she did. Langham was flogging the stuff he'd stolen in the pub on Sunday night according to Jago and he left home on Monday afternoon bright and breezy. He wasn't seen again. He didn't return to finish off Borland or to cover up a crime.'

'*He* didn't, no,' Horton said with emphasis.

Cantelli looked puzzled for a moment then his expression cleared. His dark eyes lit up and a broad grin crossed his face. 'Of course!' he cried. 'His hand returned. That's why it was amputated. It was used to implicate him.'

Horton nodded. 'It was why it was placed in a container, which probably contained grease in order to keep some of the prints waxy so that they would leave an impression. It would explain why those particular prints under the electric fire were smudged and more difficult to identify, whereas the others in the hall and on the bannister were crystal clear. Langham entered that house, which, as I said, was in darkness, with the intention of robbing it. He crept up the stairs and he heard voices. Borland had admitted someone who he was confiding in about what he had witnessed through his binoculars.'

'Why wouldn't Borland have turned on the light in the hall when he'd shown this visitor upstairs?'

'Maybe he did and quickly turned it off again.' Horton didn't know. 'Perhaps he needed the house in darkness in order to show this person what he could see through his binoculars. Instead of running away, Langham stayed put, glued to the spot, his ears flapping and he heard something very interesting.'

'Probably the word "smuggling".'

'Yes. And he thinks, I'll have a piece of this action. He steals out of the house but loiters outside and confronts Borland's visitor when he leaves—'

'But hang on, how does he know this visitor is in on the smuggling? Borland could just have been reporting what he'd seen to someone he knew and trusted, and he's still alive when this person leaves. He's also still alive and kicking on Monday when Mrs Samson saw him, so Langham couldn't have witnessed the visitor assaulting Borland or admitting to being a smuggler.'

'Maybe Mrs Samson is mistaken. We need to check if anyone else saw him on Monday.'

'I thought you said it's not our case,' Cantelli said.

'Just a few questions, an hour or two's not going to hurt,' Horton said quickly. It would be his neck on the line if Bliss found out or if DCS Adams discovered they were investigating despite his orders. Horton knew that Sergeant Trueman wouldn't say anything to Adams or to Uckfield, unless either specifically asked him and he had no choice, but Dennings might tell Uckfield he'd been in the incident suite asking about the case. Horton wouldn't put it past Dennings to tell Bliss, just to drop him in it. Uckfield though would say nothing, not unless it backfired on him in some way then he'd hastily deny all knowledge, or wriggle out of it somehow. He said, 'I'll take full responsibility.'

But Cantelli dismissed that with a smile. 'Go on.'

Horton recalled what Mrs Samson told him. *He'd research everything, go to the library, read books, write it down, weigh up all the pros and cons.* 'OK, so let's assume Mrs Samson is correct and that Borland left on foot on Monday, looking smart. He often visited the library. He wasn't carrying any library books but check with the library to see if he called in there, and ask around the bus drivers and at the train station to see if he travelled anywhere.'

Cantelli nodded and said, 'Langham might have been seen by Borland's visitor as he left the house and this person, our killer, confronted Langham. He told Langham he had to keep quiet about the smuggling, it was a big operation and they had to put the evidence before the police. Langham said he would keep shtum for a fee. The killer pays up until he can think of a way of getting rid of Langham and Borland, and implicating Langham in the murder.'

'There is another possibility,' and Horton didn't much care for it. He said, 'Borland is a cautious man. He weighs up everything before making a decision. He's compiled a dossier of evidence and he waits until he has enough to show it to someone he respects and trusts.'

'A police officer,' Cantelli said, then added with a troubled expression, 'Not DCS Adams surely?'

Horton didn't like to think so but it had to be considered.

'How would Borland know DCS Adams?' asked Cantelli

'That's what we need to find out. Maybe he rang NCA and asked for the man in charge.'

'The call would be on file.'

'Not necessarily. It might not have been noted or it could have been deleted. Maybe Borland saw Adams' picture in the newspaper and read an article that said Adams was responsible for investigating serious and organized crime, not realizing that he was actually involved in one. Borland admitted Adams because he'd already contacted him and had arranged a meeting. Adams tells us that Langham is an informer and spins this yarn about Jacob Crowe to throw everyone off the scent and make it look as though Graham Langham is our murderer working under orders from Crowe. It's a flimsy story to say the least.'

'But would Adams place Borland's body over an electric fire and leave him to burn to death?' Cantelli said solemnly and with disbelief.

Horton found it hard to believe too. But then they were often called upon to believe the incredible; horrendous crimes carried out by seemingly ordinary and sane individuals.

'And would Adams kill Graham Langham and hack off his hand and plant it on Westerbrook's boat?'

'Not personally, no. Whoever he is working with does that.'

'I can't see that being Nugent,' declared Cantelli.

Neither could Horton. 'I think it's someone much higher up the criminal food chain. Not Crowe, or any of his confederates, that's a blind, but someone who is behind human trafficking.' Horton completely discounted the drugs theory Adams had spun him. 'Someone who Adams has come into contact with or been groomed by during his time in NCA.'

'I hope to God you're wrong, Andy.'

'So do I,' Horton said solemnly, then after a moment added, 'So if we discount him for now. Who does that leave us with?'

'Someone Borland used to work with, or someone he knew through work.'

'He retired some years ago.'

'Perhaps he kept in touch with a few past colleagues. Or it could be someone he has got to know since his retirement. He might have joined a club or taken up a hobby, apart from covert surveillance that is.'

There had been nothing in his house to suggest hobbies although clearly Borland had liked to read judging by the charred remains of his bookshelves and his library visits.

'Perhaps he went to church,' continued Cantelli. 'He might have trusted a priest or a vicar.'

Horton considered this with growing interest. 'We talked about the amputation of a hand being mentioned in the Bible. Oh, I know not for the reasons of theft, as you explained, but it is in the Good Book.'

'But could a priest have done such a thing?' asked Cantelli, troubled.

There was one who sprang to Horton's mind. The padre who had discovered Westerbrook's body. A very fit, strong man, who although religious was also a soldier. A man used to seeing death and slaughter. And a man who would have the strength to kill and to carry a body if needed down that cliff to the bay. Not that he'd have had to because Langham would have descended into the bay willingly. But certainly a man strong enough to throw a body over the side of a boat, possibly his own boat, into the sea and drag another body and place it over a fire. But could he kill?

He recollected what Gaye had told him about the types of knives that could have been used to hack off Langham's hand. One of them had been a Khukuri knife, a weapon used by The Royal Gurkha Rifles also known as the Gurkha knife. *Better to die than live a coward.* Was that how Jeremy Dowdswell, the army padre, would have seen Langham – as a coward? He was a soldier. He'd have witnessed his colleagues being maimed and killed. He'd have seen supreme acts of bravery and self-sacrifice so when a whining, skinny, lowlife thief like Graham Langham had sidled up to him, he'd have felt no compunction over killing and mutilating him – a man who, in his mind, was beneath contempt. Neither would he see anything wrong in framing the dead man for a murder. Did

Dowdswell have connections with the Gurkhas? Had he been stationed at either of their bases at Shorncliffe in Kent or at the British Garrison in Brunei? Or perhaps he knew or had known someone in the Gurkhas.

But then being a yachtsman Dowdswell could have used a boat knife. He'd be bound to have one on board. Or perhaps he enjoyed fishing and had used a fishing knife to hack off Langham's hand. Then there was the fact that Westerbrook had headed for the Thorney Channel – to tell Dowdswell he wanted out? It would have been easy for Dowdswell to launch a dinghy, kayak or row boat from the shore. Why wasn't Westerbrook's boat seen? Because someone had sanitized the CCTV or knew the way to avoid being seen on camera. But why would Dowdswell be smuggling illegal immigrants or girls for sex trafficking? For money?

Horton relayed his thoughts to Cantelli, adding, 'Are you sure the army base showed you all the security footage?'

'The dates and times tallied.'

'And there was nothing on it?'

'Nothing showing Westerbrook's boat arriving or any other boat getting close to him.'

But someone could have done so by using a small tender which had come from a larger boat. And a boat moored close by. Dowdswell's boat.

'I'm going to talk to the padre.' And Horton decided to take the scenic route, by sea, following the same one that Westerbrook had taken after leaving Portsmouth Harbour. Horton was also keen to get away before Bliss appeared. And the time was fast approaching when she'd show.

He rose, picked up his helmet and jacket and entered CID with Cantelli following. Walters ambled in, biting on a bacon roll, with his face buried deep in a tabloid newspaper. Horton quickly told Walters that he was reprieved from trawling the bookmakers, which cheered him up. He added, 'But contact the probation service, find out everything you can about Westerbrook.'

'Where shall I say you and the sarge are if DCI Bliss asks, which she will,' Walters called out after them.

'Dentist,' answered Cantelli.

'Opticians,' replied Horton.

'Didn't know there was anything wrong with your eyesight, guv.'

'There is every time I look at you, Walters.'

'Ha, ha.'

Outside Horton called Elkins and asked him to meet him at the port on the police launch. When he arrived a short time later he noted that Westerbrook's boat was still secured there. As the police launch headed out of Portsmouth Harbour in the clear cold morning Horton's thoughts travelled to his first and only encounter with Jeremy Dowdswell. He tried to envisage the padre as the kind of man who could bludgeon a man in his mid-sixties and then place his body over a fire to burn, and the type of man who could kill Langham and then hack off his hand with a knife. It didn't seem likely but then killers didn't go around with it stamped on their foreheads.

Why use Westerbrook and his boat for smuggling? And why Fareham Marina when there were far more isolated spots around the Solent and Chichester Harbour to bring in illicit goods. But maybe the latter was too close to home for him. It was a point but it still didn't explain how Dowdswell would know and be able to enlist the services of Clive Westerbrook, or Lesley Nugent come to that, or how he might know Borland. None of them had been in the armed forces or had relatives in the services, or at least not as far as he knew. But perhaps Westerbrook had advised members of the armed forces before his prison sentence. He might even have given Dowdswell financial advice. And Dowdswell knew that Westerbrook would have done anything for money to feed his gambling habit.

Horton's thoughts had taken him into the long rolling waves of Southsea Bay. He glanced to his left as the launch sped past the apartment where Carolyn lived. Ripley handed him a mug of coffee. Taking it, Horton went below and rang her.

'Sorry about Saturday night,' he apologized. 'I was tired. We'd had a pretty gruesome murder and I—'

'Say no more. It's fine. About that dinner? Any chance of rescheduling it for tonight?'

'Not at the moment,' he tried to sound apologetic. He didn't have to try too hard.

'I'd still like to see you, Andy. Could we meet for a drink or just a talk?'

He left a short pause before saying. 'OK. Lunchtime today, at

Oyster Quays, the Millennium Walk on the residential side, on the route round to the ferry terminal.'

'What time?'

That depended on what he got out of Dowdswell. 'I'll text you when I'm heading there.'

'OK.' She rang off.

He climbed back up on deck. She hadn't sounded upset or disappointed. Perhaps she was just happy they were still seeing one another. He gazed across the harbour. They were approaching the small U-shaped nature reserve of Pilsey Island and his thoughts turned to his daughter. He and Emma had come here often in the summer, just the two of them on his small yacht. They'd always had the island to themselves not counting the seabirds. There was a landing area on the eastern side, and they'd picnicked in the sand dunes. He hoped to God there would be more days like that but after experiencing the sunshine of the continent on board a luxury motorboat he wondered if this would now hold any appeal for her. With a heavy heart he thought not.

As Ripley tied up on the pontoon at Thorney, Horton addressed Elkins, 'Ask around in the sailing club, see if anyone recognizes or has heard of Clive Westerbrook.'

On shore Elkins turned left while Horton headed to his right and through some lichen-covered gravestones to the heavy wooden doors of St Nicholas Church, the patron saint of children, sailors and pawnbrokers, more widely known as *Santa Claus*, the original Father Christmas. Maybe he should ask Santa Claus for a Christmas present. Or perhaps he should pray. Not for discovering the truth behind Jennifer's disappearance but for him to be with his daughter. And as he pushed open the door he wondered with a jolt if he'd made a big mistake this last year. Instead of looking back he should have been looking forward. Jennifer was the past. Emma was the present and the future, and maybe it was time he focused all his efforts and his attention on that. He'd consider that later because, ahead, staring at a plaque on the wall, was Jeremy Dowdswell.

NINETEEN

'The Royal Arms,' Dowdswell said, gesturing at the wall in front of him. 'It was ordered to be displayed in each church of the realm on the accession of King George I in 1714. The strap or belt around the shield carries the motto *Honi soit qui mal y pense* – "Evil to him who evil thinks", the symbol of the Order of the Garter.'

Horton glanced at it and then at Dowdswell's strong-featured face. And evil to him who *does* evil, he thought. Was Dowdswell feeling guilt over what he'd done? Had he been praying for forgiveness? Maybe he was about to confess to murder. He showed no surprise or alarm at Horton's arrival.

'How can I help you, Inspector?'

Horton asked if he knew or had heard of a man called Leonard Borland. He watched Dowdswell's reaction carefully.

'No. I can't say I have,' he answered, looking puzzled and worried.

But Horton told himself this could be an experienced liar, a cold calculating murderer. He showed him Borland's photograph while again studying his reaction, noting interest and curiosity but nothing more.

'I'm sorry I've never seen him before. Why the questions, Inspector?'

'He's dead. He was beaten until he became unconscious and then his body was placed over an electric fire. He burnt to death.' Horton spoke the brutal words harshly, his intention to prompt a response but Dowdswell didn't flinch. Neither did he appear shocked but Horton thought a touch of weariness crossed his rugged features.

Evenly Dowdswell said, 'And you believe this Mr Borland is connected with the man I found dead on his boat here.'

'That's what we're trying to establish.'

Dowdswell studied Horton closely. In those dark eyes Horton read strength and confidence but did he also see compassion and innocence?

'You're wondering if Mr Borland's killer might have come from here.'

'Do you hear confession?' Horton asked, avoiding answering the question.

'Not in the usual sense of the word. There is no confessional here, but people come to me in private and confide in me. No one has confessed to murder though if that's what you're thinking.'

It wasn't but he let Dowdswell believe that. 'If they had would you tell me?'

'I might.'

Horton examined Dowdswell's intelligent face and studied the big strong hands and arms. Would he beat a man? Would he kill? Would he drag a man over a fire and leave him to die? He'd been trained to kill. But he was also a man of God. That didn't mean he couldn't kill and hadn't killed.

Dowdswell eyed him shrewdly. 'You think I have some information or knowledge of this murder.'

Horton wasn't ready to answer that question. 'Have you preached or attended a church in Fareham or Portsmouth?' Borland could have attended a church in the city where he had worked for years.

'Portsmouth Cathedral, yes. I've also led services there, and funerals, sadly.'

And could he have met Borland there?

'How long have you been in the army, sir?'

'Seven years.'

'Always a padre?'

'I took a master's degree in Theology and became ordained. My ministry was in Norfolk but although I enjoyed it I found it wasn't enough. I come from a military family, Inspector, and I wanted to serve my country but not as a soldier like my father and grandfather. I joined up and have never regretted it. I provide spiritual support, pastoral care and moral guidance for those in my unit. I, and my fellow padres, go into operational zones but we don't carry weapons. It's a challenging vocation.'

Horton wondered how he could square killing with his religious beliefs. Perhaps there was a way and it was that which had assisted him in killing Langham, Westerbrook and Borland.

'Where were you Wednesday night?'

'Here, helping the vicar. We had a nativity service for the children and parents.'

'What time did that finish?'

'If I'm to be questioned and suspected of a crime, you do suspect me, don't you, Inspector? Then I'd rather we discussed it outside the church.'

He turned and set off down the aisle leaving Horton to follow him. Outside Dowdswell made for the small clean neat gravestones that Horton knew were part of the Commonwealth War Graves Commission, they marked the graves of both Allied servicemen and German airmen of the Second World War. Horton couldn't see Dowdswell's expression and wondered whether his action was a delaying tactic to give him time to disguise his emotions and to get his thoughts in order.

They walked the short distance to the old low flint wall encompassing the church grounds where, beyond, Horton could see Ripley on the police launch talking to two men on the landing stage, army by the look of their build. Across the narrow channel was the shore and low-lying land of Chidham and in the distance Horton caught sight of the steeples of the ancient churches both of Bosham, where Larry Egmont told him he lived, and the spire of Chichester Cathedral. It was two hours to high water and the gulls were circling overhead. Horton could also see the buoy where Westerbrook had moored up.

Dowdswell turned to Horton. 'The nativity service finished at seven thirty and was followed by mince pies and coffee. I helped the Reverend Davies, who is the vicar here at St Nicholas's, clear up. I chatted to a few people then left about nine. I returned to my quarters where I spent the night alone, so no alibi, Inspector, if I need one.'

'Just routine.'

Dowdswell studied him candidly. 'I'd rather you be honest.'

Horton returned the gaze. 'OK then, why would you beat a man and then leave him to die of a heart attack, kill another man and sever his hand and then leave a third man to die in a fire?'

Dowdswell showed no emotional reaction, perhaps because he'd seen too much carnage in his career and had heard too many harrowing tales of death and destruction. Solemnly he said, 'I understand your anxiety now. I'm not your killer. Someone who could do that is either desperate or troubled, or both.'

'Or psychotic or greedy or thinks he's superior or has what he believes a justifiable reason for doing so. Where were you last Monday and Tuesday evenings?'

Dowdswell didn't protest either at the question or at the harshness of Horton's tone. 'In London. I attended a two-day seminar which started at four thirty Monday afternoon. I stayed over in the armed forces club at Waterloo, attended the seminar on Tuesday, met up with some friends Tuesday evening and returned here on Wednesday morning, arriving at midday. I'd happily give you contact details.'

They could check his alibis and they'd be cast iron. With relief Horton knew that Dowdswell was not their killer. He hadn't wanted to believe he was. He turned and stared out to sea. 'I have to check.'

'Of course you do.'

'But you still might be able to help me. You mentioned earlier that Clive Westerbrook's boat was moored up on a soldier's buoy.'

'Yes, Hugh Maltby. He's in Cyprus.'

'You're sure about that?'

'Positive and the Station Commander will confirm it.'

So Maltby couldn't be the man who Westerbrook might have come here to meet, and who could have been his assailant. Unless Maltby had a son or brother that Westerbrook had known. He asked Dowdswell.

'Hugh's divorced and has no children, neither does he have any brothers or sisters. His father is a barrister with chambers in London and wanted Hugh to be the same and although Hugh went along with it and qualified for the Bar he threw it all in as soon as he could to join up as a Military Police Officer. Something his family and his former wife couldn't understand. He was very talented and would have been making a fortune had he stuck to it but he found the law tedious. He wanted a more challenging environment, and life is not all about money, is it? Not for some. I can put a call in to ask him if he knows of Clive Westerbrook or you can make a request to call him direct by going through the Station Commander but either way you might not be able to get the information quickly, because of his job. He might be engaged in activity that prevents him from making contact outside his usual channels.'

Horton frowned with irritation knowing it could take days to get hold of Maltby and then the answers might not lead them anywhere in the investigation. And it wasn't his investigation anyway.

Dowdswell added, 'Hugh's father might be able to assist. His chambers are in High Holborn, Maltby and Stone.'

'Thanks. We'll contact them. Have you ever seen Westerbrook's boat on that mooring before?'

'No.'

'Or any other boat moored there?'

'Only Hugh's motorboat.'

'You mentioned that it was laid up, where?'

'Here in the compound.'

'Can we check?'

'Of course.'

Horton wasn't sure why he wanted to know if it was there but there was that niggle at the back of his mind that said the killer could still be connected with someone from here.

Dowdswell quickly located Hugh Maltby's boat in the nearby compound.

'Do you know when Mr Maltby took it out of the water?' Horton asked.

'Just before he went overseas, three weeks ago.'

And Horton could see that it hadn't been used since then. Westerbrook must have come here for peace and quiet, to reflect on what to do next and had chosen one of the spare buoys at random. Horton thanked the padre for his help. He didn't apologize for suspecting him and Dowdswell didn't expect him to. He'd know it was all part of the job.

Horton returned to the police launch where Elkins told him that he'd managed to speak to a few people in and around the sailing club but none of them recognized Westerbrook or Borland. And no one had seen Westerbrook's boat moored there before.

Horton gave instructions to be taken back to Portsmouth and as Ripley got underway Horton went below and rang Trueman. He asked if DCI Bliss was loitering about, she'd go ballistic if she knew what he and Cantelli were expending their energy and time on. But Walters hadn't called to say she'd been demanding to know where they were, which was unlike her. Trueman informed him that she was at a one day conference on domestic violence. Good, that gave them a breathing space. He relayed the gist of his interview with Dowdswell. Trueman made no comment about him not being on the investigating team as Horton knew he wouldn't.

Uckfield though might feel differently, unless they came up with something that could lead to a result and Horton thought the Super wouldn't be averse to getting one over on DCS Adams. 'Can you look into Borland's background and see if there is a link to Hugh Maltby? He's in Cyprus and has nothing to do with Borland's death but I'm wondering if Borland knew the family, contact Maltby's father at his chambers and ask him. Also see if he's heard Clive Westerbrook mentioned.'

Trueman said he would.

Horton asked if Borland had ever worked with Nugent.

'Not according to Nugent's employment history. He's had several jobs, no convictions, but his short length of time as an accounts clerk for a variety of companies makes me wonder if he had his hand in the till but left or was chucked out before anything could be proved, or the company decided it didn't want to go through the hassle of reporting the crime and taking him to court. We've picked him up by the way.'

'Where?'

'Returning to his flat. He said he'd stayed overnight with a friend and had overslept. Dennings and DCI Neame are interviewing him now.'

Horton rang off wondering how Nugent would react to Dennings. He recalled the thin stooping, shuffling man. In Horton's opinion Nugent was not very strong either physically or mentally. If he was involved in this then Dennings would crack him wide open.

He checked his emails on his phone to find that Guilbert had sent over the photographs of the Ducale twins. With his heart hammering he called them up. First his eyes fell on a teenage Eileen, it was unmistakably her and his heart felt heavy with grief. He missed her intelligence, her gentleness and her kindness.

In the second photograph she had her arm tucked into that of a man. Horton stared at him, his heart knocking against his ribs. He had the same features as his sister, keen eyes, an angular face and wide mouth. Horton studied him as the boat rocked and plunged in the swelling sea. Was it the same fit and tanned man in his mid-sixties he'd talked to on his boat in Southsea Marina in June? He recalled Ballard's intelligent grey eyes, his craggy face, his rich well-educated voice, and the air of command about him. And if there was any doubt the third photograph of Andrew Ducale alone on a yacht confirmed it. Horton was certain he was staring at Edward Ballard. Ballard was Ducale.

He let out a long slow breath, trying to ease his racing pulse. Was Ducale also his father? Had he been named after him? Was he the man Jennifer had seen in the casino and had thought dead? It was looking that way. Horton knew – although he had no proof – that Ballard had been in the intelligence services. Perhaps he'd been at Fort Monckton in Gosport and had taken the ferry across to Portsmouth and the casino, not expecting to find Jennifer there. Had MI5 been operating at Fort Monckton in 1978? Or perhaps, Horton thought, with a pounding heart, Ballard had been visiting the Royal Hospital Haslar questioning someone who had returned from a trouble zone, Bernard Litchfield, recovering from a bullet wound incurred in Northern Ireland. And Ballard, or rather Ducale, had discovered – or perhaps had already known – that his twin sister, Eileen, was in love with Bernard. Yes, it certainly fitted. Perhaps Ballard had discovered that Jennifer was working at the casino, or he'd been told she was and had been ordered to make contact with her. But if Ballard had killed her why then rescue him from those God awful children's homes and place him with Bernard and Eileen? Conscience? No, he didn't think so. Perhaps he was ordered to meet her on the 30 November 1978 but someone else kept that rendezvous because Ballard had been sent away, overseas on another mission, only discovering on his return four years later that she'd vanished and been killed. Ballard had tried to put things right by making sure that he was fostered by his sister. And then, this year, in June Ballard had returned and, deciding it was time for Horton to discover the truth, had left that photograph from 1967 on Horton's boat. God, he wished he'd told him more instead of letting him stumble around in the dark trying to piece together the past. He needed some air.

He climbed up on deck. The weather was worsening. The sky had deepened to an ominous dark grey and it was blowing a gale. The police launch was bucking in the heavy waves. It didn't bother him, he was used to it, so too were Elkins and Ripley, but Cantelli would have been hanging over the side, a peculiar shade of green. Horton was glad to let his thoughts return to the case. He wondered how Cantelli was getting on with Mrs Samson.

Dowdswell was out of the frame, along with his friend, Hugh Maltby. Aubrey Davidson was also off the list. That left Nugent.

But Horton didn't believe that Borland would have trusted Nugent enough to admit him to his home and show him his evidence, even if Trueman unearthed a link between Nugent and Borland. There was still the possibility it was DCS Adams but there was someone else that linked Westerbrook, Nugent and Borland, and whom Borland could have confided in and trusted.

Turning to Elkins, Horton shouted above the roar of the engine and the wind, 'What do you know about Julian Tierney?'

'He's been the marina manager at Fareham for three years. Friendly, well liked, good at his job.'

'No hint of scandal or any criminal activity.'

'None. He's a bit vague and forgetful at times but that's not a crime. I can't see him as a butcher and a killer,' Elkins added following Horton's thought pattern.

Horton recalled the round friendly face and tried to imagine Tierney as a killer but like Elkins he couldn't. But Borland had been watching that marina and there was that discrepancy where Tierney had claimed in a previous interview that he'd seen Borland in the car park talking to Aubrey Davidson, but Davidson had denied it. Horton thought Davidson was telling the truth. Maybe Tierney was mistaken if he was as vague as Elkins claimed. Or perhaps he'd said that to throw him off the scent and point the finger at Davidson. Horton told Elkins to head for Fareham Marina but it was twelve fifteen and there was someone else he'd promised to see. He asked Elkins to stop off at Oyster Quays and sent a text to Carolyn.

TWENTY

She was leaning over the railings looking out across the water. He thought with sadness how things might have been different between them.

'I can't stay long,' he said.

Her smile faded and she pushed back her hair as she registered his serious expression and abruptness.

'This is the brush off then.'

'I didn't think we had a relationship.'

'No?' She looked hurt and he felt a stab of guilt, perhaps he was wrong. But no, he knew what he'd seen.

'Not when you're already in one with Rufus Anstey.'

'Ah.'

He kept his steady gaze on her. Her eyes fell and she turned away to look out to sea. 'How did you know? No, don't tell me you saw him arrive at my apartment after you'd left. I don't think I like being spied upon.' She swung back at him, her eyes angry.

'And neither do I, Carolyn,' he calmly replied.

She looked surprised then puzzled. 'Why should I spy on you?'

He didn't answer but searched her face to see if she was telling the truth. She held his gaze without flinching and with what looked like genuine bewilderment.

Rather harshly he said, 'Was sleeping with me the only way you thought I'd agree to you probing me about Jennifer?'

'No!'

'Did you think that I'd be so smitten and infatuated with you that I'd pour out my heart? Is going to bed with your subjects a usual trick of yours to get people to confide in you?'

'How dare you.'

'I dare because that was what it was.'

'My God, you honestly think that's the way I operate?'

'Isn't it?'

'No, it bloody well isn't. I was . . . am very attracted to you.'

'Poor bloody Rufus,' he sneered.

Her face flushed. Tight-lipped she said, 'Rufus and I have been dating for a month. I met him when I first came here for the project. He's divorced. I like him but I . . . look it just happened with you. I didn't mean it to and I certainly don't make a habit of jumping into bed with every man or any man come to that the second time I meet him.'

Maybe that was the truth, maybe not. 'And does Rufus know about us?'

'Of course he doesn't and I'm not going to tell him, unless you are.' Her eyes narrowed.

'Would it matter if I did and he chucked you over?'

She opened her mouth to speak then closed it again. Slowly with a sigh she shook her head. 'No, it wouldn't matter.' She turned back to stare at the sea. 'He's a nice man but rather dull. And before you say it, I know, not dull enough that I didn't want to sleep with him. And you're right I did call him after you left.' She spun round. 'I was pissed off with you. I could see in your eyes and hear in your voice that you didn't want to see me again. I was hurt. It felt like *I* was being used. To you I'd been just a one-night stand, one of many I expect, though I had hoped that what had passed between us was special. You obviously thought not. So I thought sod it, let's see if I've still got it, so I called Rufus and he came running. But then he always does. That's probably why I treat him so badly.' She took a breath. 'Andy, I'm sorry. Can't we start again without Rufus?' She eyed him beseechingly.

He so wanted to but he knew he couldn't. 'It wouldn't work, Carolyn.'

She said nothing but held his steady gaze. After a moment her shoulders slumped. 'No, you're right. I can see that. It wouldn't.' Then she pulled herself up. 'But it was nice knowing you. Good luck with your search for the truth behind Jennifer's disappearance.'

His muscles tensed though he made sure not to betray his thoughts. 'I'm no longer looking,' he firmly replied, but she smiled.

'I don't think you have much option but *to* keep looking.'

He watched her walk away. He let out the mental breath he'd been holding. He still didn't know if she'd been primed by Eames to discover what he knew. And now he didn't care if she had been. Knowing that Ballard was Ducale and Eileen's brother was a giant leap forward and there was more swirling around in his mind. Maybe he'd misjudged Carolyn. Maybe everything she'd said was true. But he could never have a relationship based on maybes.

He returned to the police launch determined to dismiss her from his thoughts. The bracing sea air in the harbour would clear his mind of her. It was time to get back to what he was being paid to do, and that was to catch criminals and he badly wanted to get the man behind Borland's brutal death and the equally brutal slaying of Langham, whose mutilated body might one day be washed up on the shore. He hoped so for Moira and the kids' sake. It was no fun living with the unknown.

Fifteen minutes later, he found Julian Tierney on a pontoon close to where Westerbrook had kept his boat. The wind was now gusting strongly and Tierney said he was checking the boats to make sure they were all well secured. 'The forecast is for gusts of up to sixty miles per hour, better to be safe than sorry,' he added cheerfully.

Horton said he wouldn't keep him long. 'You mentioned before that you'd seen Mr Borland in the car park but did you see him in the marina, on the pontoons for example?' He had to raise his voice as the wind howled and moaned through the masts.

'A couple of times. I think he might have been angling for a trip because he asked me if any of the berth holders did boat trips. I told him he'd have to go to Portsmouth for that, unless someone here fancied taking him out. I said he could put an advert in the office if he liked. But he said he wouldn't bother, he just wondered because he'd seen people arrive with Clive. Fishing, I told him. Clive was a keen angler.'

Not as far as Horton had discovered. He trawled back through his mind to his previous conversation with Tierney. 'I thought you said when I came here before that you hadn't seen anyone go out with Clive except a thin stooping man last Wednesday.' Lesley Nugent.

'*I* haven't. But Mr Borland thought he had.'

Horton's interest quickened. 'Did he say who?'

'No.'

Was this a fabrication to deflect interest away from himself? Was Horton looking at Borland and Langham's killer? His vagueness could be an act to disguise a clever ruthless killer.

'You mentioned before that you saw Mr Borland talking to Aubrey Davidson by his van.'

'Did I? Yes, he was talking to someone.'

'Not Mr Davidson, according to him,' Horton said sharply, watching Tierney.

He shrugged and said casually, 'I assumed it was him, Mr Borland was by Aubrey's van.'

'Where was it parked?'

'Next to Clive's car.'

Horton suppressed his surprise and growing interest. Maybe Tierney was on the level and Westerbrook's car had been the real focus of Borland's interest.

'Was Mr Westerbrook there or inside it?'

Tierney's face creased up as clearly he tried to remember. After a moment his expression cleared. 'No. I remember now I saw his boat go out.'

How sure could Horton be that Tierney was telling the truth?

'It was about two weeks ago, I think. I can check the diary because Aubrey came into the office to collect the keys for a boat engine he was servicing.'

'Please.' Horton followed him back to the office. He was pleased to get out of the temperamental wind.

Tierney retrieved his diary from under a mountain of paperwork on his desk. 'Yes, here it is, Monday, two weeks ago.'

Horton quickly checked the tide timetable which was displayed on Tierney's office wall. High tide had been at 14.10 so Westerbrook had gone out some time between midday and 4 p.m.

'Do you know when Mr Westerbrook returned?' he asked, not really hopeful that Tierney would be able to provide the answer. And he was correct.

'All I know is his car was still in the car park when I left just before five o'clock and his boat was moored up on Tuesday morning when I arrived. His boat was on the pontoon when I did the rounds just after midday.'

It sounded as though Westerbrook had been away overnight. This was a week before Langham had waved goodbye to Moira and had travelled to the island. And eight days before the fire that had claimed Borland's life. It could have no bearing on the murders but it might on the investigation. Horton tried to remember if a journey for those days had been plotted on the GPS he'd viewed on Westerbrook's boat but he couldn't. Was Tierney making this up to throw suspicion off him? But if he were then he'd have picked the day of the fire. Nevertheless Horton asked him where he had been last Tuesday.

'At home.'

'With anyone?'

'My girlfriend.'

'And last Monday night?'

'At home again. But Ella was working. She's a receptionist at a hotel at Whitely.'

A large modern conurbation of houses, offices and a retail park just off the motorway between here and Southampton.

'We'll need to check.'

'Be my guest.' Tierney seemed unperturbed. Either he was supremely confident or completely innocent. Horton was beginning to think it was the latter.

He took down the details of the hotel and Tierney's address, which was a few miles to the west, and returned to the police launch where he asked Elkins to wait for him. Then he headed for Borland's house. He stared at the blue and white crime scene tape flapping frantically in the howling wind wracking his brains to see what he had missed. The mobile incident unit was in place. Had they got new information? Had Cantelli? If he hadn't then they'd have to leave the case to Uckfield and his team. Horton hadn't got anything new that could help throw light on why Borland and Langham had been killed. Only painstaking research, checking and rechecking statements, interviewing and reinterviewing people would get to the truth unless Nugent held his hand up for two murders and Horton didn't think that was likely.

He looked up at the fire-damaged house and saw in his mind Borland being hauled over that fire and left to die. His muscles stiffened but somewhere in the back of his mind something registered. Was it a word or a phrase? He couldn't put his finger on it. Perhaps it was connected with what Tierney had told him. Perhaps Tierney had misheard Borland or misinterpreted what he was saying. Borland, up at that front window, had spied on the marina with his binoculars and on Monday, a fortnight ago, he'd gone down to the marina and stood by Westerbrook's car, why?

He turned and made for the police launch, calling Cantelli as he went.

'Where are you?' Horton asked.

'Just alighting from a bus in Portsmouth.'

'A bus!'

'Yeah, haven't been on one in years,' Cantelli said brightly. 'It was the bus Borland took last Monday.'

'Go on,' Horton said eagerly.

'Firstly Mrs Samson couldn't tell me anything more than she told you about Borland's hobbies but the librarian was very helpful. She was very upset when I told her Borland had died in a fire. He was one of the library volunteers. He had a passion for the law. She gave me a list of the books that Borland borrowed, most of it true crime and famous criminal trials. He also spent some time viewing reference material and newspaper articles on criminal trials. He used to attend some of the big trials or rather the ones he found most interesting whatever the crime was. He went to the Old Bailey, the Royal Courts of Justice, and other courts around London, Winchester and Portsmouth. He told her that he'd always wanted to be a barrister but his family couldn't afford it. They were just ordinary working class. He did well though, went to grammar school and then passed the civil service entrance exam and worked his way up. He came in every day during the last week of his life, except for the Sunday when the library was closed.'

Why did Horton think of Hugh Maltby? He was in Cyprus.

'Last Monday he caught the nine thirty-one from Fareham Bus Station to Edinburgh Road.'

The city centre then, perhaps to do some shopping, thought Horton disappointed, but he caught the excitement in Cantelli's voice.

'He was a regular on the service. The driver knew him well, in a passenger driver relationship way,' Cantelli added. 'I could only talk to him at the bus stops or when we got held up in traffic. He told me that Borland used to moan that he had to walk from Edinburgh Road through the civic centre to the courts and he continually asked why the bus route didn't go that way, but in a light-hearted manner. The driver used to joke with him, saying "what are you up before the beak for now? Forging your bus pass," that kind of thing. Borland told the driver that he liked to attend the more interesting trials and he went there on Monday, which was why he was wearing his suit.'

Horton's interest deepened. He didn't remember seeing Borland in court but then he would only have noticed him if he'd been known to him or a relative of the family of the accused or victim. No one from CID had been in court last Monday.

'Find out what was being heard?'

'On my way there now. I'll also see if I can find out what other trials he attended but that might be difficult if no one remembers seeing him and we wouldn't get a complete list. You know what this could mean though?'

Horton did. Cantelli didn't need to spell it out. The list of trials would give them the names of the police officers involved but as Cantelli said it wouldn't be complete.

Cantelli continued, 'I'll check with Tim Shearer to see if he remembers Borland.'

Horton told Cantelli that they'd pulled in Nugent. He rang off and made to climb on the police launch then hesitated. 'Dai, are you needed anywhere?'

'Not desperately, no, why?'

'Come with me.' Horton headed back to the green, relaying as he went what Cantelli had reported. He found Marsden in the incident suite and asked him if a safe had been found in Borland's house. It hadn't been. Marsden also confirmed that no new information had come to light. Horton asked for the keys to Borland's house. As he climbed the stairs with Elkins, he said, 'Borland might have used a computer to keep a record of what he had witnessed going on in this marina and of the trials he attended. If so the killer took it and Borland being a thorough man would have backed it up but that might also have been taken or destroyed in the fire. He's also old school though and, as Mrs Samson said, very thorough and cautious which means he could also have kept written notes.'

'Belt and braces job.'

'Yes.' They entered the burnt-out bedroom.

Elkins eyed the destruction. Horton saw his gaze fall on the remains of some books on the floor and then those still in the charred bookcase. The fact that there were books on the floor now struck Horton as unusual. They couldn't have leapt out of the bookcase on their own, and the bookcase, although badly burned, was still upright beside the fireplace. It seemed likely then that the killer had searched through some of the books in the bookcase and tossed them on to the floor before dragging Borland over the electric fire. Or perhaps some of these books on the floor had been on the table and the killer had rifled through them then thrown them down. If so then the killer was searching for written evidence and would have taken it with him if he'd found it. Or would he? Horton's spine tingled.

He said, 'You take the bookcase, Dai, I'd hate for you to get your uniform trousers dirty. See if there is anything in those books that might tell us what Borland saw and who he confided in.' He pulled on his latex gloves and applied himself to the books on the floor. There were a couple of biographies, law books, factual books and a few police procedural novels. Some were nothing but charred remains, some crumbled to his touch, but others were remarkably untouched. Horton considered what Cantelli had said about Borland's reading material.

'Anything on famous criminal trials?' he asked Elkins.

'There are a couple on cold cases, Jack the Ripper, crime

investigation and evidence and one on famous unsolved mysteries, crimes and disappearances in America.'

'Flick through them to see if Borland left any notes.'

Horton continued picking up the books. There was nothing in them but as he moved to the seat of the fire there was a pile of plaster that had fallen from the ceiling. Carefully he lifted it and a slow smile spread across his face. There were a few books badly burned and the remains of what must have been paper but underneath there was what looked like an exercise book. SOCO might have looked under the plaster for blood or other evidence but not for books. The killer had tossed Borland's written evidence on the floor next to the body on the electric fire in the belief that it would be destroyed. He'd piled other books on top hoping to fuel the fire but the heat had caused the plaster to fall and protect some of what was underneath, as sometimes happened. With eager anticipation Horton lifted the blackened exercise book and eased open the pages. Elkins crossed to him.

'Found something?'

'Yes. It's a notebook and although many of the pages are burnt there are some that are intact with handwritten notes.' He showed Elkins. 'Borland's writing. It looks as though they're notes from a trial he attended and some reference to research material, newspaper articles if his shorthand DT refers to the *Daily Telegraph*.' Horton didn't delve any further. This was important and he couldn't afford to damage what was vital evidence. He placed the notebook carefully in an evidence bag. He needed to get it back to the lab.

He handed the keys back to Marsden. As the police launch headed into Portsmouth Harbour Horton ran over what he'd discovered and what Cantelli had told him. The threads were coming together and a pattern was beginning to form. If DCS Adams really believed that Langham was involved with Jacob Crowe then someone had told him that. Someone who was reliable, someone who knew that Crowe was in prison and who also knew that Crowe and Langham could be connected because they'd both been in the same prison at the same time. His thoughts were interrupted by a call from Walters.

'Westerbrook's offender manager was Dennis Popham.'

'Is he the only one working in the probation service?' asked Horton. He'd been Alfie Wright's and Graham Langham's offender manager.

'He said that Westerbrook attended Gamblers Anonymous and did some voluntary work with the Citizens Advice Bureau giving financial advice. He was by all accounts very astute.'

'Not astute enough to avoid gambling.'

'Popham says it was the thrill of it that got him hooked, not the money. He kept his nose clean for a year as far as Popham is aware. Hasn't seen or heard of him since then.'

So as soon as the term of his sentence had been served inside and on probation Westerbrook had got himself a boat, a car and a lucrative sideline and returned to gambling. Had he met someone during that year who had waited until he'd served out his sentence and had then enlisted him? Or had it been someone Westerbrook had met inside who had only been released a year ago? Horton believed it was the former.

He rang Trueman. 'Have you managed to speak to anyone at Maltby's Chambers in London?'

'Yes. The Clerk says they've never heard of Leonard Borland or Clive Westerbrook and Hugh Maltby's father doesn't recognize either name and neither has he heard his son mention them.'

'Check the cases Hugh Maltby was involved in before he left to join the army. See if there is any connection with anyone in our investigations, and check his background, school, university, who he trained with.'

Horton's thoughts returned to what Julian Tierney had said, that Borland had asked about fishing trips especially those under- taken by Westerbrook because he'd seen people arrive with Westerbrook and go out on his boat. But Tierney had never seen anyone go out with Westerbrook except Nugent. He could have missed them though. Davidson had said that Westerbrook had wanted to rejoin the angling club so that he didn't have to go out on his own. That had been a lie then if Borland had been right, and the fact that he had been murdered meant he must have been.

Horton's brain raced as the launch pulled into the port. What was it that was niggling at him? What had he heard or seen that was significant? Tierney's words rang through his head. Borland had seen people arrive with Clive Westerbrook. *Fishing I told him. Clive was a keen angler.*

But he wasn't. Tierney had only seen Nugent go out with

Westerbrook, why? When had Borland seen others? In the evening, at night, early morning?

A newspaper article he'd read the day after Alfie Wright had absconded flashed through Horton's mind. An article written by Leanne Payne, the local crime reporter, who had ridiculed the police for letting dangerous criminals escape sentencing. The courts was where Borland had spent a great deal of time both physically and mentally. Snatches of conversations came to Horton. Now he thought he knew why Westerbrook had headed for the Thorney Channel, not for the fishing, not to escape, but to moor up and take his own life, only he'd died of natural causes before doing so. He might have intended leaving a written suicide note, Horton would never know, but his choice of where he'd picked up a buoy, on Hugh Maltby's mooring, was note enough. Westerbrook had left a message which pointed to the killer. Maybe the exercise book would reveal who that was. But Horton didn't need that now because he knew who it was and he knew what had been plaguing him. He smiled. Borland had seen people *arrive* with Westerbrook but he'd never seen them *return*. That was why he had been hanging around Westerbrook's car, he'd been waiting for Westerbrook to return to see if his fishing buddies were with him. They hadn't been. They never would be. Westerbrook hadn't been bringing people *into* the country – illegal immigrants or girls for sex trafficking – he'd been taking people *out*, people who could afford to pay generously for their escape.

TWENTY-ONE

'We've got nothing on him,' Uckfield said, rubbing his neck. They were sitting in a quiet corner of the canteen. Horton had called Uckfield from the launch not long after Cantelli had rung through to tell him that Tim Shearer had often seen Leonard Borland in court and had spoken to him.

'Nice man but a bit of an anorak, very keen on the law and always keen to tell me where I had gone wrong,' Shearer had told Cantelli. Shearer had given Cantelli a note of the trials he'd seen Borland attend, including those when he'd worked in London, which was where Borland had first made himself known to Shearer. One of those trials had been that of Jesse Stanhope, convicted of fraud, who Leanne Payne had pointed out in her article had skipped the country before being sentenced. It was a name that after very careful handling of the exercise book, Horton had seen written there. The exercise book was now at the lab.

Horton had asked to see Uckfield alone, not away from the station, just away from DCS Adams and DCI Neame. Uckfield had readily agreed, having already got the heads up from Trueman that Horton and his CID team had continued to work on the investigation, despite Adams' command. Uckfield wasn't going to bollock him about that if they'd got new information that could lead to an arrest. And Horton knew that Uckfield would be only too ready to claim any glory, especially if it gave him the one up on Adams. Uckfield said that Adams was with Dennings and Neame going over the interview with Nugent who was still being held in custody. He'd confessed to nothing and was sticking to the story he'd given Horton and Cantelli. Because it was true Horton had said. Bliss, thankfully, hadn't returned to the station from her one day conference on domestic violence and Cantelli was in CID working alongside Walters researching into the convicted criminals who had escaped sentencing and those who had absconded while on bail. Horton had told them to concentrate on only those cases where the accused and convicted had wealth and to get details of who had represented them both for the defence and the prosecution.

Horton now said to Uckfield, 'And we're not likely to get any evidence for some time even if you get a full team working on it, Steve.' Which had been Uckfield's first thoughts but Horton had stalled him. 'He could skip the country by the time we amass enough to charge him. He's done it for others without us even noticing, he can easily do it for himself. And he must have enough money stashed away to evade being caught. The people he's been getting out of the country have coughed up big time if what Westerbrook spent on gambling is anything to go by, and he was given cash to buy his car and the boat with all its expensive equipment. But then our killer would only help those who could afford to pay generously for their passage to Europe courtesy of Westerbrook's sturdy rather ordinary motorboat.' Which was why it had been chosen. A flashier more expensive and larger model would have drawn more attention from the Border Agency, who weren't necessarily looking for people being smuggled out on what by all appearances looked like a day's fishing trip, but people and contraband goods being smuggled *in*.

Uckfield looked gloomy.

Horton continued, 'But if we put it around that I'm convinced Nugent is not our killer and I think I know who is then he'll have to find out how much I know. He can't afford me shooting off my mouth.'

'We set a trap.'

Horton nodded.

'So what have you got in mind?'

'Call Tim Shearer, ask him to come over as soon as possible to discuss the case against Nugent. When he's here get Trueman to ring through to me. I'll then call you and say you've got the wrong man in custody. Argue with me, say that as far as you're concerned you have the killer in a cell, Lesley Nugent. Say something along the lines of you can believe all you want but that you—'

'No need to spell it out, I'm not fresh out of cadet training,' Uckfield said acerbically. 'I'll tell Shearer you're adamant you know who the killer is.'

'Make sure DCS Adams is with you when this takes place.'

Uckfield nodded solemnly.

'Let me know when Shearer leaves. You leave shortly after. Then I'll head home to my boat.' Horton rose.

Uckfield picked up his coffee cup and scooped up the keys lying beside it. Horton eyed him for a moment. Uckfield sniffed and nodded.

Horton returned to CID where he updated Cantelli and Walters on what he'd arranged with Uckfield. Cantelli urged caution. Horton promised it. Cantelli reported that they had found a handful of cases that had made the national newspapers and a couple of high profile local ones that Borland had followed in the Portsmouth courts.

'There are two men who have absconded before being sentenced, Nigel Tamar, in November last year, convicted of wine fraud, selling fake vintage wine when what was really decanted into the bottles was cheap plonk, two of the bottles he sold totalled forty-five thousand pounds, can you believe that!' Cantelli said incredulously.

'Enough to buy Westerbrook that boat,' Horton said.

Cantelli continued. 'Tamar has never been seen since, neither has

Stuart Broadman who also absconded before being sentenced in September this year, holiday fraud. He set up a fake website, had all the credentials listed, all phoney, and took thousands of pounds off punters who thought they were going to be basking in the sunshine topping up their tans when none of them got further than Heathrow Airport.'

Walters chipped in. 'Then there's Gordon Penlee.'

Horton recognized that name. 'The phoney art dealer.'

'That's the one. Had an exclusive art gallery tucked away in his very expensive house in Old Portsmouth and was flogging off paintings that were supposedly by some big art geezers only they were fakes. The trading standards office caught him. He was granted unconditional bail on the 26 November and was due to appear before Portsmouth Magistrates on Wednesday 5 December only he'd vanished into thin air along with some of his paintings.'

Horton said, 'Taking with him a lot of the cash he had stashed away. That's who Leonard Borland saw arrive with Westerbrook on Monday 3 December but not return. It's the day Tierney saw Borland standing by Westerbrook's car.'

Cantelli said, 'There are three others, one is Jason Gracewing, a millionaire property dealer in London, who was charged with murdering his wife, granted bail but failed to report in. It's too late now to check with the Chambers that represented them, they'll all have gone home, but we'll access the full case files and that'll give us more.'

Horton's mobile rang. It was Trueman. 'Tim Shearer's in with the Super.'

That was quick, but given Cantelli's enquiries around the court and in the CPS offices maybe Shearer had dropped everything when Uckfield had called him to hurry here. In his office Horton rang Uckfield's number and went through their pre-arranged routine. He then called the marina where he kept his boat and gave instructions to Eddie in the office. Then from his window he watched Shearer leave twenty minutes later after Trueman had given him the nod. Next came Uckfield a few minutes later with DCS Adams.

Walters stuck his head round the door to say that he was off for a kebab.

Horton didn't envy him that. He glanced again at the clock. It was seven twenty-five. How long would it take, he wondered?

He called John Guilbert in Guernsey. When he came on the line Horton thanked him for the photographs.

'Glad to be of help.'

'Did Violet Ducale say when she last saw the twins?'

'When their father died in 1967.'

'Not since then?' Horton said, disappointed. 'Has she heard from either of them since then?' Not Eileen she wouldn't have done but Andrew, yes, he thought so.

'I didn't question her, Andy, I just listened to her talking about Guernsey of old and it wasn't a chore. I can go back if—'

'No, you've done more than enough. I'll come over to Guernsey. I'd like to talk to her.'

'Great. It'll be good to catch up. When are you planning on coming?'

'As soon as Christmas is over,' he said, then quickly added. 'Is she in good health?' He didn't want her to snuff it before he could make it.

'Not bad but she is eighty-nine and has health issues. Her mind's as sharp as a razor though.'

Horton said he'd let Guilbert know when he was coming. He would probably fly from Southampton to Guernsey, it was less than an hour flight, and would be quicker than taking the ferry from Portsmouth, which took seven hours. In spring he might return there under sail.

He glanced up at the clock, the hands seemed to be moving at dead slow speed. He had to check the time on his computer screen several times to make sure the clock was working. He rose, restless.

'Nothing yet,' he said, entering CID where Cantelli waited. 'We can't be wrong. It all adds up.'

Then his mobile phone rang. It was Eddie from the marina office.

'You've got a visitor,' he told Horton, as instructed. 'Just seen him head down the pontoon.'

'Thanks.'

Cantelli nodded and slipped out.

Horton returned to his office, switched off his computer and pulled on his leather jacket. Picking up his helmet he flicked off the light and went to meet the man who had killed Leonard Borland and Graham Langham.

TWENTY-TWO

The air was crisp. The wind was gusting violently. Horton swung into the marina and noted the figure on the pontoon. He gave a tight smile of satisfaction. The killer had taken the bait. Before he reached his boat the man turned, an anxious frown on his smooth fair face.

'I've heard that Lesley Nugent's been apprehended for Graham Langham's murder. I understand you don't believe he did it. I think you're right.'

'You'd better come on board.'

Shearer had done his job well. Horton climbed on first and turned his back on Ewan Stringer in order to open the hatch. He knew Stringer wouldn't attack him yet. Stringer had to find out how much they knew and if DCS Adams was satisfied that Langham's death was connected with Nugent, and Borland's death with Langham.

'Why do you think I'm right about Nugent not being a killer?' asked Horton conversationally while leaning back against the work surface of the galley, causing Stringer to take up position in front of him. There wasn't much room. It had been dangerous to bring him down here. But it was the only way.

'Because Langham knew about Jacob Crowe's smuggling operation.'

'How do you know that?' Horton asked.

'I overheard Crowe telling his girlfriend. I was visiting the prison to see someone on remand.'

If they checked Horton knew that they would find that Stringer had been at the Isle of Wight prison at some stage but he doubted if he had seen Crowe or heard him say anything like that or anything at all. Stringer could easily have found out about Crowe, and his girlfriend's visits, from someone at the prison and he'd have had access to his criminal record, or at least the trial notes, from his work with the Crown Prosecution Office. But Horton thought that Stringer had seen someone else at the prison, someone he thought perfect for his purpose.

'What did he say?' Horton asked.

'Something about it was business as usual despite Langham sticking his nose in. He'd have someone deal with Graham Langham.'

'When was this?' asked Horton.

'Two weeks ago.'

Another lie but then Stringer didn't count on him being around to repeat it.

'Sit down, I'll make you a coffee,' Horton said.

'No. I'd rather stand.'

Not good, thought Horton. Sitting, Stringer was far less of a threat. It was difficult to react fast when you had to wriggle your way out from behind a galley table.

'I was concerned,' Stringer continued. 'I approached DCS Adams and told him what I'd heard. I don't know what he did next, maybe he got hold of Langham who decided to inform on Crowe, or perhaps DCS Adams had his officers watching Langham. But even then, from what I've heard, Crowe has some very ruthless contacts on the outside. I'm guessing that Westerbrook must have been part of a smuggling operation and Langham was killed and his hand planted on Westerbrook's boat to warn him to keep his mouth shut. I think Nugent just happened to be there.'

'And Leonard Borland?'

Stringer didn't look surprised or baffled at mention of the name. Uckfield had told Shearer and Shearer had relayed the information to Stringer. 'Clive Westerbrook must have killed him under orders from Crowe when Westerbrook told Crowe through his contact that Borland had seen them. It must have made him sick to his stomach and he suffered a heart attack as a result.'

Horton seemed to consider this. 'And one of Crowe's operatives must have beaten up Westerbrook.'

'Did they? I didn't know that. They might come after me because of what I overheard. I hate to admit it but I'm rather scared.'

'Not as scared as you were when Langham told you that he'd inform on you unless you cut him in.'

'Pardon?' Stringer looked dazed and shocked. That wasn't an act thought Horton. He had hoped to get away with it.

'Don't look so surprised, Ewan. It's why you're here, you want to make sure that I don't know what really happened. But I do know, so are you going to kill me too?'

Stringer stiffened and eyed Horton keenly but not nervously. Horton tensed but forced his voice to sound casual. His ears were straining for any sounds but all he could hear was the wind howling through the rigging and the sea slapping manically against the yacht.

'I'll tell you what really happened,' Horton continued. 'You approached DCS Adams about Langham but not in the way you claim. And certainly not two weeks ago. It was after Cantelli and I interviewed you and asked you if Alfie Wright had ever mentioned Graham Langham. That gave you the idea that you could link Langham's death with a criminal and therefore Westerbrook's too, because he was getting to be too much of a risk and you might need to dispense with him. But Alfie Wright wasn't a big enough crook to take the blame for Langham's death, you wanted someone bigger. You trawled through the cases to find a suitable villain, someone who wouldn't name his confederates or give information away about his drugs routes, who NCA would be very keen to get more from. The trial information gave you DCS Adams, the officer-in-charge of the arrest. Crowe was perfect for your purposes because when you checked the files you discovered that Crowe had been in Winchester Prison three years ago when Langham was serving time there and had then been transferred to the Isle of Wight prison where Westerbrook was serving time. It matched perfectly.

'You contacted Adams and spun him that fairy tale about Langham possibly being involved with, or having information on Crowe, which could be why he was killed. Adams took the bait. He didn't want the Major Crime Team or CID muddying his waters, which was why we were pulled off and spun a yarn about Langham being an informer. The only informing Langham could have done was on you but he was too stupid and greedy to do that.'

'This is fascinating, do go on,' Stringer said with a bewildered air.

'Oh I will, Ewan. After you'd spoken to Adams who said "thank you" and "we'll look into it" you needed to be sure that line of inquiry was being pursued which was one of the reasons why you came into the station and gave Superintendent Uckfield that information about Alfie Wright being with Barbara. You thought it was best if he was caught and removed from the picture as far as Langham's death was concerned. The second reason was that by admitting you had this information later rather than immediately he'd gone on the run, you looked foolish and weak, which is the opposite of what you really are.'

Stringer continued to look puzzled but it didn't fool Horton.

'Uckfield had already dismissed you as a dozy-minded do-gooder, now you seemed inept, confused and muddle-headed. Whereas you're clever, clear-headed and ruthless. And won't hesitate to kill again. So how are you going to kill me, Ewan? There are no buildings to set fire to here so you can't drag my body over an electric fire and leave me to burn to death. And it's not a secluded cove on the Isle of Wight, or the Solent where you can throw my mutilated body overboard. Oh, I see it's stabbing is it,' Horton said calmly though his heart was racing as he looked down at the curved boat knife. And into his head flashed Gaye's words, *it has a curved blade . . . about four and half inches and the blade just over three inches . . . it could have been used if the victim was restrained and unable to defend himself or was dead or unconscious.* He'd already recalled the conversation he'd had with Shearer and Stringer outside the bar when he'd learnt that Stringer was going out on Sunday on Shearer's boat. Stringer knew how to handle a boat. But he didn't own one or rather he did because he had bought Clive Westerbrook's boat for him. And on Monday night he'd borrowed it, and Westerbrook's knife, and motored to the Isle of Wight to rendezvous with Langham.

'I take it that's the knife you used on Graham Langham to cut off his hand. You then put that hand in a container and kept it hidden on Westerbrook's boat until you could use it at Borland's house on Tuesday after dark, just in case Borland's death was discovered to be suspicious and you knew Langham had been there because that was when he approached you. Did Borland let you in?'

Stringer didn't reply.

Horton continued. 'You probably told him on Monday, when you saw him in court, that you'd come over on Tuesday and review the evidence he'd compiled. You were carrying a rucksack or sailing bag with the container inside it and once in that bedroom, when Borland turned away to gather together some information for you, you viciously struck him several times on the back of the head with a powerful torch, which had been inside the bag. You then took Langham's severed hand out of the container and pressed the fingers on the metal under the electric fire, to complement the prints Langham had already left in the house when he broke into it on

Saturday evening believing it to be empty, which was when he overheard Leonard Borland telling you what he'd discovered. You switched on the fire and dragged Borland's body over it, making sure to open the window before you left in order to fan the flames. You also put the written evidence Borland had compiled on that fire.'

'I see you have all the answers.'

'Most of them.'

Stringer frowned. The knife remained gripped tightly in his right hand.

Horton continued, 'Leonard Borland, watching through his binoculars, had seen at different times, individuals arriving at the marina, being met by Westerbrook or arriving with Westerbrook in his car. At first Borland probably thought nothing of it, they were just fishing trips. But something made him suspicious. He recognized someone who, from his keen interest in criminal investigations, he'd seen before, either in the newspaper, or on television or in court.'

Into Horton's mind came a picture of Borland, a bereaved husband, a man who had loved his wife and whose only child was far away. A lonely man, who, having retired, had time on his hands and probably wanted to feel he was doing something useful. And he had something to prove to himself and others; that he could have made a better life for himself and his family as a barrister or lawyer if given the chance.

'He kept watch and saw more of this happening over a period of time. He should have come to us but perhaps he thought we'd dismiss him unless he approached us with evidence that was watertight. So he asked you, who he'd met in court several times, to come and review it with him. It was bad luck for him. Until then you had no idea your scheme had been uncovered. You told him to keep the information to himself and that you would approach someone in the right quarters, someone in the National Crime Agency who would really appreciate the tremendous work he'd done. How long had he been watching?'

'Six months.'

'Jesse Stanhope,' Horton said, recalling the article that Leanne Payne had run after Alfie Wright had absconded. Tried at the Royal Courts of Justice in London, he had evaded a bankruptcy charge but was wanted for fraud on a massive scale. His family in

Portsmouth swore blind they hadn't heard from him and had no idea where he was. And seeing this first individual was enough to make Borland curious. If only Borland had come forward. But perhaps he thought he was mistaken. He began to take a keener interest in the marina.

'So who did Borland spot next?' Horton asked.

'Stuart Broadman.'

'The holiday fraudster.'

A flash of irritation crossed Stringer's face. He was obviously peeved that they'd got so much information. Horton said, 'And of course there was Gordon Penlee, the phoney art dealer, and probably Jason Gracewing, a millionaire property dealer in London, charged with murdering his wife. You must have made a lot of money, what have you done with it? Put it into property in London, bought for cash? Is that how you were able to approach Gracewing and offer to get him out?'

'There are plenty of people willing to pay a handsome fee to escape conviction or apprehension.'

And Leonard Borland had sat at that window in his upstairs bedroom day after day on or around the high tide, recording people arriving, waiting for them to return, particularly those who went out with Westerbrook. He probably discovered that Westerbrook had been convicted for fraud. With his keen interest in the law, Borland would have researched the criminal cases archive. Borland saw individuals going out with Westerbrook, ostensibly to fish, only they never returned. And that made him very curious indeed. So curious it cost him his life.

'You paid Westerbrook to take people out of the country.'

'He gambled heavily. He was desperate for money.'

'You did your research well,' Horton acknowledged.

Stringer looked rather pleased at the compliment. 'I was looking for someone who could handle a boat and who wouldn't say "no" to being given one, no questions asked. I gave him the money to buy it in cash in return for doing some errands for me. Not drugs I assured him and not smuggling, just helping some individuals to make a new start in another country.'

'Did you give them false papers?'

'Of course not,' Stringer said, shocked. 'All I provided was a route out.'

'And it was going well until Graham Langham showed up on one of his robbing sprees. So he had to be eliminated along with Borland who knew far too much and had photographs and details of the times of departure and return. And when Westerbrook discovered that you'd killed Langham and Borland he wanted out and got a beating for his troubles.'

'Langham was an idiot and a thief. It was easy enough to string him along. I told him we had a trip arranged for Monday night and to meet the boat in Pelham Cove on the Isle of Wight and that we'd need his van. I said that not only were we taking people out but we were bringing them in, a lie, of course. I said we could use his van to bring those Westerbrook dropped off on the island over here to the mainland. There are no checks on the Wightlink ferries as you know. I told Langham that someone would meet him at a drop-off point, a lay-by on the A3M heading towards Petersfield, to take them off his hands. He had no qualms about it.'

Stringer's hand was steady, the knife only a foot away from Horton. He knew he would be able to react quickly and dodge from the main and first impact but there was little room to dive completely out of the way without it possibly causing some damage to him and not much room to disarm Stringer.

Horton said, 'Was Westerbrook with you when you met Langham on the Isle of Wight?'

'No.'

Horton eyed him steadily. He thought that was the truth.

Stringer continued, 'The cove was in darkness and deserted. Langham came down to meet me as arranged. I told him to climb on board and that the cargo was below in the cabin. As he bent to look I struck him on the back of the head—'

Horton's knuckles gripped the work surface in anger.

'Langham fell on some tarpaulin sheeting I had already placed underneath him to catch the blood. I hacked off his hand, and popped it into a container to keep it as fresh as I could. I knew that there has to be some kind of moisture or wax on the fingerprints for them to take.'

Horton stiffened with fury at Stringer's callousness and his casual dismissal of Graham Langham but then he knew from what he'd done to Leonard Borland that here was a man who would think nothing of killing to suit his own purposes.

'I didn't know that Langham had already left his prints in the house.' Stringer frowned as though annoyed with himself for not knowing that. 'I should have noticed he wasn't wearing gloves but I thought a crook like him would know how to cover his tracks.'

'Why do you think he's been in prison so much?' Horton scoffed.

'Yes, but it worked to my advantage. You, or rather I should say, the police think Langham killed Borland.'

Not for long, thought Horton.

Stringer resumed. 'I wrapped the tarpaulin sheeting around the body and took the boat out. I hauled Langham into the cockpit and then dumped him overboard. It took some doing, but I managed. Handy things these knives, and sharp.'

But Horton needed more from Stringer. The wind howled around the marina and through the masts, rocking his boat.

'Why did you start helping villains get out of the country?' he asked, hoping that Stringer was filled with the desire to show how clever he was and believing that he, Horton, wouldn't be around to repeat it. But he knew why Stringer had chosen his route. He recalled what Tim Shearer had told him: *he takes his work seriously . . . but he gets a pittance for what he does.* Stringer had a master's degree in criminology and he'd trained for the Bar but had diverted into forensic mental health in order to help others. And Horton knew that Stringer had trained with Hugh Maltby, it was the message Westerbrook had left them by mooring up on Maltby's buoy at Thorney, but unlike Maltby, Stringer had failed to be called to the Bar. And when Hugh Maltby had chucked it all up to join the army that must really have stuck in Stringer's craw.

Horton continued, answering his own question. 'It's not about justice though or even money, is it, Ewan? It's about you getting one over on a system that rejected you. What went wrong? Did you fail?' He knew that word would goad Stringer and judging by the tightening of his mouth and the whitening of his knuckles as he gripped the knife Horton could see he was correct.

'Is that what happened to you, Ewan? Hugh Maltby made it and you didn't, why?'

'Because he spoke with the right accent, he came from the right schools, he had money and contacts,' hissed Stringer. 'My dad worked on the railways and my mum was a waitress.'

'And they worked hard to put you through college and university.'

Stringer gave a hollow laugh. 'Of course they didn't. They thought education was a waste of time and that I should get a "proper" job like a plumber or builder, or work in the civil service for forty years like Borland. But I knew I was destined for more than that. My parents wouldn't hear of it. So I had to apply for grants and take any work I could during the holidays and at weekends and evenings while my fellow students were pissing it up. Everything I achieved was through my own efforts. After my law degree I got a grant to support me through the Bar Professional Training Course. I was in pupillage to Maltby's father's Chambers in London with Hugh but they dispensed with my services. They said I wasn't cut out to be a barrister because I didn't have the right approach. I wasn't clever enough to reason and I couldn't think laterally. I was too attached to the clients, not detached enough,' he scoffed.

'That must have stuck in your gullet.'

'It did for a while. Then I thought as they wouldn't let me become a barrister to defend I'll help in another way.' He smiled. 'I took a degree in criminology and then a master's while working part-time and voluntarily in the courts in London.'

'Which is where you met Tim Shearer?'

'Yes. And I worked for victim support. I saw many offenders sent to prison when they shouldn't have been because of their severe mental health issues. I applied for a positon as a forensic mental health practitioner and got it. I was very successful in putting across the offender's mental health issues, and managed to refer many for medical help rather than sentencing.'

'But that wasn't enough.'

Stringer's expression clouded over.

'What happened to make you change tack?'

Stringer stiffened. 'Gerald Maltby.'

Horton eyed him curiously. 'Hugh Maltby's father?'

Stringer nodded. 'He was so bloody smug. Thought he could get his client, a rich and successful businessman who was equally cocky, off a charge of fraud. But he didn't.' Stringer smiled. 'He was convicted, and released pending sentence. I approached him. I offered him a route out. He grabbed it and was very grateful.'

'You had a boat before you bought one for Westerbrook?'

'No, I borrowed Hugh's.' Stringer smiled. 'That was two years ago. It was so easy. I took him out from right under everyone's nose, no one, not the police, the army, knew what had happened and where he'd gone. He paid handsomely. Now if that's not clever then tell me what is,' he declared confidently.

'It didn't fool Leonard Borland.'

The fist on the knife tightened.

'When did you give Westerbrook that beating? Tuesday night? Was that when you told him Langham had been dispensed with and he said he wanted nothing more to do with your scheme?'

'I met him on the beach here, or rather the other side of this marina on the shore, by the lifeboat station. It was dark and cold, there was no one about. Clive wanted out but I persuaded him he had no choice but to continue, otherwise he was looking at a very long prison stretch, and I knew he couldn't face that again. I told him on Saturday after my little chat with Borland that he needed to start taking people out fishing to make it look less suspicious, in case the marina manager, Tierney, began to ask questions, although he probably hasn't got the brains for that.'

'Which was why Westerbrook went to the angling club on Sunday and asked Nugent to go fishing on Wednesday.'

'Yes. I left the hand on board Clive's boat on Tuesday. I had no more use for it. I have keys to the boat. He saw it, panicked, tried to get rid of it not thinking to throw the hand out of the container, he tossed it in the sea, Nugent's line got caught on it and—'

'Westerbrook had to go through the charade of reporting it.' And realizing that things had gone too far he went to Maltby's mooring to point the finger at Stringer.

'Lucky he had a heart attack,' Stringer said lightly. 'I can get someone else to take his place.'

'I doubt it. It's over Ewan. There's nowhere else for you to go and no one else for you to kill.'

'There's you.'

'And if you kill me do you think that will be the end? Detective Chief Superintendent Adams might think that Lesley Nugent, or even one of Crowe's men, killed Leonard Borland and Graham Langham, but I know different and so too does Detective Superintendent Uckfield.' Horton looked beyond Stringer.

'I won't fall for that old trick,' Stringer said smugly.

'It's not a trick, sunshine,' came a gruff voice.

Stringer spun round to face the cabin behind him. In a split second he swung back and lunged forward at Horton with the knife outstretched, his face contorted with fury. But the delay had allowed Horton to side step the impending attack. Swiftly he grabbed Stringer's wrist and, with a cry of pain, Stringer dropped the knife and Horton twisted Stringer's arm up his back. Behind Uckfield was a sour-faced DCS Adams.

'Did you get all that?' Horton said.

Uckfield nodded. 'All nicely recorded too.'

But it was Stringer who answered. 'You can't use any of that. It's not admissible. I haven't been charged or cautioned.'

'Then we'd better do it now.' Uckfield nodded at Horton who formally charged Stringer while Uckfield spoke into his radio. The boat bucked as Cantelli climbed on board. The cabin now was very crowded. Horton handed Stringer over to Cantelli who looked sombre.

'I have no idea why you're doing this,' Stringer declared airily. 'I haven't done anything.'

'Tell that to the jury,' Uckfield quipped.

Stringer smiled.

'I think you've just made his day,' Horton said, watching him being led away by Cantelli. On the pontoon there were two uniformed officers.

Adams replied. 'He's right, though, none of this will stand up in court. And he'll claim he didn't put Leonard Borland's body over that fire but insist that Langham did, and that he was nowhere near Westerbrook when he died—'

'Which happens to be the truth.'

Adams went on as though Horton hadn't spoken. 'Even if we can place Stringer in that house with Borland he can say he went there at Borland's request because he had suspicions but that he didn't take them seriously. Or claim that he went there on a social visit having met Borland in the courts. He's probably scrubbed down Westerbrook's boat and even if evidence is found on it that shows Langham was on there and killed on it, Stringer can claim he knows nothing about it. Langham could have got on board and been trying to rob it, and Westerbrook or Nugent killed him.'

Even Uckfield was beginning to look depressed. But Horton addressed Adams, 'Then tell him he's right and that we have got nothing on him. Say you're going to release him and that he's too clever for us. That no one will know about his scheme. If I'm right he'll give you something to arrest him, perhaps he'll even give you Jesse Stanhope or one of the others, because he'll want a trial. It will be his chance to show the legal world what a brilliant advocate they've lost. Now that we know about his scheme Stringer will want to put all his legal training to use. It's what he's longed for. And he is very clever.'

'Then we'd better show him we're smarter,' Adams snapped and climbed off.

'He doesn't like being wrong. Or being used,' Uckfield said, beaming.

'Do any of us?' Horton replied thinking of someone who had used him. Or had she?

He told Uckfield he'd join him at the station shortly. He descended into the cabin and felt the rise and fall of the pontoon as Uckfield headed for the marina car park. He heard the sound of car doors slamming and vehicles moving off then he reached into his trouser pocket and withdrew the black and white photograph taken in 1967 at the London School of Economics' first sit-in protest.

He ran through what he'd been told since deciding to investigate his mother's disappearance a year ago; that she'd been involved with a diamond smuggler but hadn't run away with him; she'd got involved with an international criminal code-named Zeus by the Intelligence Directorate and had run away with *him.* Horton discounted both.

She'd worked for British Intelligence and had played a part in informing on the plans of the Radical Student Alliance in the 1960s and early 1970s; that was the truth. And Guilbert had told him that Eileen Ducale had left Guernsey in 1961 to work for the civil service in London. Horton wouldn't be surprised if it had been there that she'd met Jennifer and introduced her to her twin brother, Andrew. And Jennifer had been recruited by Andrew to work for British Intelligence in the days of the Cold War.

He'd discovered something about all six of these men in the photograph and he'd been left a code by the man who had taught five of them, which Horton believed indicated she'd been heading for Gosport and a rendezvous with someone from the intelligence services, possibly Eames or possibly the man she'd seen in the casino, who was also working for British Intelligence and whom she believed was dead. Susan Nash's words reeled around his head: *she went deathly pale as though she'd seen a ghost.*

Then there was the story that she'd been connected with the IRA in the mid to late 1970s either to help foil terrorist plans or to aid them; he thought both were unlikely and Dormand had told him this in October to distract him from what was really the truth. And that brought him back to the brooch, which PC Adrian Stanley had stolen from his mother's flat. He'd seen her wearing it. The fact that it wasn't listed anywhere on the stolen art and antiques database meant that it had been given to Jennifer by someone she had loved and who had loved her. Someone who had come back from the dead.

So who was the ghost Jennifer had seen? A ghost that Eames was so desperate for him not to find? One who Eames was going to great lengths to protect or rather to prevent from ever being found. Andrew Ducale aka Edward Ballard?

Horton poured himself a glass of water which he drank thirstily in one go. He stuffed the picture back in his pocket and locked up the boat. The marina car park was deserted. He climbed on the Harley and headed for the station, but on the deserted seafront he pulled over and silenced the engine. He stared at the black expanse of sea that stretched before him. In the light of the moon he could see the flecks of silver on the waves as they rolled on to the shingle beach.

Trueman's words on identifying Borland's burnt body rang through Horton's troubled mind: *although a formal ID and finger-prints are impossible given the fire, his dental records were accessed shortly after he was taken to the mortuary and they matched.*

Horton took a deep breath; was it possible the ghost that Jennifer had seen was Zachary Benham and he hadn't died in that fire in the psychiatric hospital? The dental records had claimed the body was that of Zachary Benham but that would have been easy to fabricate. So where was Benham now? Had he killed Jennifer? Had he run off with her? Had someone else killed them both? Why hadn't Benham perished in that fire? And if he hadn't then who had in his place? Two men could give him the answers to these ques-tions. He knew where one of them was, Lord Eames, except he never would tell. The other man would.

Horton started the engine and headed for the station. The answers lay with Andrew Ducale, and now that Horton knew what questions to ask he also knew that Ducale would reveal the truth. All he had to do was find him and he'd begin by talking to Violet Ducale in Guernsey.